FREYA THROUGH THE VOID

LUCY E.M. HUNTER

Cover artwork and design: William Ingham

ISBN 978-1-916529-73-1 Paperback
ISBN 978-1-916529-74-8 Ebook

The Unbound Press
www.theunboundpress.com

Endorsements

"This is a fascinating story of inner and outer journeying, touching on themes of cosmic energy, personal enlightenment and healing. It also has some stunningly beautiful descriptions of nature."

Sophie Cooke, author

"This is a great piece of writing…I read it in just three days. Anyone who has visited, or who wants to visit Peru, Cuba or Scotland will love this book as it introduces traditions and rituals that weave well into the storyline…The depth of emotion portrayed through the characters experiences is etched in truth and reality: shamanic journeying, trauma, difficult personal decisions, confrontations and solutions will all draw readers in just as I was drawn in.

The Author has shared something that has arisen from deep within their heart, expertly touching on the really important and relevant subject of the Void or Abyss and how it can and will affect people. The addition of the angelic realm conversations brings a wonderful dimension to the story. The book ends in a beautiful and positive way that has left me inspired and hopeful, touching me in a very positive and healing way."

Rory Duff, founder of the *Sacred Path Network*, Geo Biologist, and author

"Fresh and vital and alive…Beautiful writing."

Frederick Turner, American poet and literary critic (1943-2025)

Hey unbound one!

Welcome to this magical book brought to you by The Unbound Press.

At The Unbound Press we believe that when women write freely from the fullest expression of who they are, it can't help but activate a feeling of deep connection and transformation in others. When we come together, we become more and we're changing the world, one book at a time!

This book has been carefully crafted by both the author and publisher with the intention of inspiring you to move ever more deeply into who you truly are.

We hope that this book helps you to connect with your Unbound Self and that you feel called to pass it on to others who want to live a more fully expressed life.

With much love,
Nicola Humber

Founder of The Unbound Press
www.theunboundpress.com

*For all those who walk in the Depths that
others don't have to...*

Contents

Disclaimer

This book is a work of fiction. While it draws inspiration from the author's personal experiences, the characters and situations depicted are a weaving of memory and imagination. Where real places, organisations, or events are mentioned, they are used fictitiously or in service to the narrative. The story should not be interpreted as a factual account of real-life events.

Prologue

What if we told you that the world as you know it is about to change, change utterly? That the Earth, like a great cat sleeping in the spray of an annoying fountain, seemingly not minding being impinged on drip by drip, is suddenly about to awake. Finally fed up with the imposition of this spray, and before being fully saturated with the offending droplets, the creature is about to stand up and, with a great roar, shake all the irritating drops from its fur, drops that will fall away like so much flotsam.

What if we told you that all that you have been told is important – productivity and rushing around being VIPs in pursuit of a lifestyle that would need 5 worlds to sustain if you were all to adopt it, a pursuit which is anyway taking you all to the very brink of extinction – what if we told you all this is about to fall away.

——

That she can be alive on Earth at this auspicious time our heroine Freya Banks is about to be born. She will be one of a collection of souls who have elected to incarnate on Earth to join in and help facilitate what will become known as The Great Shift.

But wait, there seems to be a problem. There is the Angel whose job it is to make sure the souls get shunted to Earth in time to be born, waiting as normal at the Sending Station. But by their side arrives the commanding Angelic presence of one of the Ophanim, which is far from normal as it is not their job to concern themselves with the Sending Station. They are part of the unfolding of the changing blueprint, and their department has been super busy of late preparing for the New Cycle that will arise out of the ashes of all that is about to fall away.

The first Angel, who is known as Jamear, is scanning a see-through Angelic clipboard where all manner of lights and flashing colours come and go on the screen, and their blue and green radiance pulsates in a flurried and irregular manner. They look perplexed.

"What is happening?" the Ophanim asks, "Where is the soul? Why is she not here now? It's time to send her to Earth." All Angels are splendid beings, but this Ophanim was of a different order, and even though they had cloaked their golden radiance in a film of white, golden sparks nevertheless shot forth as they spoke. The Ophanim are an order of Angels concerned with the blueprint of creation and do not usually concern themselves with the niceties of the Sending Station.

Naturally, Jamear is not insensitive to the honour of this Angel's presence, if somewhat overwhelmed.

Seeing this, the Ophanim softens a little.

"Beg pardon, dear Jamear, you may call me Galgaliel. Pray, what is the delay?" All this said in a voice of one not used to inefficiencies.

Jamear has no time to answer before they both become aware of a commotion.

A flurry of guiding beings flock around the two Angels as a third Angel comes into view, unaccustomedly also a little flummoxed. They say, as they approach Jamear, all the while glancing in surprise at the presence of the Ophanim,

"She doesn't want to go; she says she isn't ready."

Before Jamear can answer, Galgaliel, becoming even more majestic, says,

"She isn't ready? What an idea! We have a 12,000-year cycle nearing completion. We have the end of a Kali Yuga cycle imminent, where finally humans, having plunged to the pits, are ready for the re-ascent. The planets are all aligning up, ready to move from the ponderous water and Earth to the speedy air and fire, in time to see us into the Great Shift which will precipitate the beginnings of a New Cycle after 2025." Galgaliel is warming to their theme and the golden sparks shoot out alarmingly. "It will be an opportunity for human beings to recalibrate and find ways to live in Peace. Become mindful of their dependency on the Earth, start cleaning up the mess they have been making so far." Remembering themselves, they stop mid-flow. "But we have talked about this already – you have attended all the briefings." This to the new Angel. "Are you not Azula, assigned as her guardian Angel?"

Azula beams in delight that so important an Angel remembers their name and assignment.

She nods, while Galgaliel decides the seriousness of the situation needs to be clarified.

"But before any of this can happen, the bridge has to be made. The bridge into the Abyss. The Abyss where the New Potential will be seeded. The Earth has to move from the path it is on into a new configuration. You know we can't do that here from the Angelic realms. It has to be done by incarnate souls."

Jamear and Azula glance at each other, they do indeed know this.

"I am Galgaliel, come from the Ophanim; as you

know, we have the job in these Angelic realms, of tuning into the unfolding of the blueprint. We have been very busy recently preparing to facilitate the Great Shift, because a new blueprint will be emerging. The blueprint has to emerge from the incarnated ones. The Ophanim have been carefully blending and combining their energies with certain carefully chosen souls who are to be born. We have been preparing them to withstand the Void, as these souls will be tasked with going into the Void. A task which would send unprepared souls into madness. The mysterious Void, the Daat of the Kabbalah. All existence must cross through Daat before it can come into being and equally all can be drawn back into its great nothingness and be undone in a moment. We are moving towards the time of the Great Undoing, which must first occur before any new potential can be released. We, the Ophanim, will stay connected to these prepared souls while they are on Earth. To help them stay on task. To stay in flow with the co-creative pulse of what is emerging."

Sensing a slight prickling from Azula, a disturbance in the shimmering soft green and lilac light emanating from them, the Ophanim adds,

"We will not in any way be usurping your role, Azula, as guardian Angel."

The shimmering around Azula smooths itself, settling back down into a harmonic flow.

"Only this soul has been prepared for lifetimes," Galgaliel continues. "They are part of an intricate plan. They have understood and accepted the task. The last time we connected with them was in the Bardo, after the life before this most recent one, most satisfactory in a Japanese monastery – very balanced. And calming after those most challenging Native American lives. They had reached a high level of understanding. All that was left was this last short life in the camps. To test their detachment in the face of horror."

Azula is trying to interject but Galgaliel is on a roll and continues.

"All this careful preparation and nurturing of these particular souls for this job has been going on for lifetimes. You know this is a specific task that has to be done at a specific time, involving drawing many souls to meet and travel to be just where they are required at just the right moment. The planning has been off the scale. We have to have everything in place for when Pluto crosses the Galactic Centre in 2007. It will be an important moment with the portals opening across all the energy grids on Earth when the new blueprint can be seeded. There are many Ophanim who have been assigned to different Energy portals across the Globe and each will be in connection with those souls assigned to them who are destined to be there for the activations that must occur across the Earth's grids – the Himalayas, Egypt, there is an important one in Murcia in Spain too. But none of this concerns us or this soul. I have been assigned to assist this soul in the Galactic activation, when the time comes, at the Earth's Navel. All will unfold in time. We require this soul to be at the Navel of the Earth at the appointed time – many years ahead, it is true – but all must be experienced first, so she will be strong enough for the task when it is upon her. And here you are telling me she is not ready to be born!!"

"Forgive me," Azula, her guardian Angel, finally manages to say. "It was very traumatising for her, that last life." Azula feels somewhat cowed by the awesomeness of the context the Ophanim has expounded, but nevertheless does not shy away from their job, to put the case for their human.

Galgaliel answers in a business-like way.

"She has had some years in the healing bays, has she not?"

"Well, yes, but hardly enough after being in the camps," insists Azula. "She was only a child. They tortured her, and in the end, she threw herself against the fence. It electrocuted her. We haven't managed to calm her system down completely yet."

The Ophanim, digesting this, softens their tone as they reply.

"It is unfortunate, we have had news of that in our

realm, it was never expected that the last Event on Earth would be quite so scarring, things got quite extreme."

But then they quickly add more briskly, "Well, it can't be helped, everything is lined up, there are too many timing issues for us to change her birth time now. The cosmic and astrological influences of her birth time must be exact. She needs to be wired into the Galactic Centre; it is this that will give her direct access to the Great Void. We only have a day or two when these exact conjunctions will be in place, we can't delay. This is all very vexing. We have at least lined up a restorative childhood for her?"

Azula looks uncomfortable.

"Well, no, as a matter of fact, some of her siblings will be survivors too. And she is going to have a lot of them. Her parents are to be good people but under a lot of stress. We have ensured she will grow up in the midst of nature in her early life and she will be able to freely roam, and we have just secured a special dispensation to allow one of our top soothing guardians in the form of a dog to be with her while she is young for her to make friends with." Azula is pleased they have managed this and can't help adding, "It is quite awkward as this particular being is always oversubscribed, but we have managed to arrange for her to have at least three or four years with the family."

Jamear, who has been waiting patiently all this while, consults their notes and makes a few alterations, muttering, "A dog, soothing spirit, three or four years…"

Galgaliel continues.

"The fact she is finely wired will work in our favour, but it will be challenging living that one out on an everyday level and staying balanced. We don't want her going over the top, so she will need to be given a wondrous capacity to renew herself while asleep. You can manage that? You have Guardian training and experience, I take it?"

"Yes, indeed," answers Azula, the shimmering lilac and green around her becoming seriously agitated as she explains.

"Additionally, we are arranging things so she will have the time she needs to sleep. She is going to be someone who is bursting with energy, contributing much to the people around her, and she will then need to withdraw and rest."

Galgaliel, the Ophanim, is considering all of this thoughtfully, as Azula continues.

"She will have a heightened ability to tune into others' feelings. This will be exhausting for her and she won't understand it to begin with, but being around people will be like being in a terrible hubbub of conflicting feelings coming from everyone around her. It will make her a great person to go to in times of trouble, but without the renewing power of sleep, we run the risk of her being drained of energy all the time."

Galgaliel is nodding with compassion. Having established the need for fixity in the timing of the birth of the soul in question, they are relaxing a little.

"These brave souls are all taking on quite a karmic load being born at this time of the Great Shift. But she is a Big Soul and with your help and intervention, where necessary, all will be well. However, you must keep a close eye on her, you will have direct access through myself to the sphere of the Ophanim. We will be ready to help as soon as there is any cause for concern. We may be able to stage an intervention in childhood if she is struggling. But we must get her safely born as soon as possible.

"An intervention?" asks Azula. "You don't mean...?"

"Yes," concurs the Ophanim, "it is occasionally done, a 'walk in' or something of the sort, if necessary. At any rate, a helping soul, and then perhaps at that point we can take home the most damaged part of her to continue the healing process?"

Azula is nodding as they absorb this plan, but then adds,

"There is something else. We need her to be outgoing in order to connect and meet the people she needs to through her life, don't we? With tapping into the emotional energy of others and sensing what they are feeling, she will process so much of this directly through her body – it will be painful for her to be around people too much unless they are pretty evolved. So, the way things stand, she is going to want to be alone a lot, to be quite an introvert in fact. How will we manage that?"

"Oh, don't worry about that. She has been given a vibrancy that will be very infectious, people will be drawn to her. As long as we give her plenty of downtime, she will be able to balance that. And haven't we seen to it that she is going to be attractive?"

Jamear, glad to have some contribution to make is scanning through their information,

"I believe she is being born into a handsome gene pool." They find what they are looking for:

"Oh yes, here it is," they scan what is written, summarising.

"Smart, bonnie, cheerful and lithe."

"So many gifts," twinkles the Ophanim mischievously, "however, she won't have the confidence to exploit any of them, so none of these attributes will spoil her. The only problem is she might want to hide herself away, as you point out... We can't have that. Well, let's give her a healthy libido, that should bring her out of her shell if she becomes too insular."

Azula looks slightly askance.

"I see I am going to have my work cut out here then, and that is for sure," they say to no one in particular.

"But what if she still refuses to go?" Asks Jamear, conscious of the practicality of the task at hand. "May I make a suggestion?" They flutter as their light field expands out in pleasing shades of dark green and sparkly river blue, as they offer,

"From what you have said, and from these notes, she is going to have a flair for the dramatic, so could we change the Sending Station to one of our Theatre exit/entry points? Take her right up high to the gods, and when she is looking down and her attention is taken, perhaps...

"A little push....?" agrees Galgaliel as Azula shimmers in agitation, knowing they can only mitigate now against the inevitable.

———

And so it is, that the soul of Freya Banks is sent to the planet Earth at the appointed hour.

Planet Earth, on its immutable journey spiralling round the sun while it follows its slow pathway through the Milky Way, in a dance, a minutely orchestrated dance with all the other planets and constellations. And the centre of this Milky Way, the still point, is the Galactic Centre, sitting at 27 degrees Sagittarius. Considered an enormous black hole but perhaps more accurately described as a pulse, gently breathing the world in and out of existence.

And with the precision of the timing safeguarded, our heroine Freya Banks, albeit unbeknownst to herself, is indeed wired to this Galactic Centre. The plan for the design of her birth has been preserved. She will be born with her natal Mercury directly opposite this potent point in our firmament. And with her north node, indicating her soul's destiny, exactly conjunct. There is no need for you to trouble yourself with planetary positions to follow this story; suffice it to say this alignment to the Galactic Centre will seem like a great plague in her life and will cause no end of travails before this story ends.

All born on this planet, whether aware of it or not, will feel at some point the effects of the cosmic influences of the outer planets. We can all recognise the archetypal stern and Saturnine character who seems to be joyless, or that Jupiterian character full of excess and bonhomie. And whether we knew the transit was happening or not, who has not experienced that inexplicable phase of good luck as Jupiter crosses our sun or our natal Venus? Or the hard slog years as Saturn transits our natal Mars; or indeed the years of sorrow and loss as Pluto crosses our natal moon?

Our heroine will stumble early into an experience as a result of being wired to this apparent great black hole in the centre of our galaxy, although she will initially have no notion of what this experience signifies. For this is to be a priming, a prelude for what is to come and of which this story will speak. Let us now look to see how her earthly incarnation plays out in her early years.

PART I

Chapter 1

A Life Unfolds

And indeed, ready or not, the soul of Freya is being sent hurtling through the beauty of a Highland dawn in May, just in time to be born the seventh child into that growing family. Her landing to Earth is problematic, the drunken country doctor has over-administered chloroform and her mother is not conscious. Freya is struggling to connect to her mother. All during gestation she has flitted in and out of the womb and been really drawn to the gentle, beautiful nature of this soul who is to be her mother.

"Wake up, damn you woman," the doctor is sobering up fast. "Push! Why don't you, your baby is not out yet!" The early dawn is just visible from the window of the room, the golden light beginning to suffuse the sky as the sun rises up between a dip in the tall mountains that surround them.

Her mother, rousing herself, dopily manages that extra push, and so Freya comes into the world. She tries in vain to catch her mother's eye as her mother, propped up by the doctor, holds her absentmindedly, not fully there. Freya's father, awakened in the early hours of the spring morning, holds his new baby girl with the delight only his romantic soul is capable of, ignoring all the practicalities of a seventh child, which fall mainly to his wife.

"Oh Leonard, I don't know if I can… manage…another one… so tired." And the soul of Freya, not yet fully embedded in the material world, is able to sense the cost to this woman of her birth and feels responsible, a weight of responsibility which will stay with her, along with a determination to protect and ease, in any way that is in her power, the life of her mother, suffering now because of giving her this gift of life.

Her father, deeply feeling and poetic by nature, will call her his Highland fairy when his good spirits occasionally surface. Burdened by the need to provide for his ever-expanding brood, he is often impatient and at times explosively angry. Nevertheless, he does his best to provide for them all, albeit it in a haphazard way in those early years. Luckily, his wife has a strong practical side, and is a very resourceful woman. She is a thoughtful and caring mother. Nevertheless, like a giant snowy owl, even when her wings are spread to full capacity, they are never wide enough to embrace all of her chicks at the same time, and despite the nudging and shoving for the prime spot, inevitably some are, at times, left out in the cold. Not only that but her mystical bent is such that she seems to have a direct line 'back home' so even while stirring the porridge it is often clear she is not present, but rather being fortified on another plane, and so, very often not available for whatever little childhood trivia any of her offspring might want to bring to her door. Fast forward the years; more babies are born in a community in the country, where Freya does indeed find great solace in the beauty of the natural world that surrounds her. When the child after Freya is born, her brother Leo, her mother's resilience snaps and a serious illness necessitates her being cared for in a hospital, all the younger children parcelled off for several months. Little Freya, barely more than a baby herself, is left in the care of neighbours who leave her to cry, and Freya then goes past the point of crying. When her mother is well enough to gather her flock about her once more, she declares Freya a stoic, though barely two years old. Surviving these very early years, we will let her speak now for herself.

———

I am calling out in the deep of the night. "Mummy... want mummy... so hot... my throat sore... can't sleep... thirsty... can't swallow..." The room is dark except for a beam of moonlight shining across the silent yard outside and hitting the wall at the other side of the room. I am aware of the bunk beds in the corner where some of my siblings are sleeping. Everything is quiet.

I begin to call out in earnest, "Mummy…" And then I remember, "Oh no, I better not, she must be tired. I know Barnie still wakes her to feed in the night."

Just then, a moonbeam hits a picture on the wall. It is one I like to look at. Jesus wearing his heart on his chest, light radiating out from it. What would Jesus do? I must put others' needs above my own, that is what Jesus would want me to do. I breathe through my pain and tears, and seem to find a relief from pain until I fall back to sleep.

Not long after this – perhaps I am four or five? – I am at home in my family kitchen, the hub of the house. The old Aga is there giving off its perpetual heat and there is a low armchair at the side where my mother is sitting, a rare moment of rest for her. A little crowd of my younger siblings are vying for the top spot on her lap, a spot, it is true, Barnie, still a baby although no longer the youngest, usually claims. I don't even attempt to compete; it is good I don't need cuddles. I notice my big sister by one year still trying though. I don't mind. I want my mother to love her. She was given away for six months on the way to a family holiday to Oma, my mother's mum. My mum was well embarrassed at having yet another baby and did not feel up to confessing to her mother, my Oma, so Amanda was handed out of the railway carriage, still a babe in arms, to a waiting friend, a nurse, on the way. Of course, this was before I was born, but I heard of this from my big sister. It was when Oma came to visit, not long after Barnie was born. My mother gave him to our neighbours to look after for those days, so Oma would not know of his birth. Elizabeth told me then how she had also hidden Amanda's birth from Oma some five years before.

I like Amanda, she is nice to me and we are close in age. Once, when I decided, as an experiment, to see if it were true that the metal iron my mother used to heat up in front of the fire before ironing the clothes, really did get hot, I put my right hand on it and scorched myself badly. Amanda was sweet at the table and wanted to feed me as I couldn't use my right hand. But my mother scolded her and wouldn't allow it, and I had to manage with my left hand. I was sorry for that because it was nice having someone fuss me. But mostly she doesn't want to play with me. She wants to hang around my mum or she is climbing trees. Like me, she loves to be outside. I prefer to go to the mermaid stone, which is in the big stream. You can get on it without getting your feet very wet and I like to sit on it and listen to the water flowing around me on every side. The trees grow on either side of the bank, small rowans and silver birches. I like to gaze at the smooth silver white of the bark of the birch trees and I especially like it in late summer when the red berries appear on the rowans. I feel protected by their shelter, sitting on that stone. I love to do that, and in the springtime, the for-get-me-nots spring into life all along the bank. I spend a lot of time on that mermaid stone just gazing.

And here in this kitchen, I am standing apart from everyone I am also gazing on. I see the big kitchen table, which has benches and seats around it and is big enough for all of us to sit around at mealtimes. Right now, my two older broth-ers are sat at this table doing their homework, the oldest two sisters at the opposite end are swapping scraps – what we did for Pokémon back then. I would like to see the scraps but they don't have room for one more at their game. My father comes in brusquely and demands my mother's attention, so the little ones are scattered from her embrace. They start complaining and scrambling once again for the top spot as close to their succour as possible. A squabble breaks out between my two big brothers – someone has the other's rubber. Suddenly, the hubbub and the heat threaten to overwhelm me. I can't bear it anymore. I cry out,

'You're all making too much noise!'

Silence. Everyone stops what they are doing and looks, first at me then at my father, waiting for his response. We all know how explosive his rages can be, how he has at times banged the big oak table up and down so hard he has lifted it and all the dishes have scattered, some breaking on the flagged stone floor, leaving all us little ones sobbing and my mother to smooth things down as he slams out of the room.

So, the silence is immense with concerned anticipation. Which way will this go?

There he is towering tall in front of me, and he says into the hushed silence of the room.

'You be quiet, who do you think you are? You're only the youngest girl.'

Not the first time he has said these words, I don't imagine, but this time the injustice of the putdown and the fact that a new baby girl recently brought home from the maternity hospital has made this statement untrue, enables me, for the first time, to push back against it. I shout back in indignation,

'No, I'm not the youngest girl, Daisy is!'

My siblings are holding their breaths at the unexpectedness of hearing from me and from shock at my audacity. They are waiting for the outburst from our father they feel sure is inevitable.

I hear my big brothers at the table whispering to each other, mouthing rather than saying, 'What's got into her?' One looking perplexed at the other, shaking their heads and shrugging their shoulders in surprise. 'We don't usually hear a peep out of her,' unspoken yet understood.

And then my father, breaking the tension, choosing his response, starts to laugh at me, and the others taking their cue from him, and with palpable relief, they too all explode into laughter.

I feel pushed out, ignored and overwhelmed as they resume their previous activities. The scraps looked over and swapped, the rubber borrowed, Amanda momentarily and triumphantly reaching my mother's lap.

It's too much for me. I slip out of the house, grateful for the fresh air and spaciousness of our yard. Crossing this, I make my way across the shared drying green. We live in a community, a huge old 15th-century castle divided up into many families, each with their own quarters. Our space is the converted stables. I meet no one. Past the big monkey puzzle tree and so on through a copse of trees towards the riverbank. I know this river so well, but I don't head left to the big mermaid stone to let the water flow around me, soothing away any agitation, no. I head to the weir where it is usually possible to cross over to the other side of the river, to the woods, where folk seldom go, and where we children like to go to build our dens undisturbed. Only occasionally is the weir quite dry, and today, as there has been heavy rain over these last days, the water is lapping a little over the edge. Nevertheless, I cross without difficulty and turn along the bank to the right. Ignoring the route to the most recent den, I walk a short way along the riverbank. I know what I am looking for, a place where it is easy to step down to the water's edge and yet where the eddy of the river creates a pool deeper than the rest of the surrounding water.

Carefully and quite deliberately, I walk into the water. I don't notice the cold as the water rises up and over me, only for a fraction of a second, that delicious smell I love, the smell of the stream. Without any hesitation, I let myself fall in and become fully submerged.

Like a Star Trek character entering a teleport chamber.

'Beam me up, take me home.'

Let it be done.

I have no recollection of how I get here, but my next memory finds me walking back to the house, approaching the communal drying green. I am dripping wet, it is true, but also something has changed. As if some part of me did not come back. Some part of me was allowed 'home' to rest. And yet I feel strengthened too in some way, cushioned and more resilient. And from then on, I am able to cope better with the demands of living in that pretty constant hubbub of competing needs.

And was it after this point that the 'knowing' arrived?

'What would you like to be when you grow up?'

That inane question well-meaning adults ask as they peer down in that condescending manner.

'Why are they asking me this, don't they know, there is no point in being anything, as everything has to change.'

And if I had not been an odd child before, I became one now with my serious penetrating gaze as I sought answers to the questions that puzzled me.

'Why is the Latin teacher always so grumpy?'

'What did the primary teacher mean when she said she was going to explode if we didn't file up two by two straight away?'

'Why do people say things different from what they are thinking?'

It must have been shortly after this incident that one joyous afternoon, I am at home with my big sister, recovering from measles, or perhaps it was mumps, on tenterhooks all morning waiting for the return of our dad. We are cricking our necks to peer out of the small wooden window with its four panes of glass, halfway up the stairs. I am on tip toes to reach the lower left pane, while my sister crouches to look out of the upper left. Yes, there he is, it's my dad, he's coming down the path towards our house and, just as promised, in his arms is a beautiful border collie pup.

I am out the door so fast and the very first in the family to embrace and welcome our dear dog. 'We're so lucky!' I beam at my dad.

Our parents are delighted to see me so happy, and from that moment, Lucky becomes our dog's name. While it was true Lucky was kept busy as a walking frame for whoever the latest toddler was who was learning to walk and who needed steadying, still, it was true that from then on, whenever I slipped out of the house to be alone, Lucky would follow me. She never let me cross that weir again on my own and she would sniff up and down the stream, apparently absorbed in the unearthing of frogs and the like, but whenever I was ready to move, she was once again at my side. One day when I'm roaming around the extensive grounds of our community, I duck down to enter into a den some of us children had been making over the last days. I am mesmerised to see a large snake with bright copper and dark zigzag markings coiled in front of me. Its head is beginning to rise when Lucky, appearing from nowhere, is pushing me out and the snake, startled, slithers away.

Having Lucky in our family makes me feel safe, like I belong. And I love to cuddle her whenever I can. The smell of her thick fur changes, depending on whether she's become damp sniffing through the uncut grass at the edges of the lawns, or if she's been running in dry corn fields, risking the ire of the neighbouring farmers. Then she brings with her that catch-the back-of-your-nose fine grain smell of summer.

Had that 'gift of healing' begun then? I remember when I was around five years old. My mother had slipped awkwardly bringing food to the table and had cried out in pain, 'Oh, my knee, my knee!' And I had, quick as a flash, darted under the big oak table and placed my hand over her knee. Something clicked. 'Oh,' she was surprised that the pain had gone, then 'thank you.' I slipped back into my place and dinner had resumed.

Lucky stays with us as we move from country to town, from town to city, following my Dad's promotions until we end up in the city of Edinburgh in a top flat tenement building. The stairs are great exercise for us, but prove too much for dear Lucky, who takes ill, and one day, when I come back from school, I am only eight, and she is gone. Put down, they said. The terrible grief is like nothing I have ever felt and I cry and cry for days. In my heart, I know I will always be a one-dog girl and there can be no heaven I would want any part of if she were not to be there to meet me when I come to die.

The hubbub of family life continues and it is harder for me without Lucky to come back to. Not having the joyous tail wagging, so happy to see me, not being able to bury my nose in her fur, to cuddle her and have her push her nose into my neck and sides as we sniff out together what kind of day we've been having.

But I enjoy learning and school, and living in a city is quite interesting. Also, life is very busy as we all have our tasks to perform. My mum, ever practical, makes a weekly rota and we take turns washing, cooking, cleaning and shopping to keep the whole operation on the road.

Then something happens to me. It is when I am twelve years old. This experience will stamp itself on me irrevocably. For it is then I first walk into the Great Void. Or, more accurate to say, when the Great Void made itself known by manifesting right in front of me and swallowing up every single drop of life as I knew it up to that moment, threatening to overwhelm my mind.

I am out at the shops gathering some groceries. Such responsibilities come early in a family of twelve children. Friday was my day and I would have been picking up the one-pound bag of haddock off-cuts from the local fishmonger, ready to be turned into a fish pie to feed my many brothers and sisters. He was friendly as ever, popping in a choice piece of lemon sole for free.

'For your mother.' He pats the top of my hand and smiles. Our family are good customers and my mother draws that kind of loyalty to her.

Only the potatoes left to buy.

As I walk under the concrete archway heading towards the Co-Op, suddenly it is as if everything has vanished: not only the buildings, the people and the number 23 bus, but time itself and – more absolute – space too, simply no longer are in existence. And I know with an awful and absolute certainty that this Great Void I am witnessing is more real than all the everyday reality which has just utterly disappeared. I am staring into the dreadful Abyss of Eternity.

All my memories up to this point seem simply a strange chimera in juxtaposition to this Absolute Reality of Nothingness.

I daresay the fish and potatoes make it home; the pie gets made and the tea eaten. And life clicks back and grinds on.

But from that point on, it is never hard for me to fall into contemplation of the unfathomable Eternal. For reality to slide away. To find my mind switching back to that Great and totally encompassing Void. It is as though a permanent fissure has opened up in front of me, which only if I walk with great care can I avoid falling into.

And so, without realising it to be the case, I carefully choose my friends and later my lovers, my activities, yes, even my very thoughts. Even so, I can never escape it altogether.

In times of stress and indecision, like a fateful curse, it is always at my back.

At university, CJ is my adored best friend and ally, a most satisfying and attentive lover. Every night for a year and a half, we nuzzle and snuggle contentedly together in our attic haven, in a bed way too small for two. And yet I leave him. He has perhaps never understood it.

It is one day I am perched on the edge of the bath, a towel draped loosely around my slim frame, waiting for the water to cool. He is reading me his latest poem, which, like the rest, is wrestling with death, the frailty and transiency of life. It is in this moment, it comes to me with great clarity. I cannot stay with him. That staying with him and the dark meanderings of his mind will be dangerous for me. And before long, I do leave him.

I go home for a while after this to reorientate myself. Barnie is up at university in Aberdeen studying law and my stay coincides with his summer break. I am so impressed with him. He is so vital and alive. On this trip home, he has decided that what our brother Leo – who is recovering from a bad breakdown – needs is some sex. To that end, he uses his persuasive powers on some of his couthie girlfriends willing to oblige, to run a veritable bordello under our mum's very nose without her apparently noticing. He is still her blue-eyed boy and I can see she is struggling with his burgeoning independence from her. At least she is realistic enough not to mark him down to be the priest in the family; that dubious calling has been reserved for the next brother down, Martin. Happily, he escapes that role by heading off to Italy in ardent pursuit of some young love.

Dear Mumma, good Catholic that she is, she closes her eyes to what she doesn't want to see. Especially if it is behaviour coming from her favourite.

'I'm leaving,' I tell her one day. She knows this is coming as she's been following the ins and outs of my new romance. In time and with a fine sense of my own survival, I have met and am heading off to live with a man of conviction and action. A peace campaigner intent on saving our Earth from the ravages of too many people wanting too much from its finite resources.

'So, you're leaving the sinking ship,' my mum says, standing there in the hall forlornly. Behind her back, I notice Barnie using this opportunity to open his door. Assessing the situation in a flash, he first lets Leo slip out to return to his own room, before ushering a particularly luscious-looking girl behind our mother's back and out the front door. Dear irrepressible Barnie, an image flashes into my mind. It is one Christmas; he must have been around ten or so. He was laid up in bed with a bad case of tonsillitis while everyone else was celebrating. Going to take him something to eat, I was struck by his cheerful good humour and optimistic outlook. He wasn't feeling in the least sorry for himself. He will keep the ship afloat once I am gone.

And what more can I do? I feel I have paid my dues, with a childhood of attending to my mother's needs, reading her every mood. She told me herself that I was like her thermometer.

'The others ask how I am, whereas you take my temperature, and then you know.'

It was true I only had to enter the house to be able to feel her mood, calibrating what I needed to do to bring her back into balance. She once told me how I used to alarm her sometimes at my uncanny ability to anticipate her needs. The glasses I would hand to her before she realised she had mislaid them. The cup of tea I had ready when she came in tired from a day's school teaching, the tasks I did to ensure the house ran as smoothly as possible. The year I took out between school and university to become the housekeeper and stay home and keep everything running smoothly. I am ready to be free of my mother's needs which seem to eclipse those of everyone near her. It seems like Barnie has everything under control. 'He'll be alright, they'll manage.' I reassure myself as, repressing a smile, I take my leave.

And so, I do. I head off with Jason and life is full, and I participate fully.

A wave of workshops, visitors, sit-ins, petitions and protests. We find a beautiful valley deep in mid Wales and rent a farmhouse. I am delighted the mountains seem to provide a psychic barrier and I am free of the constant awareness of my mother's needs. We form a mini commune with a couple of friends and it is one day when we are playing around with a pendulum hovering over my swelling belly, trying to decide the gender of my baby, when the post arrives with a letter from home. A newspaper cutting. Barnie has gone crazy. He took a dose of magic mushrooms and was found naked climbing up a statue of some Scottish worthy or other in Princess Gardens. He's in the psychiatric hospital.

That night of dreaming is a night of rage. Rage towards my mother. I put the blame at her door. She can't let go of him. I feel an anger I've never expressed to her in person. Is this what you want now? A son who is incapacitated in some way and therefore always going to need you? Aie Barnie, you were flying so high, now crashed to Earth. I am so sorry.

But gradually, sleep by sleep, I let myself surrender back into the deep of the valley, and the protection of those Welsh hills reinstates itself. The seal is back intact and I let it all wash away. It is not my concern right now. There is nothing I can do for Barnie right now. I must concentrate on my world, my life. My baby has turned breech and that is foremost on our minds. That and the network we are busy creating, building threads amid the cut-and-paste on the kitchen which that was the activist way back then to create a newsletter. We're talking the 80s here; nearly 15 years have to pass before the electrifying spark occurs that activates the internet into existence. And then, joy – our beautiful boy is born in the farmhouse with our fabulous local midwife in attendance. And worries about my family recede firmly into the background.

A few days after the birth, I am alone in our upstairs room. Jason has gone down to make me something to eat, he has taken our little boy with him. I hear him chatting and the other's cooing.

'Jason, Jason, come up, please, I need you.' An unaccountable wave of desperation has hit me. I am fighting for control, breathing slowly and carefully against a tide of abandonment that threatens to overwhelm me. After five minutes or so, Jason arrives peeping his head through the door and asking cheerfully, 'Do you want some soya sauce on your pasta?' But it is too late. An opportunity for part of me to come back has gone. I look at him dispassionately and nod. And later, the friend who has come to meet the new baby sits by me and will not stop talking to let me speak. I want to release myself from the intensity of the birth experience. I want someone to listen to me, to give me the chance to get some words out. To express myself. But I don't know how to get even a word in edgeways, and I am glad when she leaves.

Was that night the first night I had the dream? That dream that is to haunt me from then on.

> *I am standing at the top of the long staircase leading up to my front door which is behind me. I am watching this awful ugly twisted creature, a kind of female elephant man, grossly distorted with weird protuberances, a dreadful hunchback, only worse, wearing huge coverings of sackcloth wrapped around their body like some hideous mummy in an attempt to hide their dreadful deformities. The creature is painstakingly climbing the stairs towards where I am standing at the entrance to my front door. The sight of the creature fills me with such shame and disgust and horror.*

But I wake to the beauties of our Welsh retreat, the sound of the birds so fulsome and alive in their song, the need to jump over the wooden fence into the neighbouring field to reset the pump which brought us our water, or the getting out of the twin tub to go through the ritual of clothes washing and the hanging them out, pegging out the cloth nappies with the sight of the rolling hills heading towards the nearby town yet out of our sight. The smell of the Welsh air so fresh and sweet. The walks down to the local call box where the pair of red kites circled. All this grounds me and brings me great joy.

And my little boy is perfect and gives me great delight in every way, and so we muddle through. And I do love so much of that time and it is with deep regret I see that my energy is starting to impact on my activist, somehow sapping him of his spontaneous life force. I can't allow that to happen. I'm not good for him. I have to protect him from myself.

And so I leave him. We make a really good job of co-parenting and the demands of being a mother seem like a cloak of protection against the ever-present vastness of Nothingness.

There is a healing interval where I meet and marry Richard, a committed man of means who gives me a stable home and security. I was working as a freelance yoga teacher by then, and this was perfect for me as it enabled me to create in my classes the environment that I could thrive in, and happily my pupils too, judging by the healthy attendance of my classes. It is shortly after our marriage, and Richard has taken me to a retreat where other young people with inherited wealth meet to share their feelings and to find practical ways to structure giving away a proportion of their money to deserving causes. I am overwhelmed when we first arrive; all these people with money, however friendly, it's not something I have come across. I have always had to be so careful with money, like most of my friends too. Finding myself quite emotional, I go and walk in the beautiful grounds of the retreat centre, to be in nature and to calm myself. On the way back, walking up an avenue of elms, enjoying the sun shafting through the intense green of the newly forming leaves, I stop and sit down in a wooded thicket, my back against a great gnarly oak. Just then, one of the participants finds me. He is a cheery, handsome fellow and I immediately put on the bright sparkly front as I greet him. Then I see Richard coming to find me, he must have seen the back of the other man as he continued on his way. Oblivious to the beauty of the surroundings, he is angry.

'Where have you been? As I supposed, off flirting with someone!' he says this dramatically flinging his arms in the air.

The calmness of my demeanour seems to belie the words as I say, 'I was quite overwhelmed, I needed to calm myself... I went for a walk... that guy just passed by...' I see by his face that he does not believe me. He sees only the sparkle, not the vulnerability. I am at a loss at what to do.

'Hi Ricky, so nice to see you, aren't you going to introduce us?' A young couple, looking dashing and rich in a relaxed, laid back way, approach us and then it is all smiles and handshakes and the moment is gone.

Nevertheless, free from money worries, I am able to embark on a two-year course of intensive energy healing training in France, which Richard initially supports. In the midst of this, our beautiful daughter is born. Later, I work with another renowned healer for many years who I trust for his impeccability.

I set up a little practice in our lovely home and begin to have success as my spiritual gifts flourish and blossom.

Placing my hands on clients, 'seeing' things about their lives present and past, taking away their pain. Although to be frank, it freaks me out rather a lot. I don't want anybody's adulation or awe. It also is impacting on my marriage to Richard, as my husband found it disturbing seeing my gifts, although for different reasons. He judges himself lacking because they were not the gifts he has. I hate to see that. So, I back off from this work and contented myself with teaching my yoga classes. And if I find myself unerringly going to the pupil who, for whatever reason needs a bit of extra care that day, and they later confide to me that their father has just died, or their man has just left them, or they have discovered they were pregnant again and not sure if they could cope, whatever the human dilemma that needs some support, well, it only serves to keep the classes full. Life goes on and I do not have to be a 'freak' as I see it. That horrible nightmare of the disfigured bandaged woman coming up the stairs towards me epitomises this need I have not to stand out. From time to time, I wake realising I've had that same nightmare, and was I imagining it or was that hideous deformed creature approaching nearer to me with each dream?

I am sad though to see Ricky beginning to measure himself against me. He is a counsellor of the kind that sees people week after week, helping them face up to whatever they need to do. My way of working is completely different. I go for the incision of the surgeon's knife and after one session, my clients do not need to come back. In vain I attempt to reassure him.

'But Ricky, they wouldn't be able to come to me if it weren't for counsellors like you preparing them so patiently over weeks and months. You know I don't have that kind of patience, I couldn't do what you do.' The sun is shining into our beautiful sitting room, which gives out onto a gorgeous garden dominated by a huge spreading pear tree that my young son loves to climb.

But I can tell he is not assuaged. We find each other at a loss to help each other. Ricky thinking me to be so full of confidence, and me unable to show the vulnerability that might save our marriage. As the security he has provided enables me to do the training that brings me to find my power, that self-same power seems to be the thing that diminishes Ricky and creates a gulf between us. I can't bear it. I feel quite defeated, to me it is as if my aliveness kills, just as my actual birth very nearly killed my mother. I don't want to see him suffer. I have a choice, dampen down my spiritual gifts or leave. As it happens, I end up doing both. Our marriage does not last. Nevertheless, with quite a lot of careful work to smooth out the initial storms, our commitment to a calm and consistent co-parenting does. I may not be very good at relationships but I am a dab hand at co-parenting and I am proud of that.

And the Great Void continues to sit there forever on my shoulder. Once, it is some years later, during a time of indecision and stress, I am sitting chatting with a group of friends at a table in a café, when I feel the fissure begin to open up before me. I go and stand in the entrance of the café, fighting to keep the door frame from dissolving into the Great Nothingness of that all-encompassing Non-Existence.

With a tremendous effort, I force my eyes to focus on the glass of the door, to focus on the details of the reflection there that is me. What do I see? An unlined face, pleasingly defined cheek bones, a slightly pointy chin, a kind of cute wee mouth. But that expression so serious, eyes so intensely solemn. I continue to fight against the pull of the Void. Forcing myself to concentrate on my reflection – what else? A bundle of light brown curls framing what they tell me is a heart-shaped face.

I force myself to feel my feet on the Earth. Is this why I have become a yoga teacher, to help me to stay grounded? *Keep the focus on your physical body*, I tell myself. I scan that body, forcing myself to see that reflection. Small boned, even delicate, nevertheless a curvy hourglass shape. And fit, a great posture, great poise, like a dancer. But hiding it with the clothes I am wearing, a loose, grey polo cashmere pulled over a close-fitting t-shirt and joggers, also grey albeit lighter in tone. Yoga teacher clothes, designed to be able to enter a room and within minutes be ready to teach, and after class pull on those same clothes to get to the next class. I close my eyes and when I open them again, there is my lover, wondering what is happening to me, catching hold of my arm, all solicitude, and I manage somehow to pull myself back to his presence with a tremendous effort and at a loss to communicate what had just happened to me.

And if I had been able to do so, I know he would have been freaked out, frightened. Why would I inflict that on him? I am fond of him.

And so once again, I move on.

And this is how Bembe eventually comes into my life.

Chapter 2

Romancing In Cuba

We meet in Cuba. The year is 1999. Bembe is a native Cuban whose father has a *finca* in the hills above Baracoa. Bembe, strong and resilient, with a penchant for hard work and getting by. Myself, self-reliant, honed and full of energy and curiosity, drawn to Baracoa for the beauty and peace of the natural world. I have been working hard on an internet start-up, a burgeoning web design business, as is all the rage in the 90s. We have gathered a small team and worked all hours and I have managed to make time for a much-needed holiday. Nina, our wonderful girl Friday, who is well clued up in the nascent internet searching, had found me a *casa particular* with my host in Baracoa and arranged for me to be met at the airport there.

It is a small airport and Bembe is waiting for a customer in his Bici-Taxi while my hosts, Ikira and her husband, are looking out for me.

Unbeknownst to me, he notices me the moment I disembark from the plane. He tells me later he is immediately struck by me, and thinks, *'Que delicado, que artista, que fino, que sensilla.'*

I don't notice Bembe but I do feel an immediate connection to this land. It grips me viscerally. The warmth, the smell of the sea below and the blueness of the sky. The line of the cliff top near the airport high up on a hill, looking down onto that clear blue ocean, seems somehow familiar and I feel tears of a strange recognition come to me. But there are my hosts waving to me excitedly. They have one Bici-Taxi and one bike and let me choose my mode of transport. They encourage me to ride the bike down the steep hill into the town, which I take great delight in doing. I feel so free.

Bembe sees all this, he tells me later, and he is really taken by my spontaneity and childlike joy in the simple pleasure of whizzing down a hill in the warm sunshine of a foreign land.

Ikira has one other guest at her *casa particular*. A long-term guest, Sudah, who it turns out spends six months of every year here. He is a slim-built man in his early 50s, a medical anthropologist, hailing from India, although mainly living the other half of his year in New Zealand. Each visit, he brings a huge case of medication with him and sets up an informal pharmacy from his room which gives out onto the street. His other side-line is photography, and he is kept especially busy photographing girls on their 15th birthday. The *Quince Años* is celebrated in Cuba, as it is in other parts of Latin America, to mark the teenagers coming of age. As a consequence of both these facts, his room is bustling from morn to night with an assortment of folks from giggling girls looking at their printed photos to those trying on the trinkets and scarves and make up they have brought, having big confabs with one another about what would look best in their upcoming photoshoot. All contrasting poignantly with the old men and women knocking on his door, hoping for a pill to bring some relief from the pains of living beyond vigorous youth.

Having myself studied some social anthropology at university, Sudah and I hit it off and are soon off on a deep discussion about Turner and liminality. From this, Sudah invites me to a dinner he is giving that night prior to his departure in a few days. As far as I could work out, he had this arrangement whereby he provided the food to a local woman who had room to host and she cooked and served his guests at her dining table. There were not any restaurants as such in Baracoa, only a desultory state-controlled café which always seemed to be out of everything. The meal is fun and friendly and there I am introduced to Mario, who is the local star. A glorious young gay man and singer whose dream is to join his boyfriend in Paris. Until such times, he is a big fish in that pond of Baracoa and rightly celebrated. He and I hit it off and he invites me to come up with him to the hotel later that evening to listen to him perform his cabaret act. We leave the dinner shortly before 10 pm and Mario says we will go to pick up a ride in a Bici-Taxi at his friend's house. Hence, barely 8 hours after Bembe first claps eyes on me, he is astonished to open his door to Mario and find me standing there!

Picture that journey in the dark and warmth of the subtropical night, sitting beside Mario with Bembe cycling us up the steep hill, hardly breaking a sweat. His muscles honed by years of agricultural labour and now the physical job of running a Bici-Taxi.

Forgive a girl from the cold and grey of the UK if she begins to be drawn in by this man.

After the show, which was wonderful, Mario shoos me away, he needs to wind down with his fellow performers. I am to wait with Bembe until our diva is ready to come home.

Bembe is waiting outside the hotel with a little group of youngsters who have gathered at the entrance of the hotel. When I arrive, they begin to share their dreams of having an opportunity to travel to foreign countries. I know how rare that is, but we talk of excelling in dance as one possible route and they take turns in showing me their moves. It's fun and then one of the lads takes off the simple wooden necklace he has around his neck and presents it to me. 'This is for you so you remember us and your time here in Baracoa.' I am very touched.

I feel comfortable with Bembe. He has a quiet strength and a gentleness about him that makes me feel safe.

The story from there? You have heard of a whirlwind romance – well, speed that up a little and you are getting close. The next few days are an extraordinary collage of sightseeing with Sudah and Castro the local guide, visiting the glorious lushness of the nearby coastal gardens. Bembe taking me to the beach, his hard stare, worthy of Paddington, keeping all other comers at bay. The extraordinary beauty and warmth of that glorious beach with the mountains in the distance and Bembe, in his element, running along the sand, encouraging me to go splash in the warm sea. Dancing in the *Casa de Trova* where Mario is performing. Climbing up a steep hill to pay respects at the statue of Hatuey, an indigenous

Taino Indian, a freedom fighter who fought to resist the Spanish conquest and was killed in 1512. Bembe, although strong as an ox, is not a climber. Having arrived first at the top, I turn and reach down to pull him up. As he takes my hand, I am given a flash of this being what our connection is about. I am quite literally going to be giving him 'a hand up'.

And all the while, we are navigating the rules of Baracoa at that time, which come down hard on any local getting involved with a tourist. There are monitors on every street corner, apparently, which of course I am oblivious to. But Ikira is terrified she will have her license revoked. She asks me not to bring Bembe inside her house and has me pretending to be going with Sudah, to the point of having to go onto the street and elaborately say goodbye to each other every time I go out. Learning about Bembe's ex Anna and catching sight of her with their little boy, still a babe in arms. Bembe wanting to take me into the hills of Baracoa to meet his father, him walking with me to the edge of town away from prying eyes in order to pick up a motorbike ride from his friend, Adonis, who is like a lot of the young men round here, strong and fit from the physical life they lead. Riding pillion up into the hills, wedged tightly between this handsome Adonis in front and Bembe, sitting close behind me. I feel I may have died and gone to heaven, sandwiched between these two splendid Cuban men, as we drive along the spectacular coastline where palm trees offer shade to those who seem to live on the beaches in basic round huts with woven grass roofs. The soft sand offers an easy run into the waters made azure by the blue of the sky, but we are not swimming today. Turning in sharp right, we double back on ourselves, a parallel road leading to a few houses right in front of the sea. And there we find the fisherman ready and waiting, a huge fish handed over, money deftly changing hands. The fish is quickly hidden in a sack brought for this purpose. Cubans have to be on it and organised, as it is illegal for locals to catch fish at this time without declaring it, and it is even more of a no-no for other locals to buy it from them. The fish safely stashed, we are back off again, retracing our path, this time to pick up the mountain road a couple of miles outside of Baracoa, which will take us up to Bembe's dad. As we putt-putt up the hill towards Bembe's father's *finca*, we pass farmers at the plough pulled by oxen, and young boys trotting by, riding bare-saddled on their nags.

Sitting under a tree on his dad's land, my back leaning against the gnarled trunk, I am sensing into the energy of the place, the pace of life slower and connected to the cycles of the Earth. His father is apologising for the simple life he lives. 'I am sorry things are not better for you.'

'Please do not apologise,' I say, 'you have something quite priceless here. Here, you have peace.' And in that moment, we are firm friends. Using his machete, which always hangs by his side, he slices open a coconut and hands it to me to drink, and it feels like a sacrament. An honouring of the Earth where I sit. Rosa, Bembe's step mum, cooks the fish, and later is mortified when I need to go to the loo – an affair of stacked up tyres you need to climb to sit atop. After we eat, we drink freshly brewed coffee grown on their own estate. Though not normally a coffee drinker, I participate, as it feels like a ritual further connecting me to them and the Land. This Land I have fallen in love with.

In the cool of the evening with the cicadas chirruping, when Bembe goes to tether and feed the nag they keep nearby, Bembe's dad uses this opportunity to take me aside to explain to me that he had not brought Bembe up, as when he was only four his wife had tragically died and he had not been able to manage all his four children, so he had sent Bembe to live with his sister and her husband. It was them who had then raised him. The uncle had been a hard man. He hadn't long been released from prison, where he had been for many, many years before adopting Bembe. He had been on the wrong side of the revolution and had been imprisoned for nearly 30 years for his part in supporting the Batista regime. He had imposed a tough upbringing on Bembe, who had been more of a servant than a son. I could tell it preyed on the man, and he was worried Bembe had been scarred by his upbringing.

'Is your late wife buried nearby?' I ask, thinking I would like to visit the grave with Bembe. But Bembe's father looks a little startled and tells me no, sadly, they do not know where the grave is.

I think this a little strange, but just then Bembe appears carrying a beautiful tropical flower he has picked and he presents it to me with a flourish and I pin it to my hair, and then we must get back to town. In a flurry of goodbyes, we are off.

I really want to get a ride in that horse and cart full of locals that is up ahead, on its way into Baracoa, as we arrive back at the main road. But tourists are not permitted to use them. Instead, Adonis and Bembe have to risk being caught with a *gringo* riding pillion as we make our way back to town. The locals coming towards us, away from town, are making elaborate signals, using a code I don't understand. Signals that Bembe and Adonis clearly interpret as indicating there is no need to worry. The way is clear. The locals understand the situation. The paleness of my skin clearly indicates I am a tourist. So happily, there is no need to dump me on the roadside to save themselves being fined!! Trying to find somewhere to be alone together, eventually Bembe organises to pay two gay friends of his, who are already having to hide their preferences as homosexuality is not encouraged at that time in Cuba. They let us have their rooms for a few hours, as finding somewhere to stay and be discreet is impossible in that tiny town. And my favourite, going to *Yumari* a bit outside Baracoa, where there is a mountain of that name. Here a local native jumped off rather than surrender to the Spanish conquest, saying, '*Yumari*,' or 'I die' as he did so. *Yumari* is a lagoon and Bembe jumps into that river and swims over when it is time to get the boat man to take us back. Emerging, like some fabulous sea god from the waters, smooth, beautiful brown skin and muscles enough to sway me his way if I was not already quite smitten.

Bembe comes with me all the way to Havana when it is time to pick up my flight and his sister, Iliana, who lives there, comes to meet us at the airport to say hello. She is married to quite a senior figure in the military, a lot older that her but providing a safe and comfortable lifestyle. I like her. She waits until Bembe has gone off to check the flight times. Then, leaning over the café table, she asks, 'Did he tell you about our mother?'

'Well, yes, that she died when you were little.'

'It's more than that. She killed herself.' Iliana says this looking at me cautiously, worrying how I will react.

'I'm so sorry to hear that, Iliana.'

'Yes, and we don't even know where she is buried. My mum was like me, she loved to read books. She came from Santiago and was quite well educated. Living in the hills around Baracoa, she didn't really fit in. She had different ways. I think there was a lot of gossip and I think she must have felt very alone.'

'It must have been so hard for you all,' I manage.

Iliana leans in to add, 'It's just sometimes Bembe, well, he can be quite... I guess you will be able to cope...'

'Quite what?' I ask as Bembe returns with some soft drinks for us all, and our *tête-à-tête* is at an end.

I want to invite Bembe to come to the UK. He really wants to see something of the world, and if it is in my power, why should I not enable that for him? So somewhere in all the whirl, we also manage to fit in a visit to the *notaria* in an old-fashioned office with an old-fashioned typewriter and blue copy paper and get them to issue a certificate of invitation that Cubans need before they can leave the country. The first of the many official and expensive hurdles we had to jump, the first of many documents that needed to be produced, translated and authenticated. All in all, it takes two more trips back to Cuba; getting married in the second and in the third, an interview with the British ambassador. Although to be honest, at that point, nearly 10 months after our first meeting, I did not know whether to say to him, 'Please let my husband have his visa to come to the UK,' or 'Please help me get out of this.' Bembe, all the while, waiting for me outside in the grounds of the Embassy in Havana.

Some have said that it was that ambivalence in me that did for the relationship. There might be some truth in that. But early on, notwithstanding being shunned by folk I had thought friends, what I bathed in, what sustained me even when transferred to the cold climes of Scotland was Bembe's grounded practicality. His large independent-minded spirit, which as it seemed to me, was unsullied and free from so many of the unquestioned beliefs we carried with us in the West. Such as judging yourself by how much money you have, for one, or by your job. So, a full year later, after tremendous hard work and effort, and those two additional trips to Cuba, I am waiting at the airport in Edinburgh for him to come through customs. He takes a long time but when he finally appears, all grins, he tells me the customs officer told him he never knew another case where someone from Cuba got their visa so quickly.

Wouldn't it be wonderful if that could be the happy ending, but the hard facts I am yet to learn are that the disparity in wealth and access to money and goods cannot help but to create a discrepancy that can lead Cubans to wear a double face. The British ambassador had warned me about this, it is true.

But Bembe is not your typical *jinentero*, being from the hills and growing up as a peasant farmer. A *jinentero*, or *jinen-*

tera, as any guidebook for Cuba will warn you, is a male or female native of Cuba, who will be nice to you in different ways, in order to obtain various outcomes, from a paid evening out, to kudos, to money, all the way to a passport out of the country. They cater for the tourist dreams, raunchy music and dancing, toned muscles and sex. Provided you can pay, it is all on tap.

Before you judge, bear in mind that Cubans at the turn of the 21st century were surviving on a subsistence economy. They were forbidden to earn dollars, and hence the dollar shops where 'luxuries' such as pasta, chicken, and tins of tuna fish were to be found, were out of reach for most ordinary Cubans.

Did that make me a gullible foreigner? I had fallen for Bembe, despite him not being an obvious kind of *jinentero*. For one thing, he couldn't dance. Well, that is not quite true, every Cuban can dance, so it is said. Music – the opium of the people – being delivered from all quarters pretty constantly. If people are grooving, they are not fermenting dissent.

What I mean to say is he didn't dance.

Jinenteros could be extremely slick, could close in on their targets and manoeuvre them round the dance floor, into bed, to the office for visitors permits, the embassy for a visa, Air France for a plane ticket – the whole merry whirl – before the hapless person had a chance to ask, is this a *bachachta* or a *merengue*?

As it turns out, Bembe is something far more dangerous. Being from *El Campo* – the country – he was strong and fit.

He had no need of the gym; those well-defined muscles and to-die-for biceps came from a lifetime of physical labour. 29 years old had found him working his Bici-Taxi in town, mainly among the locals, as you need a license to transport tourists and that took connections and money, which he didn't have.

As I later understood it, *campesinos* were pretty low status, even if they were working their own land. After the revolution, from 1953-59, those farmers like Bembe's dad who had land were allowed to keep it provided it stayed in the family. They grew coffee and cocoa for chocolate and kept pigs and hens, they even had an old horse. They did alright, sort of tropical crofters, they were never going to be rich, but neither were they going to starve.

I suppose because of the connotations of the African slaves who used to work those self-same *fincas* for their Spanish masters, the stigma of agriculture work persisted, and Bembe had a big chip on his shoulder. He told me years later of his burning humiliation when, as a 16-year-old old, he had come down from the hills into town to be mocked by some towns-folk from Baracoa calling him a *guagira* – a peasant. It stung deep.

So, I must have seemed like a prize, an instant status lift. Can we blame him if it subsequently went to his head?

If Bembe was not your stereotypical *jinentero*, neither had I gone to Cuba looking for love, romance or sex. I don't deny there were plenty of women going to Cuba for exactly that, and the exchanges were at times rather in your face and sordid, however much the woman might want to dress them up as romance.

But I was not looking for a lover, indeed that was precisely why I had chosen Baracoa, this out-of-the-way sub-tropical part of Cuba. If I had been after the frisson of romance, I would have stayed in Havana, with my friend Joan, an ethnomusicologist. She was in Havana on world music business and she always got the hot tickets to any musical event. Mind you, she wasn't the best company at that moment, as she was in the midst of an absorbing and torrid love affair with a married Cuban artist.

At any event, I could have stopped off in Santiago de Cuba, where my pal Terry was running one of her Spanish language and Salsa dance holidays. You would be assigned your very own personal one-to-one professional dancer to bring on your salsa dancing, and whatever else might be brought on. No, I kept well away, because I was already aware of the possible scenario, swarms of hopefuls looking for a European to lift them out of the trap they saw their country as.

And it wasn't as if I was short of male attention either. I might have been on the wrong side of 40 back then in 1999, but it was a case of the proverbial moths around the flames. Call it the allure of the yoga teacher, and getting out there on the salsa dance floor, plus inherited genes that seemed not to show the years, I was working it and having a lot of fun. It was so great to feel confident, unlike during my insecure adolescence and 20s. But I needed a break, the peaceful mystic side of me craved nature and I was not on the lookout. Bembe caught me off guard. And I hadn't reckoned for 'the force of nature' that he was.

Oh, it was easy to see what Bembe had to gain from me, a home in a place where he could earn money to send to his ex for the support of his small son. The class system in Cuba placed those who were able to earn in a Western country and send regular remittances home – even if to a Western reckoning, they were very modest amounts – up there with the state-licensed taxi drivers who had access to the tourist dollars. And they were high-class, trust me.

But me, what did I get from it all? The black hole that seems always at my shoulder means faith in life did not come naturally to me, and Bembe's grounded relish in his physicality and non-cerebral approach to life was a relief to be around.

Apart from contending with the Great Abyss, as if that was not enough for a girl, I had been haunted by dark dreams and nightmares since childhood, of cattle trucks and death camps and the whole ghastly scenario of the European heritage of the Holocaust.

I wasn't even Jewish, although I had chosen to specialise in Judaism as part of my religious studies course, and I had grappled with and studied some of the philosophers and mystics and learnt Hebrew, but even before that, I seemed to have imbibed the great schism of our time – our European trauma.

This was graphically illustrated to me once when flying back from a trip to South America. There my mind felt free to expand. But while heading home on the aeroplane I suddenly felt as if I hit this energetic density. I didn't like it, I wanted to go back.

Glancing up at the route map on the screen above me, I saw we had just hit European landmass.

That is the kind of density we are living in every day over in the Old World, without even realising it.

Over in the 'developed' world, we seem more bound by our minds, rationalising the life out of ourselves. But can you understand this? Bembe embodied a faith in life. He never questioned his existence. He wouldn't have known an existential angst if it had hit him. And if it had, he'd probably have skinned it, roasted it and eaten it whole and then shat it out with equal relish before you could say Jean Paul Sartre.

And that is what I used to bathe in, his great faith in the goodness and pleasure of being alive.

Chapter 3

Home In Edinburgh

Fast-forwarding a couple of years finds us at home in my Bruntsfield flat. Bembe's initial lack of English isn't so much of an issue, as it turns out he has an unerring knack of finding Spanish speakers whenever and wherever he needs to. Apart from that, his English improved every day. He had found work in a local sawmill. Every day, he got the bus to the other end of town, where he met up with his boss, who then gave him a lift out to the sawmill, and then the reverse to get home.

This particular morning, it is the weekend and we are having a lazy breakfast. My 10-year-old daughter is staying over at her dad's house this weekend, and Javier, our 17-year-old Spanish lodger, is still blissfully sleeping when the post arrives.

It is a brochure from Celtic Hall, a New Age shamanic retreat centre in the wilds of Scotland, north of Edinburgh, telling us about their upcoming courses.

I'd got on the mailing list by meeting Patrick, who ran the place, at a holistic health fair. Before the Internet blossomed, these were great hubs for showcasing and networking the burgeoning complementary therapies and practices which were in their infancy then. This was back in the early Nought-ies. I used to take a stand at them to promote my *Holistics* website. I was in a self-employed web design partnership with two others and we had dreamt up and created this portal for managing complementary practitioners. Though at that stage, trying to switch them on to the value of a web pres-ence was a losing battle.

It was at one of these that I had met Patrick at his stall from Celtic Hall. I liked the rugged masculine energy of the Celtic shamanism he was promoting, which sat authentically with the working-class Glaswegian he was. I had not been so taken with his high-flying wife, Antonia, a 'reiki master' and would-be High Priestess of Scottish New Agers. I had seen it before with people presenting themselves as spiritual leaders, the glamour of the presentation, but scratch the sur-face and something darker and unintegrated seemed to lurk.

I am definitely wary of this new movement, the so-called *New Age*, especially when people set themselves above oth-ers as gurus. It wasn't a blanket aversion, and it wasn't a cynicism. Like I have explained, I am myself a natural healer and have in the past studied intensively over many years with several gifted and trustworthy spiritual teachers. But as far as I understood it, it was that side of myself that had caused my marriage breakdown and so I kept it all in a tight rein. Working hard not to be a freak. That recurring night-mare of what I call now 'the elephant woman' is never far from my consciousness, and this image has impressed itself indelibly on me, and not standing out has become a bit of a mantra: hence my decision – despite much study into the metaphysical side of life – not to pursue the 'energy healer' role.

But let us return to the Bruntsfield kitchen on that Saturday morning in late August 2004.

Bembe has cooked up some fried plantain and egg, a childhood dish that gives him comfort, and I am sipping Darjeeling tea and nibbling on sourdough toast and marmalade. Glancing through the leaflet, I dismiss the Master Reiki course but my attention is struck by a 5-day Ayahuasca retreat with a Peruvian shaman over from Lima, a Dr Chakaruna.

For some reason, I am drawn to this course and I am really interested to meet the shaman himself. But it is £365, well out of my budget. Since Bembe has arrived, everything is more or less out of my budget. He arrived with pretty much the clothes he stood up in and I needed to buy him cold-weather clothing for his arrival. Initially, he was always cold and he would put on more clothes to sleep in than he wore in the day, including thick, long wool mountaineer's socks. Bembe was so shocked at all the waste and excess he saw around, and perhaps it was this that gave him the idea that there was an endless supply of money over here in the West – that money truly did grow on trees. He certainly seemed to think my own supplies were endless. And compared to what they had to manage on in Cuba, I did feel I couldn't say no to some of his requests. For instance, when that essential fridge of his sister's packed up, how could I not help out? Or when his lovely dad, who I knew would be mortified to be toothless, needed money for a set of false teeth – not available for free, even in Cuba's generous healthcare services; again, how could I not oblige?

So, I put the leaflet aside and get on with my day, heading down the allotment to pick beans and harvest some potatoes. Bembe shuns my allotment. The fear of becoming the *esclavo negro*, as he puts it, he prefers to take himself off to Portobello to browse in a super-size tool shop. This is his favourite haunt, as in Cuba, tools are prized and hard to come by. Every piece of equipment is carefully studied and appraised for its possible usefulness back home. Over the years we are together in our on-and-off fashion, he takes suitcases full of *equipo* back to Cuba, most of which he sells off in order to keep himself and his family in the high style expected of those who work and live abroad.

However, the following week, on an evening I'm not teaching a yoga or Pilates class, the phone rings. This is in the days when mobiles are not ubiquitous and people are still using each other's landlines. Bembe has cooked up a typical Cuban dish of *frijoles con arroz* – black beans with rice – and I am wondering how come such foreign smells have pervaded my world. I am lying in some relaxation pose on the futon, trying to ease the pain that seems constant in my back. The pain of having taken on more than I can handle, as it turns out.

It is Patrick from Celtic Hall.

'Freya? Listen, I need a favour. We're hosting a Peruvian Shaman here next month.'

'Chakaruna? Yeah, I read about that in your leaflet a few days ago.'

'Problem is, he doesn't speak one word of English, we need an interpreter, can you do it?'

'Woah, slow down,' I am thinking, my mind is racing. My friend Anke studied to be one of them at university and it had been a slog involving several years of study.

'What would you need me to do?' I nevertheless find myself asking.

'Well, there'll be 24 participants for both the two ceremonies, and they'll all need a one-to-one interview prior to the first ceremony, plus a follow-up one afterwards, all of which you'd need to translate for. That includes during the two ceremonies themselves plus there'll be an introductory group explanation and a round-up Q&A at the end.'

I run through my mind my level of Spanish. I have been studying for maybe five or six years. I'd achieved A* in the night class exams I'd studied for. The few years Bembe had been in my life had accelerated my fluency and I could have an argument and get my point across with the best of them, and also, more importantly, I knew the terrain. The world of the healer, which explores and sees into the places where invisible currents can give rise to problems seemingly unrelated to any presenting issue. So, hey, what the heck, why not give it a shot? Thus, the deal is struck. I am to arrive on the evening the day before the main event to meet Karu and translate between him and Patrick while they put in place the last-minute details for the five-day workshop. Then basically I have to be with Karu whenever he is working: to translate both ways for him and the participants. In exchange, I would go to the workshop for free.

If I had known what hard work it was to be and that the final tally of participants would rise to 36, not the stated 24, then I might have driven a harder bargain. But I am too pleased that a way has opened up for me to meet Karu and for me to be able to attend the course that I do not quibble. All of which, no doubt, Patrick has bargained for.

In due course, I make the necessary co-parenting arrangements for my daughter to be with her dad for extra days. Bembe is not too happy for me to go, his English is still very rudimentary, he relies on me for so much. But he and Javier will have each other. Javier, it has transpired, is an excellent cook, and for my part, I am glad of a break from the responsibilities that seem to have landed heavily on me since Bembe's arrival.

Chapter 4

Driving North

Thus it is, on a bright late summer morning a few weeks later, I find myself driving north from Edinburgh, through increasingly uninhabited land, past cute villages and forest cabins perched strategically to overlook a scenic lake.

I am still worrying about how they will manage back home. My daughter, staying over with her dad and stepmum, will be fine. But I have not left Bembe to fend for himself before. Javier will be company for him, it is true, but he is also a liability. He has only been with us a few months so far. A 17-year-old Spaniard with an attitude. 'Cool on sticks,' as one of his teachers dubbed him on first sight. His mother had thought it wise to remove him from Madrid for a while since Javier's attempts to become a dealer had ended badly and he was being chased by some unsavoury characters back in his native Spain for not having the readies ready at the right moment. All this he had freely volunteered to me on the drive back from the airport when he first arrived in the UK, and I'll admit it, I had warmed to him and wanted to make sure he would be okay.

I have a job getting him to school on time, although generally he refrains from smoking his weed when I am around. I have to hand it to him, though, he is very resourceful and I am not sure how he even manages to get hold of the stuff, given that his mother has given his allowance into my hands to distribute weekly. This is before internet banking, folks, so that was an effective strategy back then. Well, they will just have to manage.

I had set off just after seven in the evening, and now, having left Edinburgh far behind, I am enjoying the long evening, the sky a beautiful clear blue.

As I approach Dunknockie, a little village, on the main road I pass the wee guest house where I had once stayed the night. It was after I had dropped off my son to meet up with Richard, his stepdad. They had a camping and cycling trip planned over the next few days, along the pathways adjoining the town which were designed just for that purpose. Myself, I had then set off to have my own adventure, but that story does not belong here.

I pull my attention back to the road. I need to concentrate. I realise I have shot past my exit. I stop the car, carefully re-reading my instructions (guys, this was before sat nav), turning off one byway into another even more remote until eventually arriving, long after I'd planned – it is by now after 10 pm – at Celtic Hall.

Celtic Hall is one of those big, grey granite, dour-looking edifices, no doubt built for some industrialist or wealthy farmer enjoying playing squire. If I have had any doubt I am in the right place, the signs are unmistakable; a large tipi is parked on the lawn and a couple of yurts can be spotted secreted in discreet corners of the grounds still visible in the long summer evening light we enjoy in Scotland.

Guided by the lights that are still on in the building, I find Patrick. The place is really quiet. He greets me, clearly relieved I have finally shown up and, it seems, somewhat desperate to head off to bed. He calls on an extension.

'Carole? Freya just arrived.

'Carole's the assistant manager, ' Patrick explains, 'she'll look after you, we need you at 8:15 am tomorrow morning. Come to our flat. Karu's already turned in. Antonia, my wife, she's resting. Baby born, a few days ago.'

Goodness, no wonder Patrick looks so shattered.

'The interviews'll begin at 9:30 tomorrow for folk already here, mainly helpers and co-leaders.' He's already moving towards the door, longing to put head to pillow. 'And actually, there are 36 people on the course now.' Patrick throws this remark over his shoulder before disappearing as Carole enters the room to take charge.

She has a caring yet matter-of-fact energy and a face that shows life has been tough at times for her. She is probably still in her forties but looks older. She has a sturdy build and wears jeans and a checked shirt open over a white T-shirt. Her hair is dyed blonde, thick and brushed back in a bushy way, out of the way yet lively. I like her straight away, and make a shrewd guess that without her, the whole shebang would collapse into chaos. She leads me back into the main building to all the dorms.

'The main body of participants are not arriving until the morning,' she reiterates to me, 'so, you can have your pick of the rooms. It's 3- or 4-bed dorms.'

'Oh, no single room I can bag?' I ask hopefully, but it seems not even for the interpreter can this be managed, so I choose a 3-bed dorm which has a bed tucked away in a corner, with the hope it would let me sleep the hours when I am not working.

Chapter 5

Settling In

I wake early, as is my wont, and find my way to the shower block. The place is cold, the heating is only just beginning to come on – it must be set for 7 am.

I dress warmly, knowing from experience how chilly these big granite houses can be even in a Scottish summer. I may not look stylish in my thick tracksuit bottoms and long woolly cardigan and big scarf but I am not going to suffer from cold. I find my way to the main dining room in search of some hot tea. It is a large dining room with rows of wooden refectory tables and long benches like something out of *Jane Eyre*. The breakfast things have all been laid out ahead. Carole comes into the room just then from what must be the kitchen entrance. Brisk and competent, holding a clipboard with her to-do list, she is clearly glad to see I am up and about – one less worry for her.

'Good morning, Freya,' she smiles, coming over to where I am fumbling with the hot water urn. She shows me how to use it. I am relieved to see that hot water will be endlessly on tap. Eschewing the herbal offerings of the house and glad of my supply of Darjeeling tea bags, I fill my flask for later – an essential secured for the day to come.

'Patrick and Karu would like you to go over at 8:15 am for a planning meeting. You'll have time for a relaxed breakfast.' Her hands sweep over the fruits and cereals laid out.

'I'll come back later to take you over to where they're staying.' And with that, she is gone.

Brilliant. It is to be the last meal I am able to enjoy unstressed for a while. I am glad there is no one else there and I can take a moment to get my bearings. Enjoying some peeled fruit, I put some muesli in a bowl and slosh boiling water over it. Letting it steep while I make some more tea – this to drink now – I settle myself at one of the long refectory tables, adding copious honey. I enjoy the warm mush, and sipping down the tea, I feel good and ready for what is to come.

True to her word and with an uncanny knack of perfect timing, Carole arrives back and leads me out of the main building across a yard and up some steps to an adjacent and recently refurbished barn. This is home to Patrick and his wife Antonia. Antonia is out of the scene in some back bedroom, tending to her newborn.

I find the two men just finishing breakfast sitting at a table in a pleasant sun-filled room, with a lovely outlook to trees. An open window lets in the sound of bird song. Carole introduces us and quickly leaves, no doubt to see to the mountain of other things that are in her province.

Patrick looks more rested, and he greets me warmly, offering me a seat at their table. I have a chance to observe him more closely. A wiry West Coast Scot with a mop of black curly hair and a restless energy. He has that slightly insecure look I have seen before among working-class Scottish men that have crossed the class divide. In Patrick's case, it is his spiritual gifts that have enabled him to make this transition, and he isn't about to mess it up. I can tell he is conscientious and wanting to make sure everything goes smoothly. And that suits me very well.

Karu is standing up from the table, smiling and taking both my hands in his. As we go through the pleasantries of *'encandado'*, *'encantada'*, our hands pumping up and down both wreathed in smiles, I notice he is a small, neatly built man, his thick hair well cut and only just beginning to turn grey. He looks like what it turns out he actually is, a professional psychotherapist. He does not come over to me as weird or scary in the least, in fact, he seems an absolute pet – and I know we will get along just fine. Karu is clearly very relieved to see me and super keen to get going. The frustration of not being able to communicate with Patrick is spilling over, and he is bursting with eagerness with all the things he needs to say. He launches into a complicated description of different possible infusions which could cater for various health conditions, for instance, for someone with high blood pressure problems.

I begin to translate this back to Patrick.

Patrick waves his hand. 'Please tell him he doesn't have to worry, everyone here has filled in a health form and are cleared for drinking the normal brew.'

Karu relaxes on hearing this.

Karu then begins a careful description of the three distinct ways of preparing the plant medicine: boiling and adding alcohol or not. But as Karu has already arrived with his brew pre-prepared, Patrick waves this aside.

'Thank you so much for taking this on, Freya,' Patrick launches in – a man with no time to spare, and plenty to communicate.

'Karu has no English and I have no Spanish. Let me explain the programme. Participants will begin to arrive this morning and some people are already here, so you will begin the interviews at 9:30 am. Everyone is to have a one-to-one interview of half an hour. This morning, it will be all folk who have done Ayahuasca before. They have arrived early and some of them are helping with the retreat. You will meet them all later. You'll keep this up all day with a short break for lunch at 1 pm.

'At 4:30 pm – by this time everyone'll have arrived – we'll be gathering the whole group for a one-hour group circle where we'll run over the programme and Karu'll go over what to expect, most especially for those new to Ayahuasca.'

Naturally, I am needed at this too.

'Also,' Patrick continues, 'we'll be doing cleansing rituals in the two days leading up to the first ceremony, which'll help prepare people for the first medicine ceremony on the evening of day three.'

Karu nods in a professional manner as I relay all this back to him. I sense his huge level of expertise and detailed knowledge of the administration and healing power of this and other plant medicines from his native homeland. I later discover the apprenticeship for a shaman specialising in Ayahuasca involves many years of training and deep immersion in the jungle with an already skilled mentor, to imbibe and, in time, embody what the plants sacred to his tradition are about – their medicine.

Right now, we have to get down to the nuts and bolts of schedules and timings. Gradually, the programme over the next five days becomes clear. Patrick, with his co-leader Daan, who we are about to meet, will work with the main group preparing a fire walk, a 'breaking the arrow' ritual, and also the setting up and conducting of the sweat lodges. Meanwhile, Karu and I will, in tandem, work our way through the 36 participants, helping them discover and set their personal intention for the two ceremonies, which will take place through the night on both the third and fourth day.

As well as each person's allotted half an hour before the ceremony, additional time will be set aside for anyone needing help post-ceremony with any issues that aren't resolved during the ceremony. Participants will also have a chance to book a special private session with Karu at any point if they need additional input.

We also cover the *dieta* as there are strict protocols of foods that need to be avoided, most significantly sugar and salt. Honey is okay, as well as fruits. I'm not planning on imbibing the Ayahuasca, but nevertheless, I am glad honey is not off-limits.

Patrick confirms we will start the interviews this morning with the people who have drunk Ayahuasca before. Two of these apparently feel they have enough Spanish to not need a translator. I am delighted I may be able to slip away for a break from what was sounding like a pretty relentless schedule.

These basics covered, Carole again mysteriously reappears and takes Karu and me to a large room, where the interviews are to be conducted. It looks like a school hall – the windows are high up and I am again glad of my big mohair cardigan. I sit at a small table on Karu's left, and we place a chair opposite us for the participants to sit. I rearrange the table in such a way that the sun shines on my right hip, which is starting to ache. My big scarf I now wrap around my middle. I'd managed to pick up some fresh tea on the way past the canteen and with a quick check that my stash of crackers is easy to reach, I'm all set. The first person arrives.

This is Daan, with rolled-up dungarees and welly boots and a fluid way about him. He is one of the co-leaders who will be preparing and running one of the sweat lodges.

The first morning isn't too bad. I even manage some free time to settle into my room. One of the helpers, a woman who I like named Morag, and another person, both speak enough Spanish to conduct their own interviews.

The main body of people have started to arrive by now and it is while I am in my room, organising my things, that I encounter one of my fellow roommates also settling in – a young woman. She is wearing earphones and comes over to me in a pushy kind of way.

Oh dear, do I have to be in the same room as her?

'I'm awake all hours,' she is saying, trying to give me something. I look down at her hands – it's earplugs and an eye mask.

'And I need the light as I potter about a lot, so these'll prevent me bothering you,' all this said brazen-faced.

No way, baby. I already knew the job ahead would take all the energy I could muster without having to deal with this whippersnapper.

'Is that right?' I counter. 'Well, I'm in this room,' my voice is dangerously soft. 'And it's already a designated lights-out sleeping room, so your translator can be fresh in the morning, so you can keep these,' I flick my hand at her plugs and mask, 'and go find another room where they don't mind your... idiosyncrasies.'

She is taken aback that I am not acquiescing. She begins to protest, but on a short reflection and seeing my implacability that trumps her thick skin, she backs off and, gathering her things, leaves the room. If she is a sample of the new-age seekers, I am not going to get on with them too well. Oh well, too tired to think about it now, just time for a quick nap before the main group introduction.

'Freya, Freya, wake up!' It is Carole who is shaking me from a deep sleep.

'It's nearly 4:30 pm, time for the main group.' I rush after her downstairs to the big hall, trying to gather my wits as I go. By now, everyone has arrived, and there they are all sitting in a circle on the floor on big scatter cushions waiting expectantly. I notice Karu and, sitting up by Patrick, there is Daan with a cluster of devotees around him. Karu waves at me to come and join him. As I walk hesitantly towards him, I am mentally calculating. 36 people, I think, 6 already done, leaving 30 people at half an hour each, equals 15 hours over the next 2 days, equals a nine-hour day, and that is before breaks. Really? Am I going to be up for this? My back aches, I am prone to migraines, and I have such a delicate stomach that I practically have the diet of a toddler. Still, one thing I do not lack is determination and grit, probably what got me into this physical mess in the first place. Where is my flask of tea? The thought is no sooner there than that wondrous Carole is at my side, handing me a mug of warm green tea.

'Thank you so much, how do you...?'

But no time to dally, Patrick is kicking off the welcome and introductions and I am back to work.

It is not too bad as Karu is already *au fait* with the schedule and only needs the odd prompt from me to know what is being said. It will be his turn to speak at the end after first Patrick and then Daan have finished running through the ins and outs of the schedule. So, I have a chance to look around at the motley crew. They are all ages: one young girl has a pretty, open face, hungry to drink in whatever life can offer her; there's an older, tense man with pianist fingers, who I later discover is a composer, and then a guy in his early forties who looks like he is already wired to the stars. I make a mental note to give him a wide berth. Some of the people look quite far out and hippy, others look like executives and business types. It is fascinating to see everyone, all of us pitching in together over these next five days.

I am brought into the present as I hear Patrick hit the group with the news that on day three, everyone will have to drink a litre of heavily salted water to purge before the main event. I can't help taking some pleasure at the look of alarm and distaste on the earphone girl's face.

After everyone starts to disperse, a shy, rather sweet-faced woman appears at my side. She has detached herself from Daan's devotee coterie.

'Hi, I'm Betty, you haven't been to Celtic Hall before, then? I've not seen you before.' She speaks with a Scottish accent – Glaswegian to be precise.

'There's a group of us here, we go to Daan's sweat lodges near Glasgow. He runs them four times a year, you know, at Beltane and that?'

For those of you not familiar with Celtic mysticism, there are four quarter day festivals celebrated in times of old: *Imbolc*, the turning of the cold Earth to spring, *Beltane*, the time of planting, *Lammas*, the time of harvest, and finally *Samhain*, the turning inwards towards the winter. So, a wonderful fusion of native American ways, Peruvian jungle medicine, and ancient Celtic paganism was going to be going on over these next days.

Betty's clear blue eyes are looking at me with an appealing simplicity,

'Daan takes a group of us out to Peru every year, for a spiritual journey of a lifetime,' her gaze looks warmly over to the limber of limb man. 'Some people go every year,' she adds, without irony.

Still, I warm to her as I go off to find Karu as we're due to fit in a couple more interviews before dinner.

When I make it to bed, I fall quickly asleep and don't even hear the person who takes the vacated bed later that evening. She must have crept in like a mouse. My reputation must be getting around – good.

Chapter 6

Working With Karu

It was clearly explained in the literature sent out to participants before arriving at the workshop how important it is to set an intention before the Ayahuasca ceremonies. By doing so, the participants will get the best outcome from the retreat. This was again impressed on everyone during that first group gathering on day one. Karu's and my job during these 30-minute interviews is firstly for Karu to connect psychically with each participant and know their intention so he can be there for them should help be needed during the Ayahuasca journey, but before that, we need to make sure each participant has clarified and set their intention for the first ceremony. Some need help in discovering what is bubbling up for them that needs attention.

Karu and I very quickly establish a rhythm of working together. It is surprising how easy it is. Each person in turn arrives and settles themselves opposite us. Karu asks them what their intention is for the ceremony.

So, one by one they come, and I translate back and forth between them and Karu, English to Spanish, Spanish to English like a three-sided ping-pong game. Karu begins by asking the person 'please tell me', but I notice by the afternoon of that first day, he has changed that to 'please tell *us*'. It is true that my sensibilities and training from the past mean I can sense the unspoken, and I seem to know which way Karu's answers and questions are going almost before he speaks. To be honest, I can also usually tell before the person answers what they are going to say. Even though I have put my healing gifts into the closet, so to speak, they are still there it seems. While listening to the way Karu explains things and comments on each individual dilemma, I am intrigued to discover how similar the teachings from the Amazon are to the teachings of one of my most gifted spiritual teachers, Mike Robinson. Although each person coming in front of us has a different issue, as Karu imparts his advice and counselling, the conceptual framework under which he is operating begins to emerge more clearly.

The first thing that is similar is the need to express emotions. Emotions are the key to uncovering what is actually going on with you. How different from a Western stance and especially a British stance of suppression of the emotions – control and ignore. No, this approach believes that by healing yourself on an emotional level, you are in that moment also healing yourself on every other level, right through from the body all the way to the soul. Karu has a diagram he draws to illustrate this point. It shows the essence of a person like a kernel but wrapped around with anger or disappointment or bitterness or regret, making it impossible for the essential you to shine forth. My earlier teacher, Mike, had a saying, 'You have the right to be Yourself.' You can throw off the encumbrance of what has been put on you by actively feeling the emotions this encumbrance is eliciting in you. It is like they are the clue to get you to the kernel, the essence of you. Karu explained that the Ayahuasca reaches into the depths of yourself and everything that is not you has to come out. This is why there is often a lot of retching and purging during the ceremonies.

One of the things that is most interesting to me is the grounded, indeed sensual way he has of dealing with issues. A way rather far from the dualistic way we have in the West of dealing with spiritual matters. With Karu, there is no split, there is no dualism. The body is embraced, as is our need for nurture. His is a way of infinite practicality and kindness. One young girl, whose issue is that she is yearning for a lover, a life partner, is encouraged to practise self-massage and self-pleasure while she waits. I am startled at times with his directness, as he would ask me to confirm to the person in front of us the delight in even the most basic of bodily functions that they might be having an issue with.

One young woman comes to us with a beautiful wolf mandala she has drawn. She is torn between the need to develop her spirituality – which she thinks would mean giving up her children to her ex's care in order to go to join some kind of ashram; or giving up her pursuit of her spirituality in order to attend to her children's needs. The anguish a separation from her children would cause her was clear to see.

Karu is a bit nonplussed that she is creating such a binary division. In his world, men and women, however spiritual, live in the world, albeit they take the time to go into retreat as required, or climb up to the *Apus* at special times of the year. But he is able to use her own animal imagery to explain that the wolf is a pack animal and she, like her wolf protector, needs to be with her tribe, including her children. That it is her job to manage the delicate task of co-parenting that is now upon her.

The Peruvian shamanic world view is very connected to the world of animals. If anyone mentions an animal, perhaps a dream animal, or a power animal they have discovered on a journey, Karu would use this as a clue to uncover the deeper processes at work for them and their journey. He seems to have an encyclopaedic knowledge of animals and their distinct habits and proclivities. By understanding the habits and needs of the animal in the animal world, this provides him with clues to understanding the dilemma the participant might be experiencing in their life. For instance, one man had been very upset by the recent open-plan office he was obliged to work in. He felt very uncomfortable and exposed. He talked about a recurring badger dream, and Karu suggested he bring lots of big plants into his space, which he could hide behind, as this would suit his reclusive badger-need-to-burrow nature more. That he should not judge himself that the new layout was against his fundamental nature, rather he just needed to take steps to mitigate the impact.

While Karu and I are busy with the interviewing, the others are all meeting in groups, going through the various activities on the programme. I catch a glimpse of one of these when I take a quick break between clients to fetch more tea and nip to the loo. It looks quite dangerous, as I stop to look. The man I'd noticed before, the one I thought wired to the stars, is attempting to break an arrow with the front of his neck. It is a ceremony designed to help you face your fear. His circle around him, supporting him. He has tears in his eyes and it is clear some huge shift is going on for him. I hear his words and feel compassion.

'To my father, I forgive you all the beatings. I choose not to be afraid.' The arrow snaps in two. His circle clap and cheer, he is smiling. I feel chastened and pause to consider how easy it is to make quick judgments on people. It is only by digging deeper that we can understand what might be going on under the surface. We don't have the right to judge anyone.

I hurry back to Karu, who I know will have that perplexed look on his face, not understanding why I could not, like him, plough on without a break hour after hour.

Chapter 7

The Pace Is Relentless

It is the afternoon of the second day.

I have gone to my room for a quick lie down. Karu is conducting an interview for Morag; the one I have made friends with; who has been to Peru before and does not need help with translation. I am so grateful for the break and fall into a deep sleep the moment I lie down. Seconds later, or so it seems, I am being shaken awake. It's Carole.

'Freya, wake up, it's 4:30, everyone is gathered downstairs, they are waiting for you to come and translate. Karu is going to be explaining about the Ayahuasca and how it works. You're needed.'

I am keeping her busy as the waker-upper of the interpreter. I grimly follow her along to the main meeting studio, swigging some water from my bottle as we go and working hard to bring my faculties to the fore. Sure enough, when we enter the hall, there is everyone, sat expectantly. Patrick looks relieved that I have shown up and Karu eagerly pats the space he has left for me by his left side. I go to sit down and Patrick tells us that we are getting closer to the Ayahuasca ceremony, which will be tomorrow in the evening. It will run all through the night. And the next day it will follow the same pattern. Karu has brought us together to explain what to expect from the journeys and to give us some context.

Over to Karu, who starts to speak a few sentences at a time, pausing to give me time to register what he is saying and translate. I don't always translate literally, as English is more nuanced than Spanish, and I don't want Karu's message to be diminished by sounding clichéd, or even worse, trite. I take the time to receive Karu's meaning before I pass on the translation.

'You cannot heal the damage caused as a result of a lack of gentleness, a lack in tenderness and love, by harshness and force.'

Thus speaks Chakarura, his words reaching into the souls of the Scottish contingent raised on the harsh Presbyterian outlook on life. 'Work hard, don't be frivolous, get on with it.' An even harsher version of the prevailing Christian mindset in the West.

It had often struck me – a yoga teacher who notices such things as posture – how sad it is seeing young girls out on a night out in Scotland. Lovely slim bodies, still lithe and beautiful, yet walking with their shoulders hunched, as if they have no belief or pride, nor are taking any real enjoyment from their beauty and their youth. It isn't that way in Italy, France or Spain, where women young or old seem to have that ability to walk proud. Whoever says the *que guapa* equivalent to a Scottish lassie?

New Agers aren't much better when it comes to denying the body and its needs. All those folk waiting for the rapture to be carried away to a world where they can ignore their primal emotions and needs. So much of it is a continuation of the dualism taught by traditional Christianity. Squash the needs of the body. But by squashing the needs of the body, we are dishonouring the feminine.

All these men, and indeed women too, disappearing into their minds and ignoring the feminine domain. I remember a healer staying with me once, a teacher of Reiki who had learned from the best in Japan. I cooked him a meal. He managed to eat the whole meal without tasting or savouring one mouthful. Apart from vowing never to cook for him again, it made me suspect his spiritual teachings.

Karu is looking expectantly at me, and I quickly shake myself back to the present.

'There is no such thing as coincidence,' Karu is repeating this statement, and I translate it to the group. As it happens, this is an important point which he mentions quite often.

'I am here with you Europeans, a Peruvian Shaman; I who have ancestry in Eastern Europe and Britain, in order to be a bridge between the cold self-punishing world of the dual-istic West, where the world of the feminine, the world of woman is seen as a distraction to the spiritual path, and denial of the flesh is seen as a way to your God.

'My full name is Chakaruna, one who is a bridge from one state to another. I am here to work with you Europeans, to be that bridge into the world of Peruvian shamanism, the mysterious fecund and spiritual world of the *selva*, the jungle – this is all part of the divine plan.'

Karu is a psychologist, psychotherapist, jungle shaman, Catholic, family man. He is indeed bridging many worlds.

He holds up the *Chacana*, the *Cruz Andina*. Used by Inca and pre-Incan societies, it is a combination of a cross of four equal sides. This indicates, amongst other things, the four corners of the Inca world: North, South, East and West. A square superimposed on this indicates the four elements of Inca cosmology: Fire, Earth, Air and Water. The cross also indicates an important precept for Peruvian shamans: 'As above, so below'. The spiritual and the physical worlds come together in the *Chacana*.

He says each person has the job of integrating these two sides of their being, the spiritual with the physical side of themselves.

The way the cross is formed creates three steps. These three steps on each side of the *Chacana* indicate the three levels of the Inca universe. The bottom step is the *uku pacha*, the underworld; the middle step is Earth, our everyday reality or *kay pacha*, and the top step represents the sky or heavens, the *hanan pacha*.

Karu is further saying that in the Peruvian shaman path, there are three things which need to occur in a particular order in order to remain in flow with what he calls the *Prima Causa*.

First is to listen to the inner voice, which gives us access to the impulses and ideas that are being born in our souls.

Secondly, we must move into action to bring these inner impulses into the light, and it is only at this point we use our head to understand these impulses and actions. In this way we allow the free flowing of *Prima Causa*, the breath of life. It is our birthright to feel the free flowing of this breath, from the top to the bottom of our bodies and back again.

Karu continues to explain that all too often, especially in the West, where we are so often controlled by our mental processes, we censor and block our impulses before they see the light of day. We rationalise away our nascent ideas, and by doing so, crush the life force before it has time to emerge.

I am struck again with how similar this message is to that of my teacher, whom I worked with for many years, Mike Robinson. He too talked about listening to our inner promptings and acting on them before we let our heads interfere with the process. Inasmuch as we can do this, Mike taught us we become active participants in the moment of creation, quite literally co-creating with God. I guess artists have understood this and lived this for all time. So we are all to be artists, co-creating our life moment by moment.

I considered wryly that this is precisely the philosophy I seem to apply to my own life, acting on the impulse and living with the consequences after. I am struck by the image of that moment when I had reached out my hand to pull Bembe up that hill in Baracoa, those three or four years ago. Giving him a hand was quite literally what I had done in inviting him to the UK from his native Cuba. My back feels achy, perhaps just at the thought of all I have taken on in inviting Bembe into my life, and I shift my weight to try and get more comfortable.

Karu is waiting expectantly, as I realise I had not caught his last words.

'Lo siento, otra vez por favor.'

'Sorry, can you repeat that?' Phew, I have to stay focused to do this task.

Karu carries on to explain, he has brought Ayahuasca, a master plant whose work it is to bring each person closer to their own soul. Overcoming the mind which puts the obstacles in the way of the free flowing *Prima Causa*. Karu explains in his precise and intense way that at the moment of birth, when the baby takes its first breath, this is the moment the baby's soul comes into its body. When the mother looks into the infant's eyes with love, the infant knows it exists.

As Karu says this, he shoots a glance at me, looking deep into my eyes, and I feel seen by him in a way that slightly startles me. Does he know that my own mother could not catch my eye after my own birth, so unhappy was she at the burden of yet another babe?

I shake these thoughts away in order to be able to continue translating.

Karu is continuing, 'When the father recognises the baby and also gazes into its eyes with love, the baby knows where it is. This serves to fix the soul into the body of the newborn infant. With the soul firmly fixed in our bodies, from thereon we can hear its messages and receive its impulses, propelling us to right action. When this process is impaired, we find it hard to hear what the voice of our soul is prompting us to do. The job of Ayahuasca,' Karu is concluding his explanation, 'is to bring our souls more deeply into our bodies, pushing out whatever may be impeding its entry. If there is any heaving or retching, it will only be what is not serving us leaving us. In these sacred ceremonies, by dropping completely into our own souls, we will have the opportunity to hear clearly the voice of our soul and so take careful note of any messages and insights that may be received.'

Finally, we are done, and Patrick takes over to go over practicalities. But no rest for me as, after the main group closes, there are still today's quota of participants waiting to be interviewed.

Chapter 8

The Intensity Deepens

Back into harness we go, Karu and I, working our way steadily through all the participants. I crash out at every opportunity, relying on Carole to shake me awake when it is time to do a group session or start again with more interviews, or when Patrick and Karu need to parley.

We are now into the third day of the workshop proper. It seems an age ago, although it was only two days before, on the first night, that there had been a fire-walk. Karu had been intrigued with that as it was not a practice he was familiar with. Any challenge that the fire-walk had presented to me seems a doddle now compared with the concentration that I require to do all the interpreting. In fact, it had been rather a joyous experience to walk over the hot charcoal ashes of the fire-walk. All the wood burned had, I knew, been prepared with conscious ceremony by the others with Patrick at the helm.

It was when I had walked over the red-hot ashes that I had consciously let any lingering worries about Javier and his weed smoking or how Bembe would be managing without me just fall away as I came more fully into the present.

Now, on this third day, Daan and Patrick are overseeing the group in setting up the sweat lodges. I am really hoping Karu will want to do a sweat lodge as I have always wanted to do one myself. I have always felt a resonance with the native American ways. So, I am delighted that in the afternoon of the day we are due to have our first Ayahuasca ceremony in the evening, Karu agrees to include a couple of hours in our schedule to experience this. We had all been drinking copious amounts of salted water that morning and people were starting to purge, so on the whole, it's best if everyone is outside, albeit near to facilities.

There are two sweat lodges on the go, one run by Daan, the other by Patrick. I wait to see which one Karu chooses and quickly line up to go in the other one. I need a break. I am relieved of guilt when I see that Morag is going in with Karu, with her level of Spanish and familiarity with Peruvian mysticism she'll be able to do any translating needed.

For those of you not familiar with a sweat lodge, all the various elements are prepared with great consciousness and ceremony, just like with the fire-walking ritual. Two hearty fires are burning outside each of the lodges and the big stones, placed in the heart of the fires, are starting to turn a reddish brown as they begin to glow in the heat. The sweat lodges themselves have been built earlier by some of the participants. Under Daan's supervision, using long willow sticks that had previously been gathered and made into dome shapes, they had created the skeleton of the sweat lodge, which they then had covered in thick layers of tarpaulin and blankets to make a really good insulating layer. In this way, the heat building up will not be lost during the ceremony, but rather will continue to build. The lodges each have a capacity of about twelve people.

And now it is time – we enter, bending low to fit through the door while a circle of folk is chanting and someone else is drumming. We sit ourselves into a horseshoe shape facing out towards the entrance. Then the flap is closed from the outside as we are sealed in the lodge. In front of us is a smaller fire pit. Daan, whose lodge I've entered, calls to the fire keepers to pass in a stone, and one by one the hot stones are transferred inside. Those of us inside have stripped off and, with only a light sarong or cloth covering us, we are connecting to the bare Earth. I feel cold, my hip is really sore, and my head feels achy. I am glad that with each additional hot stone added, the temperature begins to rise. A few people get panicky and one woman has to leave. As it heats up, I start to relax and begin to enjoy the feeling of being really warm and so close to the Earth. The more the sweat lodge heats up, the more I enjoy it. I would like it to be even hotter.

Meanwhile, Daan is calling out the attributes of the four directions in turn. A talking stick is being passed around and we are each taking it in turns to speak about something in our own life that is relevant to these attributes.

First, the South, symbolising the past, and the snake, and we are invited to contemplate what we are ready to let go of. The image comes into my mind of Karu laughing at me earlier, as we were preparing the separate lodges. We had been collecting the stones to place in the two sacred fires in front of the individual lodges. A big pile of them has been gathered ahead of time, I imagine from the nearby river, and

I had chosen a particularly large and heavy one to carry over to one of the two fireplaces.

'There you go,' Karu had shaken his head looking at me wryly, 'you can't stop lifting those heavy burdens, can you?'

And now, in this moment, I get a shocking and quite distinct image of Bembe quite literally sitting on my shoulders. He is a big, chunky, strong man, and I am quite petite. So, the image itself is quite absurd. When it is my turn to speak I do manage to say, even if a little unconvincingly, 'I put down my need to carry other people's burdens.'

We move on to the West. The end, the setting sun, courage and integrity, represented by the jaguar or puma. We are invited to consider where we may need to call these attributes more into our lives. The thought crosses my mind that perhaps a little less courage, or shall we call it foolhardiness, might not go amiss with me. One of the women appears to be overcome by the heat and being enclosed, and asks to go out. The ceremony continues, we call in the North, the present, represented by the hummingbird, associated with joy and effortlessness and where we can most easily connect with the spiritual world. We are invited to ponder where that is for each of us. One woman says it is in her knitting, her choosing of colours and how she loses herself in her craft, another walking in the forest above his house. What comes to me is the love of playing with little children, how easily I can be in their world, and what fun that is for me. Finally, we reach the East, representing new beginnings associated with the eagle: the direction of wisdom and clarity. We are invited to consider what new beginnings we are moving towards. My aches have very slowly begun to dissipate as with each direction, a new hot stone is called into the lodge and the heat has built direction by direction. Gradually, as it permeates every inch of the sweat lodge, I feel an easing in those stubborn tension points in my back and hips. When the talking stick comes to me, I ask for freedom from constant back pain and aches.

I enjoy the ceremony of the sweat lodge a lot and all too quickly it is over, and we are being helped out and into the arms of those waiting, who are wrapping us in blankets and nurturing us with warm drinks. My hip feels so much easier and I even start to look forward to the first Ayahuasca ceremony, which will be held that same evening

Chapter 9

First Ayahuasca Ceremony

It is around ten in the evening when we enter back into the main hall. It is dark outside. The big room is all prepared. The hand of Carole no doubt has been at work. Rows of cushions and rugs have been placed around in a big semi-circle, all facing five low seats at the front of the room. One by one, people are entering: clutching water bottles, blankets thrown over their shoulders, thick socks on their feet. The temperature can drop at night in Scotland, even in summer. As they settle into their place in the semi-circle, I notice some folk arranging rescue remedy and essential oils, opening a vial of who knows what, taking a reassuring sniff. I could do with a sniff of something reassuring myself as I wait for Karu to enter. There he is now, wearing a traditional ritual poncho over white chinos and a crisp white shirt, showing up his brown healthy skin to advantage. He gives me a reassuring nod. 'I am with you,' my returning smile seems to say. 'We've got this.'

I am not quite sure how we are going to do this, so I hang back as Patrick, Daan, and Morag take up three of the five seats on the right facing into the group. Karu goes to sit on the chair second to last on the left, and then he motions to me to come and join him in the empty seat. As I sit down in my grandstand seat, I take in the thirty-plus souls gathered before us. My eyes sweep round the faces, and bits of their stories jump into my recollection. I glance along to my right, seeing Patrick beside Karu and to the right of him Daan, and then far right is wonderful Morag, who I am so grateful to for carrying some of the slack at meal times by sitting next to Karu to help him communicate. She catches my eye and we exchange a 'here goes' sort of look and a wee smile.

Two large Bailey's whiskey bottles have been placed in front of Karu. They are filled, however, not with Baileys but rather with the carefully prepared brew of Ayahuasca. Alongside these bottles are forty or so small *copas* or glasses, the size of a shot glass. After some introduction by Patrick and some housekeeping from Morag, Patrick leads us into a meditation and we all become still and expectant. Daan and Morag are drumming a distinct yet unobtrusive beat. I can feel my focus coming into the present – into the room. Then Karu stands up and, without any further ado, he drinks a cup of the liquid. Next, he is giving each of the facilitators on his right a glass of the brew. He then invites the first person in the semi-circle on his far right to step forward. It is one of the participants who knew enough Spanish to not need my translating services. He is quite a tall man, Michael, with his slightly greying hair long down his back. He is wearing a poncho and a deeply reverential expression, his hands over his heart as he approaches. I had been told this is not his first Ayahuasca ceremony. Karu, appraising his size and the fact he is not a first timer, pours a generous libation. Michael quaffs it mindfully, though swiftly; apparently, the taste is bitter and it is not a drink you would want to sip. I notice the liquid in the glass is thick, a whitey brown creamy looking concoction, indeed, actually very like a Bailey's. He returns to his space and the next person steps forward. Again, Karu is appraising them, I imagine he is clocking what came up for them in the setting-the-intention interview. He offers an exact measure as he sees fit for each. This continues one at a time, each person carefully assessed before Karu offers a dosage. I notice this varies from a half measure to one *copa* full to the brim. People then return to their seats, and then they settle one by one into meditation poses and wait for the medicine to take effect. Some lie down on the floor, cradling themselves into blankets. The drumming to my right is becoming more intense, the atmosphere in the room more charged. Finally, the last person has been given their dose. Karu pours another glass nearly to the brim and offers it to me. I was not planning on drinking the brew, but what the heck, I take the glass and with a swift movement swallow it down. Patrick turns towards me and giggles slightly, the drug's influence having had some time to take effect on him.

'There goes our translator,' I glance towards him and he gives me a somewhat rueful smile.

But in the event, it doesn't work out that way.

Karu stands up now and indicates he wants me to follow him. He begins to walk round the semi-circle of people singing what are called *Icaros* – sacred songs – which help to invite the spirits in, spirits who will help the participants on their journey into the inner plains.

I trot after him obediently.

'*Luz, ho Luz,*' he sings, '*Luz de Amour.*'

'Light, oh Light,' I intone in response, trying to follow the cadence in his voice,

'Light of love.

How long I am waiting for you.'

Karu continues to intone, his voice reaching in, so it seems, to the very spirit world, calling on those who will to be with us, to help us in our journey today, in our quest for insight and healing. I am very soon caught up in the beauty of his voice, emulating it as best I can, translating his words as I can…

'Rising so beautifully
Music oh music
That inner music
Bringing silent harmony.
Confusion and depression
They melt away before you.
Oh, voice internal
Silently breathing
Union and separation
That is your name
Nectar, oh nectar
Perfume of the soul
You transform our suffering
Harmonising our life into service.'

I stop trying to translate and simply echo his intoning in Spanish. I can feel how, with the help of the Icaros – these sacred songs – that Karu is helping carry us deep into the hearts of our own beings, where we can experience our own beauty and exquisiteness, our own innate connection with spirit.

The atmosphere in the room seems now to thicken and quieten. People are immersed in their inner worlds. Karu scans the room for those who might need help.

I am taking the chance of this lull to enjoy the physical effects of the brew. I lie down on my side on the mat, with pillows supporting me in a way that feels optimally comfortable. For the first time in ages, I sense my body easily relaxing. I feel the tensions beginning to drain away. I am amazed my body actually knows how to do this. It feels so wonderful. I just want to carry on lying there, going deeper and deeper into this wonderful feeling of release from discomfort and pain. My lower back starts to feel warm and is radiating a warmth into my normally sore hip. My hip starts to warm too, it is such a delicious feeling, I want nothing more than to give myself up to it. But no, dear Karu is signalling to me, and so I join him as we do 'the parish rounds', moving from person to person, hearing what is coming up for them, offering adjustments, suggestions. My knowledge of animal words in Spanish is tested and luckily, what with my miming and Karu and my good communication, he seems to understand even when the word for dragonfly or hummingbird escapes me. How I manage, I don't know, but we keep going until well past dawn. The whole ceremony has lasted over six and a half hours, and I have maintained my focus throughout. But for now, the circle is drawing to a close and I quickly find my way to my bed and sleep.

Chapter 10

Betty's Trauma Emerges

It is mid-morning of the next day. We are due to have the second Ayahuasca ceremony later this evening.

This time has been reserved for those people who have booked a private slot to come talk to Karu about what might have emerged for them during the ceremony the night before.

Right now, it is Betty who is here sitting in front of us. Betty was the one who had gone out of her way to make me feel at home before the first opening circle. She is still young, perhaps early thirties, and pretty in an open, fresh kind of way. A shadow seems to cross her face as she answers the question I translate to her. Karu had spoken it with utmost gentleness, and I try to convey this in my voice,

'What issue would you like help with, to be resolved?

Tell us what has arisen from ...?'

When she speaks, her voice is barely a whisper.

'It came up for me during the ceremony... I must have buried it... I wasn't aware...'

Her sweet blue eyes brim with tears, she seems almost apologetic to put this ugly, buried memory in front of us.

'I was ten, the same age as my daughter Jessie is now. We used to call him Uncle, he was a friend of my mum and dad's – he seemed to be in our house a lot, then all of a sudden we never saw him again...' her voice trails off.

Karu's kind, attentive face waits for my translation.

'I came home from school one day, I was excited, our team had won at netball, and I had scored two of the goals. It was a warm day, my shirt sleeves were rolled up, I noticed the golden hairs of my arm were glistening in the sun.

I was wearing white ankle socks. My skirt was rolled up at the waistband so it was really short, we all used to do that, when we got out the school gates, you know we'd roll it back down when we went into school.'

Karu looks a bit nonplussed – I am thinking maybe it's a British thing.

'*No importa,*' I shake my head at Karu, 'it doesn't matter,' and I say, 'Please continue,' to Betty.

By concentrating on the minute details in this way, she has slowed time down and brought herself fully into the memory, and we can see the flushed and excited school girl before us.

'I come in the back door. He is there in the kitchen. He looks at me in a funny way, like he is seeing something else, not me, not "Wee Maggie".

'I feel a bit worried, there isn't anybody else home.

He moves towards me, and he takes my bag and blazer off me. I feel kind of mesmerised, I am like a rabbit and his stare is like the headlights that prevents me from running away.

"It's alright", he is saying, "your mum and dad will be home later – I'm holding the fort."

He moves towards me, and as I step back, I shut the door, you know, as I step back.' Betty's words convey this had not been intentional.

'And he steps forward, he fills the space I had been in and as he does so, he also opens the larder door. He must have planned it. The door blocks the view in through the window, so no one can see us.

"We've got the place to ourselves," he says to me as he puts his hand on my shoulder and he pulls me in tight against him – he smells of beer.'

I pause – I am starting to feel uncomfortable. You don't need to be a shaman to know where this is heading.

Karu impatiently demands the translation, which I give slightly automatically.

Betty continues to speak.

I don't want to hear anymore.

'He starts to rub his body on mine, saying I am bonnie, a bonnie lass.'

Betty hesitates, she seems embarrassed at having to put this memory on the table between us.

I force myself to be detached and to do my job. She relaxes a bit.

'I felt – you know – his thing.'

'Su cosa – su pinguita.' His thing, his penis. I have to be explicit, Karu demanded clarity.

His face is pained now, like a father who hasn't been able to protect his daughter.

'...sort of knobbly,' Betty continues, looking more like a child and at a loss than ever.

'Oh please, keep it simple,' the thought comes into my head – and is a welcome distraction from the horror of the tale unfolding before us.

How do I translate 'knobbly' into Spanish?

I decide on 'hard'. *'Duro,'* I relay to Karu.

Betty continues,

'I can feel his thing, hard, rubbing against me, he starts groping under my skirt. I am thinking that it is my fault because I had rolled my skirt up.

'There was an old sleeping bag my mum used to keep by the door in the summer, to sit on out of doors when it was warm. He throws it down now, then me on top of it, my skirt is well up, around my waist.

'He yanks down my pants, he is on top of me, he stuffs his thing into me.

'I don't remember feeling anything...

'I don't remember...' her voice trails off, she looks very small and vulnerable.

Karu begins to speak, clearly, professionally.

I adopt the same manner as I translate his words to her.

'He says he can help you – he says in times of great trauma, part of the self splits away. It is our way of dealing with something that is too horrific to face. But that part which leaves also takes with it part of our vivacity and joy, and we must recover this lost part of ourselves in order to fully reclaim our full vitality, which is our absolute right.'

Karu tells me emphatically to say to her, '*No era tu culpa.*'

'It was not your fault; you were not to blame. '

Karu tells me to say it to her three times.

I look directly into her lovely, soft, tear-stained eyes and repeat twice more,

'It was not your fault; you are not to blame.

'It was not your fault; you are not to blame.'

Then Karu changes tack again. In his professional 'let's get this done mode' he asks me to check with Betty,

'Do you have a boyfriend here?'

'Yes,' the girl is nodding.

My '*si*' is somewhat redundant, yet automatic.

'Can you come back, together with him, after supper?'

Karu explains we are going to do a special ritual. The first part will be an extraction to take out the bad energy that has been left inside of her. Then we are going to do what Karu calls 'a soul retrieval', where we will invite her traumatised child to come back to her. I am familiar with the concept of extraction. This is when someone leaves a bad energy inside of you. Something that does not belong to you but weighs you down or holds you back. This too is quite common and can be a negative parental voice, for example, telling you, 'You will never amount to anything,' or a violent encounter, whether physical or emotional. The job of the extraction is to pull from out of you these intrusions which are not part of your being, giving space for what is you – your soul – to come more fully back to you.

The concept of soul retrieval, I am also familiar with. The idea is that when something deeply traumatic happens in your life, some part of you, finding it too dangerous or frightening to stay present, comes out of your body and the job of the soul retrieval is to go find that piece of the lost soul and call it back, letting it know now it is safe to return. Each person needs to have 100% of them intact and present as they move forward in their life. Yet so many of us have been scarred in one way or another and are only functioning with a proportion of ourselves. I start to feel a bit unwell. I'm not worried about the extraction or the soul retrieval, in fact they are both things I have trained in and carried out quite a few times myself before I hung up my healer's hat.

I look down at my list, still four more people to have their post-ceremony debriefing before suppertime. Then the extraction and soul retrieval, followed in short order by the second Ayahuasca ceremony. It is going to be a long night.

'Sorry, Karu, give me a minute.' My throat feels dry, I gulp down a glass of water, my hands feel clammy and my head is beginning to ache.

'I will back in a moment, I need to go to the loo.'

He looks perplexed at my need for a break. He is like a machine: as long as he is stoked up regularly with three square meals, he can continue indefatigably with the same level of intensity sixteen hours a day.

In the loo, I splash my face with cold water. I look pale. I swallow a couple of aspirins, take some deep breaths and then I go back to work.

We get through three or four more people before the supper gong. The sessions go well and are fairly straightforward. Karu interprets the symbolism of any animal imagery that has arisen and applies it to the person's unique circumstances in an unerringly helpful fashion. Imbibing the first dose of Ayahuasca seems to have released a plethora of animals into the dreams and imagining of our enquirers. Every individual, each one with their own unique and intricate problems. When you look at a bunch of people, what do you see? A bunch of people, but here, as one by one they come individually and sit down in front of us and open their innermost hearts and souls to Karu, what is striking me is how great is the delicacy of being human. And yet how brusque and careless we so often are with each other and yes, also with ourselves. How good then that here is this opportunity for these souls to be listened to; to experience the infinite kindness and attentiveness of dear Karu, having given themselves this opportunity to take time out to connect with their own selves.

It is 7:30 pm. I am fast asleep and Carole is gently shaking me,

'Freya, supper is ready.'

I must have found my way to my bedroom and crashed out for twenty minutes.

I follow Carole down to the dining room. I look in dismay at the foods on offer. I am feeling weak and know I need to eat something, but my stomach rebels at even trying any of the complex vegetarian nut roasts and roughly chopped raw veg and green salads on offer.

Perhaps if I had the leisure and tranquillity of a cow, I could munch my way through a meal, but my brain is on overdrive. We still have to prepare the room before Betty returns for her ritual healing, and I have no idea really what to expect when it comes to that, so really, there isn't much digesting of food able to be going on.

It doesn't help that I am too late for the lentil soup, which I could have managed, especially when the cook comes out and tells me he just tipped the last of it down the sink as they thought everyone was done.

Before I dissolve into tears, a sweet lad, one of the kitchen volunteers, Nick, takes pity on me. He agrees to boil me some plain noodles.

I sit myself down on a different table from Karu, who is sitting stolidly and happily munching his way through everything. I steadfastly refuse to catch his eye when he wants me to translate a remark from his neighbour at table. Happily, Morag, comes to sit beside him and picks up the slack by asking Karu about a forthcoming trip to Peru she is planning. Gulping bancha tea – a Japanese twig tea that helps in times of stress – I calm myself, waiting for Nick, who soon arrives with a big plate of the noodles. My job right now is to eat something. I splash some olive oil on top of them, add a dash of soya sauce, and readily swallow them down. Great, enough to get the blood sugar up. I am ready to go again. With perfect timing, as ever, Carole appears beside me to tell me everything we asked for in the way of blankets and cushions is ready for us to go and set up before Betty arrives. And also that tonight the second Ayahuasca ceremony will begin around 10 pm and go on through the night. No time to weaken. Plough on.

Chapter 11

Shamanic Healing For Betty

It seems like Karu has enlisted Morag to help out, as when I arrive in the hall, she is there with him. I am glad of her cheerful and competent presence. Karu gets us to set up the station before Betty and her boyfriend arrive, and we have organised the piles of mats and blankets all ready when she and Barry, her chap, arrive. He seems attentive in a gentle and supportive way.

We settle her onto the floor, making a cosy nest for her, and cover her with blankets to help her to feel as safe and comfortable as the strangeness of the situation is allowing, none of us knowing quite what to expect.

Morag now stands opposite me, with her welcome calm-in-an-emergency air.

I feel as nervous as Betty seems, and Karu keeps glancing at me from the corner of his eye in that disarming, shamanic, seeing way of his.

Standing over Betty, Morag and I glance at each other, making a 'what have we got ourselves into?' grimace. Now Karu has started to give this spiel in Spanish, so I begin to translate to Betty and Barry. He is saying about how he's had the good fortune to do this self-same ceremony of extraction on his own dear mother. Betty and my trepidation increase. You can just hear her thoughts, 'Oh yeah, and spin me another one, anything to get into my pants.' The thought shoots between us like a crackle of electricity. But then, still looking at each other, we both shake off this thought. Whatever might have happened to either of us in the past, this is a situation and a person we can trust. We smile reassuringly at each other.

Betty cosies into the nest we have made for her. In front of her is her boyfriend Barry and to the left of him Karu, and to the left of Karu, myself. To the right of Karu, Morag. His professionalism and self-assurance begin to ease the tension.

He asks me, in Spanish, to tell Betty to take off her underclothes. I am so pleased we have cleared away any remnants of suspicion as I translate this request, and she complies, modestly swathed as she is by a huge towel. Karu then gets me to explain to the couple that he is going to work through Barry. Barry is to place his hand under the towel over her private parts, in that moment, it has to be said, none-too-private.

Karu, holding onto Barry's shoulder, starts his singing and is looking off into space, his voice intensifying – there is a charge in the air. He starts gabbling – I am sure it is Quechuan he is speaking. I stop trying to translate and we all just close our eyes and focus. It is like a great vortex of energy is sweeping down from the ceiling and circling us all, centring in on Betty, but we are all being included. Karu gets that translucent glow and starts to look like a saint. I swear there is light radiating out from him. His intoning is getting stronger and tighter. It is like a tugging, like trying to get a bone away from a terrier. A very stubborn one, who doesn't want to let go. I feel myself swaying, my mind is starting to blank out. I am struggling to stay focused. A great shudder rips through my body. In the same moment, Betty gasps involuntarily and Karu is hurling something high and out – he later tells me he was sending the dark energy he had extracted into a huge fiery volcano from his native country that he uses for this shamanic purpose.

I feel faint and clutch at a nearby chair. Morag is chaffing Betty's hands. Betty looks like I feel, drained of colour.

Karu has not finished, he starts to intone again, this time a different sound, like the sound of a father searching for his lost child. Encouragingly warm, his tones are rich, like the sound of a lantern in a dark place.

Betty's chest starts to heave, it is as if she is about to have a seizure. I glance at Morag; she is crouched down beside Betty and staying calm. Karu carries on, then in a sudden movement he clasps his hands together as though catching something in the air and deftly he stoops down and places his cupped hands over Betty's heart. Again, the tone changes and he starts blowing through his hands into Betty's heart. She gives an almighty heave as her chest goes up to meet Karu's hands. He gives his final blow through his hands into Betty's heart, and in that same moment, Betty falls back, totally still and relaxed. Now it is her turn to look like a saint.

Karu looks drained. He smiles at Betty, who has tears in her eyes. She reaches for her man, they are hugging. She has tears of joy now.

Suddenly we all start laughing, slightly hysterically, it has to be said. Betty is covered up with umpteen blankets, cosy and protected.

And then I have to excuse myself. I must, must sleep. I have to be on it again in no time for the second ceremony.

Chapter 12

Lion Emerges

I feel refreshed after a brief nap, a flask of tea and some crackers. Once again I am by Karu's side, on his left, in the big hall where everyone is gathered ready for the second Ayahuasca ceremony.

It feels different tonight. I feel I am following Karu more deeply into the world of spirits. I sense what he is going to say in response to the enquirers before he says it. It's as if I am walking in the same terrain as he is, and therefore, I too can see the same things in that world. The fecundity of the forest has begun to more fully enter our space, wrapping us all in the tendrils of its warm embrace. Animals are popping unbidden into the subconscious and dream worlds of all of us participants. We prepare to give ourselves once again to the magic and mystery of this world. Once again, Karu begins by carefully administering the dosage person by person, starting on his right and sweeping counterclockwise around the horseshoe of people facing us. Again, each person gets a different dose according to what he judges best suits their needs in that moment. And again, as the last in the circle, he offers me a dose, full to the brim and I drink it down in one without hesitating.

He gets up to walk among everyone singing his Icaros songs, this bridge into the world of spirit, enabling us to enter more fully into the place of healing. This also gives time for everyone to settle into their interior world. I take my chance and go and lie down on a mat. I so long to recreate that wonderful feeling of relaxation I remember from yesterday. My body aches have come back big time. I begin to breathe into the aches, willing them to fall away. Karu seems to be managing without me. He is overseeing his flock with attention.

It is too good to last though, and soon he gestures to me that it's time to work again. A young lad is twitching uncomfortably. Karu and I move towards him in synchronicity. We are crouching down, one on either side. 'What help can we give you?' I ask. 'What is it that is disturbing you?' I translate this from Karu.

I am thankful that the majority of the people in the circle are sitting in meditation poses, legs crossed, some with frankly beatific expressions on their faces, and do not seem to need any help.

My body is becoming more and more uncomfortable, crouched as I am by the young lad, and I find myself sinking onto all fours. My back instantly feels relief, so I carry on following Karu around the room, administering to folk where needed, without standing up again. There is a blessed lull. Everyone seems good. I take that moment to return to my place and, lying on my side, I start to sink into the luxurious joy my body begins to experience of blissful release from pain. My arms and legs are out to the side, my head resting on a cushion. My total awareness is in my body as I realise my body knows how to release any aches and pains, how glorious, as I sink deeper and deeper into this bliss. I feel so joyous. I am content to remain here.

I am no longer a human; rather, I have become a lion. I need to go to the loo and without even thinking about it, I head for the loo on all fours. It is the most comfortable position for me. I see Daan glancing at me, unable to respond with more than a slight half smile from the depth of his own inner experience.

I pad back. It takes some time, and gives me a break.

Returning to the room, I see Karu has gone back to the front and is offering a top-up dose for anyone wanting one. A young girl stands near the front of the queue. She looks to me like someone who is overflowing with bliss. Her face reminds me of nothing so much as a baby stuffed so full of breast milk it has started to trickle down their cheeks. She is in front of him now. She wants more. Karu offers her a small amount. He is being indulgent, I sense. He must see more is not necessary. This young girl could be a symbol of consumerism gone rampant, not even noticing when we have all we need, always unsated, always reaching out for more.

But Karu is on the move again, indicating to me to follow him. I pad after him, still on all fours. A lady is describing her vision to Karu and he needs me to translate. She has seen a dragonfly. I make a fierce face and pretend to breathe fire while flapping my arms like wings, all the time still down on the ground on all fours. Our communication has become symbiotic and it is as though we are reading each other's minds as he catches my meaning, even when my vocabulary falls short. There is a lad who is seeing frogs. *Rana*, I am pretty sure, but I hop about just to be sure. Thus, the night wears on.

As the six and a half hours of ceremony draw to a close, the participants are invited to share their visions if they wish. A lot choose to be silent, which gives me less work. So many vines and anacondas and visions of the Blessed Virgin Mary. No one has been sick. Most seem in a state of bliss. Some ask to come and speak with Karu the next day. I want more than anything to sink back on my cushions and release all the tension from my body. It's time for bed, though, and one by one we slip away to sleep.

—

I fall into the deepest of slumbers. Next morning, I wake early as normal and head for the communal shower. Mid-shower, I suddenly have this clear memory.

> *I am back there on that Cornish beach. I am on holiday, sixteen years old. Splashing in the water, enjoying the unaccustomed feeling of the August sun, warm on my skin, the freshness of the water. I am with my boyfriend, completely off guard. Suddenly, he is manoeuvring me onto a rock, climbing on top of me, pushing my swimsuit out of the way, shoving himself into me. I am utterly in shock. I don't react at all.*

I must have breathed in some water from the shower. I start to retch. I am trembling and coughing like I've been underwater and only just emerged. I stumble out, wrapping myself in a towel. A startled girl looks scared. It was the same one who tried to give me the earphones.

'Go get Morag,' I order her urgently. And to do her justice she complies without demur.

And then Morag is there and is leading me back to my dorm, which quickly empties. Morag stays with me as I relive the rape. It all comes spluttering out.

'He was a fucking bastard, had a full-time girlfriend I didn't know about. He played the poor hero, misunderstood, what a fool I was to give him the time of day.'

I am shivering wildly and Morag wraps the duvet around my shoulders.

I had blocked it out all this time. I'm trembling.

'I'm so angry, I never knew I had this huge anger in me,' I tell Morag. 'I feel like one of these many-armed Hindu deities, you know?'

I feel my hands turning to knives, and in my mind, I am chopping him to pieces without mercy. My hands cut the air in front of me as I continue to cough and retch in a frenzy of emotion. Until finally, the emotion is spent.

Morag has stayed completely calm and centred throughout, and she is now handing me a bunch of hankies, which I take, wiping away the snot and tears. Suddenly, at the same time, we both start to laugh uproariously. The emotions now cleared from my body, I am filled with energy and we hug each other joyously.

'Oh my goodness, Freya, talk about the vengeance of Kali, the force of anger and retribution. I sure wouldn't want to be your enemy!'

However, there is no time to dwell on anything. I have to get dressed and eat something, my job here is not yet through.

Carole, no doubt having been briefed by Morag, comes to find me. I'm still at my breakfast, forcing mushy muesli loaded with honey down my throat, swigging down Bancha tea. Time to process at the end of all this. Morag casts an experienced eye over me, checking I have sufficiently recovered. I grin at her somewhat ruefully.

'Last lap now.'

She returns my grin, placing her hand on my shoulder in a way that manages to be supportive and comforting, before handing me the day's schedule. Six clients are booked for privates with the indefatigable Karu. We have to fit them in between now and 4 pm, when we will have our closing circle. There will be a short lunch break. Well, I better get on it, Karu is sure to be already wondering where I am, champing at the bit to get going on the sessions with those people needing help unravelling their visions of the previous night.

———

Somehow, I stay on it. Thankfully, none of the sessions are as intense as Betty's and we make it to lunch time on this last day without any difficulty. Managing a bite to eat, I unexpectedly find I have some free time. There are still two interviews to do before the closing circle at 4 pm, but halleluiah, Karu doesn't need me, as these are people who have enough Spanish to not need a translator. I head up to my dorm – good, no one is here. I lie down on the bed and crash out fast and the very next minute, so it seems, I am being shaken awake. It's Carole.

'Freya, they are waiting for you.' Slightly dazed, I follow Carole downstairs, willing myself awake as we go, so by the time we enter the hall, I am back in harness. And sure enough, there they all are, everyone gathered in a big circle, time for any last-minute questions before we do the closing ritual.

A closing ritual is an important part of the whole process. After going so deeply into the world of the spirits, into their interior worlds, it is crucial to bring people back into their everyday awareness before they head off on their separate ways. I find a space, a quarter circle from Karu, who is sat looking quite happy. Morag is next to him. He is not as dependent on me as he was at the beginning. Having identified the Spanish speakers of the group, he has some other allies.

Patrick opens the circle and invites questions. When someone asks Karu something, they look at me, give the question to me. I then translate it into Spanish and pass it to him. He then looks over to me to make his reply in Spanish, which I then translate into English, giving the answer to the questioner, as well as to the whole group.

Then something odd happens. A lassie asks a question, she is sitting opposite me with Karu on my right, sitting halfway between us. This time, Karu, when answering in Spanish, does not look at me but turns to speak directly to her. Something strange occurs, I can hear his words, but I can't understand them. Finished speaking, he turns to me, waiting for me to give the translation in English – but I am at a loss. Then it dawns on me what is happening: he has to give his words to me. It is only in this way that I can catch the meaning behind them. It is not enough to simply hear the words. Unless he throws them directly to me, I can't make any sense of what he is saying. I need 'the illocutionary force'. This phrase jumps into my mind from when I studied language development in Psychology. It means not so much the words, as the meaning you are sending out when you speak those words. It is how we can understand what a toddler means well before they are able to articulate actual words properly. 'Dah gah,' 'sausage hot,' 'muh uh,' 'mummy gone' or whatever. Wow, it is almost as literal as catching a ball. I actually need to catch his meaning – the illocutionary force – or I am at sea.

'No, Karu,' I say, 'you need to speak it to me.'

He seems surprised but duly repeats what he has just said, this time looking directly at me. I gather it all into me, making sense of it, putting it into an English that will register with the questioner and not sound stilted. Only when that process is done am I ready to then throw the reply back over to the questioner.

And now it is time for the summing up. This is important for all of us to hear as Karu reiterates the need for gentleness. How trauma cannot be healed by harshness – only by gentleness. He reminds us of the importance of loving our bodies – of being kind to ourselves. Karu is explaining the fundamental concept of 'as above, so below, as inside, so outside'. The symbol of the Chacuna, the equal-sided cross so important to the Quechan tradition, is a statement of that premise. He is explaining that the internal and external fauna are one and the same, and therefore, if we as woman or man allow ourselves to be treated harshly with a lack of respect, we should realise and be very sure that in that very moment we are despoiling the natural world – the living flora and fauna. This is because, quite literally, there is no separation. Therefore, we have to honour the qualities of compassion and gentleness and protect them from being abused, starting with ourselves and moving out from there. I am thinking this is simple to say, but hard for a woman or indeed a man with those receptive qualities to do. The design of the feminine energy, whether in a male body or female body, is to receive, to be generous, to be open to the masculine energy. No wonder then that the feminine energy is so easily run roughshod over. How can we stand up for ourselves, not allow the grabbing and taking that can be so easily done by a man, for instance, who has superior strength? A scene from a movie comes to my mind featuring one of my favourite movie icons – Mae West. 'Slow down, what's the hurry, you got a train to catch?' She drawls in one of her films when a man she has invited to her room gets too snatchy and grabby. I smile to myself. 'She can teach us a thing or two,' I muse.

But we are winding down now, and Karu is thanking me for translating for him.

'You have translated not just my words, but my meaning,' he says with real appreciation.

The group are all clapping warmly their agreement. They seem genuinely pleased and grateful.

However, Karu's next comment brings things back to Earth and causes a giggle in those who speak some Spanish.

'It's amazing you've done such a good job since you've mainly learnt your Spanish on the salsa dance floor or in the arms of your Spanish-speaking *amantes*.'

This actually isn't true. And I don't translate it; rather, I content myself by giving him the evil eye.

Then follows an overlong gift-giving and sharing, which I opt out of before the end as I am done. Patrick looks shattered too, I imagine, with his new babe, he's had interrupted sleep. Then, just as everyone starts to disperse, Antonia, his wife, makes an appearance with their newborn in her arms. It seems like a nice illustration of how things should be when things go right with our entry into the world. Antonia seems really content and her wee baby totally at ease and relaxed. They seem to be in a little love bubble of gentleness and safety.

Ah, if only it were so for everyone, how easy could it be then.

Karu and I are to have an early supper before being driven to Glasgow's Theosophical Society, where he is due to give a talk which I am to translate for him. Patrick drives and I suspect he is rather glad of a wee trip and to escape his many duties at home. Daan comes along too for the ride and we are all in a merry mood. On the way into the building, Karu stops to gaze at the photo of Madame Blavatsky in the hall. He recognises a fellow traveller in the world of spirits, no doubt. The talk goes really well, and I am able to translate so well and quickly because by now I have really started to get a grasp on Peruvian cosmology. Karu talks of the inner essence overlaid by what now needs to fall away.

At the end, a lady comes up to us asking when we are returning to Peru. She clearly has the impression that Karu and I are a team of long standing. And then it is over, my job is done. The four of us find a restaurant, a cosy Italian trattoria, and suddenly I am ravenous. Finally, I can relax. Indeed, now we all can relax. We are quite euphoric with the success of our joint teamwork and we have such a fun meal together. Promises are made to invite me to translate when next they do their 'trip of a lifetime' to Peru.

We drive back to Celtic Hall and have our final night's sleep there, myself in the now deserted dorm. It has been arranged that I will drive Karu back to Edinburgh the next day, where he will have an overnight stay at my place before I drive him the next day to catch his flight to London and from there his connecting flight to Lima.

———

As we journey home, back along the scenic, tree-lined roads, occasional flashes of the sparkling loch-side or the reflected light of a dancing stream bounce into my peripheral vision. Once I notice the flash of a buzzard's wings catching the sunlight. It is a relief not to have to translate to a third party, and to be able to just have a simple conversation with Karu in Spanish. However, what he tells me troubles me. He shares with me that he is out of pocket by doing the workshop. He tells me that the number of people who actually attended far exceeded what he and Patrick had originally agreed on. Karu explains to me that had he stayed in Lima, seeing the same number of private psychotherapy clients, he would have made almost twice as much. The sum agreed upon with Patrick had been based on there being twenty-odd participants, not the thirty-four who had actually been there.

'Didn't you say anything to him, Karu?' I feel outraged on his behalf.

'I had given my word, I had to carry through my part of the agreement.'

'Even if the other party breaks theirs?'

Karu nods.

The shamanic code of conduct, it seems.

I am upset by this; it seems to me that the Western consumption of the spiritual traditions of other cultures in less developed economies can cause Westerners to behave in a high-handed way. Almost assuming they are doing a favour in the first place by hiring them at all. From the little Karu has shared about his home circumstances, and from what I have gathered from other people I have come across, working in Britain yet coming from less developed economies, I have realised that those in a position to earn money abroad generally have a lot of dependants relying on this income back home. Bembe and his remittances home being a case in point.

As we head towards the Forth Road Bridge, Karu gently puts his hand on my arm. 'Always remember you are a refined woman. Never allow anyone to treat you roughly or basely. You must bring others up to your level, not lower yourself to theirs. Remember what I told the group. Everyone has within them their own internal flora and fauna. This can be despoiled by callousness from another or because of the casual way we treat ourselves or allow ourselves to be treated. The truth is, there is no separation. The outer despoliation of the Earth, of our waters, is simply a reflection of what we are doing to ourselves internally.'

I ponder this as I enjoy the beauty of the view up the Forth. The sun sends a shaft of light through the clouds, which catches a lone seagull as it lifts off from the water. I suppose then if we can't take care of ourselves for our own sakes, we would most certainly want to do it if it meant we are thereby protecting the Earth herself.

Chapter 13

Kali Energy Figures

Before we head home, I give Karu a wee drive round the centre of Edinburgh, so he can pick up the vibe and enjoy the beauty of the city. The welcome sunshine continues, so he is seeing everything at its best, it is true, but he loves the city. When we do arrive home, Bembe is out at work and Javier has gone to spend a few nights at his mate's house, so I am able to settle Karu into his room and organise for him to make that quick necessary call home that is pressing. After a bite to eat, we are both keen to sleep. I settle Karu in the guest room and go to sleep in my daughter's room, as she is still at her dad's and I need the space.

I am dreaming.

> *An intruder has gotten into my house and the police have him on the run and are chasing him through the streets. A meat van finds him and hauls him in the back, where he is hacked to pieces. I am glad and exalt in the punishment.*

I wake up, somewhat appalled at the violence of my dream. I never knew I had so much anger in me. This intruder in my home – was it Bembe?

There is no time to consider this point, as we must get Karu to the airport on time for his plane. We are both still in a weird headspace coming down from our Ayahuasca, and I read the time wrong on his ticket as 3 pm, instead of 1300 – 1 p.m. Bembe wakes early with us and stays close to me and wants to come too to the airport. When we get there, we realise we have just missed the flight to London. We manage to get him on the next flight, which will still get him there in time for his flight to Lima. And he is gone. And the whirl is over. I turn to Bembe, who is looking a bit hangdog.

'Did you miss me, *querido*?'

He nods, his big brown eyes so appealing; uncharacteristically, his guard is down.

'Come on, let's go home,' I say.

Back home, we both take time to relax. I realise Bembe has been afraid he would lose me. It is true that Karu was not a fan, he thought Bembe should be more grateful to me for giving him an opportunity to work in the UK. But I don't want Bembe's gratitude, and I am beginning to understand, too, that the more I do for Bembe, the more he resents me. Fundamentally, he is a provider, a man used to doing-for-others, and he does not want a free ride; it doesn't agree with him. He hates being beholden. However, that doesn't alter the fact that he has responsibilities in Cuba and I understand that. It was me, right at the beginning, who encouraged him to send regular money to his ex for his wee boy's upkeep.

We go to lie down together. It is so sweet to see Bembe's vulnerable side for a change. He had a really tough upbringing and it is not easy for him to let down his guard. Perhaps the rampaging bully of my dream is disturbing him in a similar way. He must have had to be so tough and hide his vulnerability after his mum died so suddenly when he was so little, and then him being parcelled off to live with such a strict uncle who treated him more like a servant than his child. He would not have been shown much kindness.

With the effect of the plant medicine still in my system, these thoughts circulate but don't stick, as we, bit by bit, find our way to rise above these limitations of our upbringings, spiralling deeper into connection. I find myself revelling in the sheer joy, delight and pleasure of being in the physical body, energetically uniting with this glorious man. Letting all thoughts dissipate, simply coming into the present, we are able to merge and blend with each other in a happy, satisfying way for both of us.

That marauding bully of my dream that needs to be cut out of my life has been a plague on Bembe too. If we can let down our guards, both of us, we have a chance.

PART II

Chapter 14

Bembe Is Homesick

But this turns out to be a short moment of togetherness which we are not able to sustain.

Shortly after this, I am walking in the Botanic Gardens. I have taken the chance of a sunny day with no wind to get some fresh air. Suddenly my back is in agony. What is happening? I feel like my kidneys are burning, I feel really ill. I sit down on a bench. A little robin hops onto an overhanging branch, watching me as I clutch the wooden bench. 'Dear Lord, what is happening?' I close my eyes and tune in. 'What is going on?' I ask my inner knowing. What comes to me really clearly is that it is Bembe's mother. She is showing me by the sensations in my body how she died. She swallowed poison! That must be what happened. What a hellish death if what I am feeling is only a fraction of that. But there is more. I tune in intently. 'I regretted it straight away. I want you to tell my son so that he knows. I am so sorry for abandoning him.' And then she is gone, the robin flies off, and I am well again, the weird symptoms quite vanished.

When I get home, Bembe is enjoying some silly cartoon on the TV, lounging on the futon on the floor in front of the gas fire. I startle him when, crouching down beside him, I ask if his mother had died by poison.

'How did you find out?' He seems defensive.

'It's okay, Bembe, it's not your fault. It's just she came to me today. She told me what had happened. She wants you to know it's not your fault. She is sorry. She regretted it instantly, but by then it was too late.'

Bembe sits up and moves a little further away from me. He is not unused to *madristas* and such like in Cuba, who are fortune tellers, and I know he has not been above consulting one at times. But he never expected this from me. I can tell he doesn't want to talk about it, so I leave it. I have to go cook the tea anyway as my daughter will be home soon.

A few mornings later, I watch him as he is sitting on the bed, about to pull on his thick socks, getting dressed for his work. I am struck by the beauty of his frame, the broad shoulders, the muscled arms, so masculine, yet his skin so smooth and such a gorgeous tone of light brown.

I sense his sadness, he is looking at his flip mobile, at a text there.

I hop behind him and wrap my legs around his body, leaning into his back, enjoying the smell of his wet hair and freshly showered skin.

"What is it, *querido*? You look sad?'

'They found my mum's grave. It was all overgrown because no one was tending it, but my dad has been searching and now he's found it.'

'You want to go back, to visit the grave?' It is very expensive to travel, and with what Bembe is able to earn, not really within his budget to take off to Cuba on a whim.

But there is more than that. The truth is, Bembe can't settle. He misses his son, he misses Cuba. He is the proverbial fish out of water. With my arms still around him, I feel a sinking in my stomach and I disentangle myself and move back to the other side of the bed. I can't hide it from myself either. He doesn't belong here. His mother's intervention is only a nudge in a direction he is already going in.

'Look, babe, if you're not happy, I don't want to keep you here. You're free to return home.'

Bembe doesn't say anything, and then I realise that as long as he is here, he is earning money – money that Anna, the mother of his son, has come to rely on. 'Look, it's okay. We can get a legal separation. I will give you some money as a settlement so you will have something to live on until you find your feet again.'

Bembe looks relieved and grateful. He gets to go home *and* he gets to take some money with him. And so, we agree.

I get my lawyer to draft up the legal separation documents, Bembe signs them, and our separation becomes official. My lawyer does not mention any need for Bembe to sign away his right of residence in the marital home. He is going back to Cuba, so I suppose the lawyer thinks it will not be an issue. Bembe seems happy to go back. He has not yet learned that the hero's welcome he will get will only last as long as his funds do. If I had understood that too, then I guess I might have played it differently as well.

Nevertheless, Bembe's return to Cuba has given me time to recover and relax. My time and attention are no longer monopolised by sorting things out for him. Suddenly, I am making plans again and meeting up with neglected pals. My back stops hurting. I have more energy. With very little planning, I take a really enjoyable trip to Jordan with an old friend, desert walking and making friends with the Bedouins we meet there.

When I am back, an old friend, Pete, visits. He is a healer and a psychic who spends half his year working the taxis in Edinburgh and the other half living in an ashram in India. He is always full of the up-to-the-minute spiritual gossip.

'Peru is where it's at, man,' he is telling me enthusiastically,

'that is where everyone is heading this year.'

I am not swayed by his hype, but nevertheless, my interest is sparked. And it would be nice to visit Karu in Peru and see something of the beautiful and ancient country. We had kept in touch by email and the occasional phone call, and he is pleased to hear Bembe is no longer living with me in Edinburgh.

Still, I dither about a bit and don't really do anything about it until one day I go and visit my sister, who has just moved into a house on a steep hillside in the border town of Hawick. She settles me into her cute little spare room upstairs. It is small, with the single bed facing out towards the window, and from out the window I can see the steep slope of the opposite hill rising up on the other side of Hawick. It is so beautiful, I leave the curtains open and fall asleep with no trouble. It is the middle of the night.

I am startled awake by a huge golden Angel who has appeared in front of me. It seems in some strange way to have come from the mountains that I am facing. The Angel's wings are outstretched and are made up of fabulous golden orangey-yellow feathers, not unlike a giant eagle or condor. They are dressed in shimmering and splendid golden robes and are holding up a big metallic staff – also golden coloured. They are holding the staff with both hands high up in front of them.

With an enormous thud, the Angel brings the staff to the ground. The impact of this thud as the staff hits the ground is what has woken me. It is like I hear a big voice proclaiming "ENOUGH!"

The shock of the reverberation of this blow seems to ricochet into my heart, and I am startled awake. I find myself sitting bolt upright, clutching my hands to my chest.

My heart is pounding alarmingly.

I slowly calm myself as the vision of the Angel disappears. I know what I must do, I have to pursue my dream of going to the mountains of Peru.

It takes me a bit of time to organise things as I need to have some lodgers to pay for my trip while I am away. I decide to

go for three months, and I take some work I want to complete with me. So, it is the beginning of October that same
year by the time I get there. I have found two students happy
to rent the house for a term. One is particularly reliable and
agrees to transfer money into my bank account faithfully,
so I feel happy about that. I find temporary teachers to cover
my schedule and arrange with my daughter's dad for him to
cover all the exeats and holidays while I am away.

And so, it is with a light heart that I throw off the yoke of all
my responsibilities and set off on my Peruvian adventure.

—

Galgaliel has found Azula taking a moment of rest,
as her ward Freya has indeed arrived in Peru and
has just this afternoon flown in from Lima and
arrived safely in the city of Cusco. She is
immediately affected and somewhat knocked out
by altitude sickness. Taking a taxi from the airport
to her digs, she has fallen gratefully into bed and
for the moment is sound asleep.

"I just wanted to congratulate you Azula on getting
Freya this far and to Peru."

Galgaliel's presence makes the small room where
Freya is sleeping seem even more tiny. They have
cloaked their incandescence but the odd spark of
bright golden orange and lilac nevertheless
escapes as the Ophanim Angel communes with
Freya's guardian.

"Yes, it has not been easy. Every time I was putting

the idea of the trip in her mind, she would find a hundred reasons why it was impractical, why she couldn't go because someone or other needed her to stay. If it hadn't been for your intervention, Galgaliel, I think she would even now still be in Scotland."

"Well, the main thing is she's where she needs to be. I will leave you now, but remember, call on me at any point if needed."

And with a great golden flurry of enormous wings, Galgaliel is gone from the room. A short swoop takes them to the top of the rounded rooftop of *Qoricancha* – the Temple of the Sun. Galgaliel turns to the East towards Marcapata. There they settle, and as they are folding their great wings about them, a shaft of light – a sharp, fresh morning, yellowy-orange light which seems to carry with it the smell of the dew-dampened dust from the previous day's heat – pierces through a gap in the encompassing hills of Cusco and catches the edge of Galgaliel's wings, perched as they are high up in the city. Golden yellow reflects golden yellow as the darkness slowly begins to give way to dawn. The first shafts of light are beginning to pick up on the ubiquitous terracotta red of the mud-baked roof tiles. Flashes of colour bounce a line of light to where Galgaliel is perched. The yet sleeping town below remains in darkness. Galgaliel speaks.

"We in the Angelic realms are excited for these times that will soon be upon you. Let me explain it like this with a simple analogy. Breath. Yes, breath. You breathe in, then you breathe out. Well, as your sages have been saying to you over all the centuries, as above so below. Patterns that occur on a micro level are repeated and reverberate through all of existence, all the way up to the macroscopic level. Imagine then the greatest breath possible, the out breath of the Creator taking manifestation to the farthest reaches possible of materiality. This is where your humanity is now, at the farthest point of the Creator's exhalation. So much so that many of you have even forgotten that you come from the Creator – are part of the Creator – as we are too, us in our Angelic realms. Coming soon will be the time of the beginning of the return inhalation. This is what your Indian sages have called the end of the Kali Yuga cycle. This age, which is about to end for you, has been one of the darkest Yuga cycles. For this is not the first time this has happened. These rhythmic exhalations into densest manifestation and inhalations back into Unity consciousness take around 24,000 years to complete, 12,000 for the in breath, 12,000 for the out breath. Your world is more ancient than you know.

It is true that the main signs of the changing shifts will occur from 2025 through to 2032. When these times are upon you, you can expect things to start shifting and changing; much will become quicker, lighter and faster.

But many things need to be put in place before then. And, depending on how these things unfold, will determine how easy or difficult the forthcoming transition will be.

From our perspective, we are able to see the way things can unfold ahead of time, but just how things will work out always depends on the actions of you humans.

At this time, your planet Pluto is having a big role to play in preparing the ground for ushering in this new Yuga over these next years.

At this moment of your Earth time, 2006, Pluto is still in Sagittarius. Financiers are partying, just as will be portrayed so well in your film, *The Wolf of Wall Street* – they are having a ball, making, as you might say, cartloads of money, your dot-com bubble is still expanding.

But come 2008, Pluto will begin to traverse through Capricorn. Capricorn, which is ruling your august institutions. Expect dramatic collapse of world money markets. The wrecking ball that is Pluto at work will expose and challenge your old patriarchal top-down structures. Over those years leading to 2024, while Pluto is still in Capricorn, any hidden corruption will be exposed, as one by one, any rot within each of your cherished organisations will be exposed. Your banks, your film industry, your church, royalty, charities. No part of your structured society, however cherished, will be exempt. What survives will be healthier and more adapted to serve the populace, rather than a corrupt few.

Pluto will then move into Aquarius at the end of 2024. You can expect to see energy of ferment as happened in France during the French Revolution. This was the last time, from your Earth's viewpoint, Pluto was aligned to the sign of Aquarius.

Because of this huge shift coming, many will fall into fear as old certainties will fall away and old ways of being and doing things will begin to collapse. Strange leaders will rise who do not follow the accepted rules, markets will rise and tumble unpredictably. The transition will not be smooth."

Galgaliel has more to say, but the Cusco dawn is gathering apace and some early souls have begun to stir in the streets below; the sound of metal shutters being rolled back, the crackle of kindling catching as a nearby still-functioning, traditional, wood-fired stone oven is being lit ready for the morning's baking. There is the smell of smoke before the damp wood ignites. Galgaliel wraps themselves more completely in a veil of camouflage – anyone looking up will see only a glint of sunlight catching the lead strutting of the rooftop.

"The Kabbalists from the Jewish mystical tradition use a wonderful image to portray this process of the continual flow of the inhalation and exhalation of Ein Sof, the ineffable Creator. They call it the Tree of Life. Imagine if you will, two pillars separated by a middle pillar. Each pillar holds circles or Sephiroth, which indicate planes of existence. The breath of creation moves from right to left to right, passing from one side of the Tree to the other, passing through the central pillar each time.

At the very beginning of this process, ready to receive this breath, is where we Ophanim reside on the right of the Tree. Our job is to catch the impulse and bring it into the great womb known as Daat by the Kabbalists. This mysterious place is represented by a non-Sephiroth in the depictions of the Tree. It is the point through which all must pass before coming into manifestations, known as the great Void. Where all is darkness. Where nothing is in existence, yet where all potentiality exists. From within this space of nothingness, the blueprint for the next impulse is born, ready to be replicated as a fractal into your world.

But we Ophanim cannot do this alone, we need souls from your planet to reach into the Void, into the very fabric of creation itself, to send an electric spark towards us so that a connection to us can be made. In this way, the new blueprint can be ignited. The electric spark will activate the New Fractal Impulse to come into existence. This, in turn, will begin the process of The Great Returning.

We have been preparing souls for this task for lifetimes, souls such as Freya, who are wired differently due to their connection to the Galactic Centre and the training she has been given in this life too. All is in readiness for what is to come.

Pluto is about to align in a close conjunction to the Galactic Centre. The Galactic Centre is the mysterious black hole at the very centre of your Universe. Every Galaxy has their own black hole and they serve an important purpose. Each black hole and, in your case, the Galactic Centre, is tethered into the Daat, the great Void of potentiality. Your Galactic Centre sits at 27 degrees 6 minutes of Sagittarius. This potent point in your galaxy is precisely the point that Pluto, as it makes its slow 248-year orbit around the sun, is about to line up with.

When this happens, a portal will be opened, making direct access to the heart of the Void possible. From this black hole, our universe is generated, breathed in and out of manifestation in accordance with a great natural rhythm.

There are others too gathering in some of the other important energy points on your planet, the First Order Nodes. There are not so many on your

Earth, seven on land – one in Japan, one on Mt Kailash, another in Spain, one on the Solomon Islands, another in Australia, and another in New Zealand, and the one in Peru. Thirteen are in the oceans. It is the work of the dolphins to see to them. A great call has gone out to those souls who have been pre-prepared for this destiny, however unbeknownst to them. They find themselves organising to visit a place at a certain time, not always being clear why, only following the inner promptings. They too will be gathering around this time, to come together in ceremony. The unique combination of beings forming a circle will create a vortex. Amongst the circles there has to be at least one who has been wired for the Centre. It will be their job at the right moment to open themselves to the Great Void. Unafraid, heart open, trusting to the complete unknown, with the vital support of the group.

When this occurs, we the Ophanim can reach through the Great Void of Daat and catch these intentions like threads and pull them in. As we do so, we are pulling back the old reality through the black hole, turning your known reality on Earth inside out. Imagine, if you like, a seamstress sewing a thin ribbon of piping that she then needs to turn inside out. She puts in a hook to catch the far edges so she can pull out the outside and bring it inside, and the inside outside. You are the threads and we are the hook. Or an Escher drawing where your eye seems to be following steps going down when all of a sudden, you don't quite know how, the steps are climbing up.

It is an onerous task. Only those already pre-primed and inured to the huge and unremitting vastness of nothingness will be able to stand it.

Nor will it be the work of a moment. The ceremony makes the connection, it is true, but after that, those brave souls must then follow the hook as it travels back up the narrow piping. This will be a path untrodden and will be done in darkness as there are no recognisable landmarks. If you like, they are creating out of nothing a bridge or a pathway that others will then be able to follow in their droves. But for the few, it will be a lonely task. It will not be the work of days nor weeks, but rather, as Pluto, the bringer of destruction and death and rebirth, retrogrades back and forth over this potent point for a full year, that full year will also be required for the making of this pathway. A pathway which once built will lead humanity away from the destructive tendencies of this Kali Yuga and into a lighter, fresher restart as the New Yuga begins and humanity begins to move away from the extremes of density back to a more spiritual understanding of existence. And that year is starting soon and will last well into 2007.

But let us not run ahead of ourselves, for a lot still is hanging in the balance here in this city of Cusco, and I must be busy about my work."

And in this moment, the sun breaks over the mountain top, sending the dazzling light of a golden dawn flooding into the Plaza de Armas. Galgaliel, spreading their radiant luminescent wings wide, notices a lone woman crossing the square. She is wearing the traditional dress still widely worn in this town, full multi-coloured skirt, wide-brimmed hat and knotted cloth slung around her shoulders. Even if she had looked up, intent as she was upon her way, surely she would have mistaken the dazzle of wings for the reflection of that glorious morning sunlight on a high-up windowpane. But a young girl glancing out of her window across the square while dressing for school sees the Angel and, telling her mother, she is told not to be so fanciful; nevertheless, the mother crosses herself to be on the safe side.

Chapter 15

Freya In Peru

Well, somehow I have pulled it off. It is early October 2006, and I am in Cusco. My flat is let, Bembe is out of my hair, my daughter is being cared for. Cusco is one of the highest cities in the world. Located way up in the Peruvian Andes at an elevation of 3,399 metres or just over 11,000 feet, the air is thin and altitude sickness a hazard for the many nationalities who are drawn like a magnet to this fascinating and beautiful place. Unfortunately, this includes me. Before I arrived here, I spent a few days in Lima, as I stopped off to see Karu at his retreat centre. However, a few nights were enough for me. Karu is busy working and his wife, a shy native lady from the *selva*, speaks no English. And not much Spanish, her *lingua franca* being Quechuan, which sadly I do not speak beyond the few words I picked up when I was working with Karu as his interpreter. Karu's house has many floors and even more rooms. Out of these, shadowy figures emerge briefly for their daily consultation or check in with Karu to perhaps have their dosage topped up – their animal imagery interpreted. Then they would vanish again. Karu had to be also taking Ayahuasca when he was working with clients taking the plant medicine, in order to meet them in their interior worlds, so he was not much company. I had not come here either for the Ayahuasca. I did enjoy making friends with his wee children, but they were at school all day, so after the second night, I caught a flight to Cusco. Lima is pretty much at sea level, so flying into the high altitude of Cusco, I only had time to briefly note and enjoy the warmth and the dryness of the air and sunny clear skies, notice the astounding beauty of the place, and get myself to my digs before I fell victim to the dreaded *Soroche* – altitude sickness. They say you can never tell who it will affect, as it doesn't seem connected to fitness. Those who take the bus journey from Lima and ascend slowly are generally okay. They would have different problems, as the journey may take as much as 21 hours. Flying in, like I did, often has the effect of laying you up for days. It is a breathlessness. For every breath you take, you are getting less oxygen than you are used to. And you feel sick and not able to eat, which leaves you weakened. Apparently, your body has to make more red blood cells; mine were obviously a slouch at the job. Still some, including a famous British DJ, die on arrival, so I guess I am being let off lightly. I read up on all this before I came here, and now here I am living it out, lying in a darkened room, sleeping fitfully as my body adjusts to the high altitude of this place. I am staying in a little language school not far off the main square, having enrolled for a course of Spanish lessons.

Not that I need many lessons, I am pretty fluent by now. Six years on and off with Bembe has consolidated my fluency, and I can row and swear and win an argument with the best of them. But my Mexican friend Daniella, back in Edinburgh, has told me that I speak Spanish like a Cuban peasant, so I was thinking some finer points of grammar wouldn't go amiss. That is, if I could ever feel well enough to get out of bed. Travelling on my own, I thought it would be nice to have a school to be part of until I acclimatise to life here. However, the place is full of a lot of young, noisy students, but one girl is being sweet and bringing coca leaf tea and barley sugars to my bedside at regular intervals, coca leaf being the remedy for *Soroche*, I am told.

———

It is my second day of being holed up in this room. There are no windows, the only furniture the metal framed bed I am lying on, a bedside table on one side of it, and a chair that I have thrown my clothes over on the other side. Opposite the bed is a table where my bags are sitting. There are a few hooks on the wall, to hang your clothes, I imagine. The nice girl – whose name is Maria, I later discover – brings me some coca leaf tea and tells me I must drink it. It tastes of grass and earth. I feel nauseous and slightly feverish but do as she suggests before falling back into a fitful sleep. Then it is back with me. That image that seems always to haunt me.

> *Oh no, not again, that hideously deformed creature, all swathed in dirty rags, is making their way ever closer up the stairs towards me. Although they are moving slowly and with great difficulty, inch by inch they are getting nearer. Standing at the top of the stairs, the front door of my childhood home at my back, I am horrified, appalled and disgusted. They have made it halfway up the stairs. I want to*

My bedroom door opens, a fresh smiley face appears. It is Maria again.

'I brought those barley sugars you asked for, I found some in the supermarket off the main square.'

I turn towards her, shaking myself into the present waking moment.

'Oh, thank you,' I manage a smile, and sit up a little. She gives me the change.

'Shall I bring you some more coca leaf tea? Everyone says it will help you get better soon.'

'Yes, yes, please, that would be good.'

She goes away on her errand. I fall back this time into a dreamless sleep.

I awake to a text message from Bembe.

'Can I stay in your flat if you are in Peru?'

Drat the man, how did he always contrive to ferret out my business and know where I am and with whom? So, he is back in Edinburgh again. Thank goodness to be here then, albeit sick. And I can, with all honesty, reply as I do.

'Flat full of paying students, sorry, no way.' I consider underlining 'paying', but decide not to be mean.

Chapter 16

A Breath Of Fresh Air

It is early morning of the fourth day, and I finally stagger out of my room. I am getting curious to know what the world is like outside what amounts to a bare cell, with not even a window from which to peer to check out my new surroundings. As I walk towards the outdoor patio where all the meals are served, I notice again, straight away, how incredibly dry the air is, and a big plus is that my body feels great – not a twinge in any bone, such as a damp winter in Scotland invariably brings on. The school is halfway up a hill and from the balcony, there is a splendid view over the mud-tiled roofs of Cusco towards the mountains beyond. Cusco is built in a basin with the main square being the bottom of the bowl, so to speak. The view is utterly stunning, the mountains dry ash colour and huge.

The morning passes pleasantly on the balcony. I enjoy being out in the fresh air and not feeling nauseous. I revel in drinking black Darjeeling tea, my favourite, with tea bags I have brought with me. As I drink the tea, I drink in the gorgeous vistas. I nibble on dry toast and begin to feel a bit more in the land of the living. The school provides some loungers on the patio and as the others are at classes, I sit there comfortably on my own, enjoying the change of scene and taking in my surroundings. I realise that the school is owned by a Dutch outfit and is more than half full of Dutch gap year kids doing 'good works' among the orphanages and street kids of Cusco. They are pretty full of themselves and noisy. Apart from this gaggle of the young Dutch contingent – mainly girls around seventeen and eighteen – there is Gianna, she stands out from the gap year gals as she is serious-looking and in her late twenties. Additionally, I spotted at breakfast a big rangy fella with long hair and a beard who looks as if he's been living in the wilds. He surprises me at this moment by appearing from the corridor and coming straight towards me to introduce himself. He has a markedly distinguished voice, even with his American accent.

He shakes hands with me.

'Hi, I'm Geoff, glad to see you're feeling better.'

I'm a bit taken aback that my state of health is something any of the other residents have noted. I smile in a welcoming way and he comes and turns the chair opposite me in a precise way so the sun is not in his eyes but yet he can still see me, before sitting down.

'I've come into town to improve my Spanish so I can understand my shaman better. I've been living with an *Ayahuasquero* in the jungle.'

Oh, so I was not wrong about that then! He says this in careful yet correct Spanish.

I am able to see past his unkempt look. It is a look I recognise from my own days living in the depths of Wales. A look that passes for acceptable when you are living away from the amenities and the mores of the city and the 9-5 life. Scruffy clothes, unkempt and matted hair, an untrimmed beard and scuffed boots are all par for the course.

I reach out my hand to his, and he gives me a warm, firm handshake.

'Hi. Freya,' I say, 'I'm brushing up my Spanish too.'

'¿Puedes hablar espanol? Es que es importante para me practicar tanto.'

'Do you speak Spanish well?' he is asking me, 'It is important for me to get lots of practice.' When I nod, he continues in Spanish, 'It's okay then if I stay here a bit and converse with you?'

He seems nice, and we nod pleasantly to each other as I turn my right hand towards him to show I am perfectly happy to acquiesce to this suggestion.

'Bueno, vamos a empezar.'

'Okay, let's get going,' I am saying to him.

His Spanish is basic, but not too bad, and I discover, as he has said, that he is an American and training to be an *Ayahuascarian*. He has already been nearly two years living deep in the jungles of Peru. He has apprenticed himself to an indigenous Peruvian shaman and has been learning about the plants and how to safely use them and work with the healing they offer. His plan is to bring his knowledge back to his native USA and to set up workshops once back home. He has reached a point with his shaman that he feels he needs to take some time out to study the Spanish language to come up to a higher level so that he can understand better the more intricate details of what his shaman is teaching him.

As I absorb this information, taking in the potency of this being in front of me, he asks me about myself.

'¿Y tu, porque estas aqui?'

He has an easy way about him and I find myself saying,

'I have taken a sabbatical from my busy yoga teaching schedule. Rented out my house for the autumn term to some mature students, which has financed this trip. I have come to get a rest, in fact. I've had some personal things going on.' I trail off, not wanting to go any deeper.

Geoff doesn't press me, but he has an uncanny way about him and I sense he is seeing deeper than the words I speak.

He gets up and gives a little bow, his tall, lanky frame towering above my chair.

'Muchas gracias y hasta pronto entonces.' He heads off.

I am left with the unwanted images of my Cuban ex, Bembe, who always seems to swamp me with his needs, his agenda, whenever he comes near me. And now he is back in Edinburgh, just when I thought he was safely back in Cuba. I suppose he ran out of money or fought with Anna, the mother of his son. Maybe he will be gone by the time I get home. At least he will have had time to sort out his accommodation and to get his job back without my involvement.

Before he left for Cuba, Bembe had found work in the kitchen of a Latin American restaurant. It suited him better than the outside-in-all-weather work at the saw mill. He liked that he would stay warm at work, whatever the weather outside, and he was very good at keeping a cool head under pressure. Not to mention, he was reliable and a hard worker. I imagine the owner would contrive to make space for him again on the rota as he had done on a previous occasion. He will be alright, I tell myself severely, not my responsibility, shake him out of your head!

Later that afternoon, to my surprise, my entrance test reveals I am advanced level, so I am put in class alongside a young woman named Gianna. It seems we have both mastered our imperfect conjunctions! It turns out she is a young Swiss lawyer with a sharp brain and chronic wanderlust. She manages to organise her life to have three months off every year to travel and learn languages. Spanish and Peru are her target this year.

All the teachers in this school, it turns out, are native Peruvians, even though the school is owned and run by Dutch people, and everyone is very friendly. They are used to that green-around-the-gills look of new arrivals, and the receptionist asks me if I feel better. I learn it was her making sure I was plied with coca leaf tea while I was laid out. Still, it was sweet of Maria to comply.

Gabriella is our teacher the following morning. She is from Lima and a sophisticate. She warns Gianna and I, in our advanced class of two, against the young men on the make, looking to hook up with Westerners.

Of course, it will always be thus in any country where you have such a disparity of wealth between the natives and the visitors. These people with so little disposable income see our things, our phones, our cameras, our wallets, as we flash notes beyond their monthly earnings. What do they know or care about the credit card debt most of us carry to pay for it? The treadmill hours most work to afford the two-week break of a lifetime – or at least of the year.

You had them in Cuba, as I have mentioned, the *jinenteros*. They cater for Cuban tourist dreams, raunchy music and dancing, toned muscles and sex. Provided you could pay, it is all on tap.

The Cusco *jinentero* equivalent caters for different dreams. For those who come seeking the mystical, desiring to be spaced out by the magnificence of the ancient stone ruins of the Inca world, perhaps seeking drug-induced visions; they will find plenty of long-haired grungy-type young men willing to hang out with them and ready to procure for them the necessary, to be their guide and bedfellow as required.

Frankly, I was in no danger; they were all kids and distinctly unappealing. Besides, they were novices compared to their Cuban counterparts. Perhaps because here, in Peru, unlike in Cuba, it was possible to thrive and even have a little business, without the State breathing down your neck, so there were other avenues for enterprise apart from gullible foreigners.

My mind wanders from Gabriella's lesson to my meeting Bembe. Was that what I had been, simply a gullible foreigner? But no time to dwell, Gabriella has moved on from her warnings to a tricky imperfect subjunctive construction. 'If I had known that, I would not have gone there.' Quite.

———

The advanced Spanish afternoon class that day is conducted by a gentle, dreamy man by the name of Rodolfo. I had read on the school notice board that he is giving a talk in a few days on the mysticism of Machu Picchu, so I am already intrigued by him.

Rodolfo, seeing that strict concentration is not on the cards, suggests taking us out to a little café he recommends where they have a fabulous display of cakes. Gianna's face lights up at the mention of cakes. She is as thin as a rake, and I guess because her brain is always whirring, she needs to be constantly stoking in the fuel.

My face, however, turns a little greener. I have not fully adjusted to the altitude yet; nevertheless, since I had missed the orientation walk while lying in my windowless cell being ill, this was a good opportunity to get my bearings down in the main square. I am going to need to get to a bank before too long, and it will be handy knowing where the supermarkets are so I can replenish my dry cracker supplies – still my current level of digestion.

So that early afternoon, we make our way through the school to the exit into the street. The way is down some stairs, past the office on the right, halfway down those stairs, and then finally by way of a beautiful oak and iron work-studded small door which is set within the much larger oak door. Ralph, the caretaker and general help, is there. He is a brown, wrinkled man, but not so old, perhaps in his early forties. As he helps us with the door, he says to me in English, 'I glad you better.'

We'd made friends when I'd first arrived, as he'd been the one to see me to my room. It had all been a blur at the time. But now we smile warmly to each other.

Stepping through the door, we venture out into the narrow cobbled street.

As we walk down the hill towards the main square, we pass some small shops selling postcards and a few little cafés offering juices and ice cream. I spot a quiet, unassuming restaurant that I decide to check out later. And then, turning sharp right, we arrive directly in the main square.

The central square of Cusco is rather like a giant cloister, two sides of which are covered walkways where tourist shops, tobacconists, and woollen garment shops ply their trade.

Wide and open with a little park in the middle, the square is full of small trees and benches, and llamas attached to traditionally dressed ladies with babies strapped to their backs, earning pesos in exchange for tourists photographing them.

We cross in a diagonal to the other side of the square. We walk unmolested since we have Rodolfo at our side. He leads us off to the right, up another street slightly wider than the one the school is in. Minutes later, we find ourselves in a busy little café peopled mainly with Cusco folk. The Peruvians, like the Cubans, like their confectionery glorious, with pinks and pastel blue layers of pastry and sponge in heady cascades. Gianna's eyes light up with glee and she is pointing delightedly to the display cabinet at what she wants. I am pleased to find some plain biscuits and we encourage our teacher to choose something – he is our guest, and even the reasonable prices of this shop could be stretching his wages too far. If he is in the same position as Karu, he might also have a lot of family members depending on his modest earnings. Whatever his situation, Rodolfo accepts with dignity, and we settle at our table.

The tea is hot and feels good, and after a few minutes, I feel revived enough to look around. The shop is in two rooms with maybe seven or eight small Formica-covered tables in each. It is quite full: a couple of small burly men, very likely taxi drivers enjoying a break; two older women with shopping bags, one complaining her feet are hurting, easing off her too tight shoes – a bad bargain perhaps bought too hastily in one of the many street markets that I find out later abound here; a young adolescent boy with his girl are sipping on a coffee in turns. An old man with a trimmed beard, wearing a wide-brimmed hat and a traditional Peruvian poncho, sits with his coffee, back against the wall facing into the café. Rodolfo greets him with deference, and the old man smiles and nods with his slightly rheumy eyes. As if he is saying, *No need to worry about me sitting here. You go about your business.*

We settle down at a table. I have my back to this man. Rodolfo commences our lesson. The conversations will be conducted in Spanish.

'So, what brings you to Cusco?'

Gianna, between mouthfuls of her whipped pinkish heaven, explains in her very decent Spanish that she has just finished her training as a lawyer in her native Switzerland. She is soon to be grounded for a whole year as an intern in order to become fully qualified. She is taking the chance she has to get away before knuckling under. Having mastered English, she now wants to become fluent in Spanish. The three things she loves best are mountain trekking, languages, and travelling. Although she has just arrived in Peru, she's already researching the various tours available for the Inca trail.

I'm put a bit on the spot when he asks me the same question.

'En realidad tuve un sueño.' Well actually, I had a dream.

Rodolfo cocks his head to one side in a tell-us-more manner; why not just tell the truth, I decide.

'He ido pensando' – there was a nice little conjugation for you – I'd been thinking about coming to Peru.

'Quite a few of my friends had been talking about Peru and Machu Picchu, and I had read some books about the mystical energy of Peru. I started to feel like I wanted to be near mountains.'

Cusco, encircled as it is by mountains, gives you all the mountains you could want.

'Time went by, and I ignored these inner promptings. Then one night earlier this year, I was staying with one of my sisters who lives in Hawick in Scotland. Her house is perched on a steep hillside. Going to bed that night, I'd left the curtains opened to take in the stunning view of the town rising up into the hills on the other side of the valley that forms the main street of the town...'

I am using my hands to illustrate my story, indicating the steepness of the mountainside facing my sister's house.

'...when I was startled awake in the night by this extraordinary dream.'

Gianna looks at me coolly, her gaze inscrutable, but Rodolfo seems to intensify his listening.

'Yes,' I repeat, 'I was startled awake by, it seemed to me, a great golden Angel in front of me. Not like the western type Angel, more like a great condor or eagle with wings straight out like this.'

I am warming to my theme and, using my arms to indicate the wingspan, I spread them out to the side, nearly catching one of the burly taxi drivers in the eye as they make their way to the door.

'Lo siento, disculpame,' so sorry, I say, but they only grin, enjoying seeing a bit of theatre in the making. The two men hang back to watch what this weird *gringo* is going to do next.

I carry on with my tale, too far into the memory of that startling dream to stop now. It is helping me, this enacting of it, helping me to feel the reality of it and perhaps make some sense of it.

'The Angel's wings were outstretched,' I continue, 'and were made up of fabulous, golden, orangey-yellow feathers, not unlike a giant bird. Dressed in golden robes, the Angel was holding a big metallic staff, golden coloured, high and in front of them.'

I mimic this action with my arms, bringing my hands together high and then I plunge them down dramatically towards the tabletop when I come to the bit of the staff being brought sharply to the ground, luckily managing not to crash into my teacup. The two taxi drivers are nodding and grimacing at each other as they follow the action.

I carry on with the narrative. 'With an enormous thud, the Angel brought the staff to the ground. The impact of this thud, as the staff hit the ground in my dream, woke me up. It was like a big voice proclaiming, "*¡BASTA!*" – ENOUGH!

'The shock of the reverberation of the blow seemed to ricochet into my heart,' I tell the gathering audience, 'and I was startled awake. I found myself sitting bolt upright, my hands clutching my chest.'

As I say this, I do clutch my chest, still sitting there at the café table.

'My heart was pounding,' I beat my hands into my chest to show this, glancing at the people watching, catching the eye of one of the taxi drivers who seems mesmerised.

'As I slowly calmed myself down, I just knew I had to pursue my dream of going to the mountains of Peru.'

The two men are nodding and clasping their hands together in that gesture that says, 'Yeah, good on you, you made the right call.'

I start to feel a little self-conscious. I have come to the end of my tale and my voice trails away slightly.

'I felt compelled somehow, so I organised myself to get here and here I am.'

At that moment, the others seem to be looking behind me, and the two taxi drivers start to move towards the door and out of the way of the person who is at my back. They are bowing deferentially as they do so. Turning around, I see the old Peruvian man coming towards Rodolfo. He starts to speak to him rapidly in Quechuan, and I can't understand a word of what he is saying. Every now and then he lifts his hand in my direction, glancing sideways at me. His manner seems a bit brusque, and his words sound emphatic, then he turns to face me fully and our eyes meet. His eyes, though a soft brown colour, have an intensity in them that arrests my attention. They have such depth. I begin to feel drawn in, as though into a spiral. Then Rodolfo breaks in, he is quickly checking to be sure neither of us pupils minds this interruption.

'This is Amuru, he is a distinguished shaman in these parts, do you mind...?' Rodolfo indicates the empty chair at our table and we both nod our agreement. The old man sits down next to me. I start to feel his energy radiating into me and look at him again curiously. He catches my look and gives a wicked smile.

Rodolfo speaks rapidly in Quechan to the old man, who nods as he listens, then sits back with a small wave of his hand for Rodolfo to continue his conversation class.

'Cuando occorrio esta sueno?"

'When did you have this dream?' asks Rodolfo.

Everyone looks at me, so I carry on with my story of what brought me to Peru.

'The dream was about four months ago, sometime in June. It took me some weeks to organise my affairs,' I explain.

As my voice trails off, the old man speaks insistently to Rodolfo; it seems like he wants him to tell us something.

'Amuru is asking if you know the legend of how Cusco was founded?' Rodolfo, in his eagerness, is speaking faster than his usual careful foreigners' Spanish. And Gianna and I, concentrating fiercely to catch the meaning, turn to exchange glances.

'No.' We both shake our heads in puzzlement.

Rodolfo continues, 'The Legend states that the great sun god Inti sent his son Huayna Cápac, who arose out of Lake Titicaca in Bolivia, to seek a new way of life and a new city. He travelled the length and breadth of Peru until he came to the site that was Cusco, this very town where we sit now sipping our tea. There he raised up his great golden staff, which he always carried with him and with an almighty thud, he thrust it into the Earth, forming the crater within which Cusco was founded.'

I am a little shocked by this information, and even Gianna is looking impressed, but there is more to come, this time from Amuru. In simple Spanish, and thankfully quite slowly, he tells us:

'To us in Peru, the mountains are Angelic beings. It is not that the beings reside there, it is that they *are* the mountains. We journey into their heights during sacred times of our spiritual year to seek guidance and to pay our respects. We call them *Apus-Angelos*, loosely translated as "Angels". They are aligned to the sacred bird, the condor.' Amuru lifts his chin and pushes his sternum forward enough for us to clearly see the pendant he is wearing round his neck. It is made of some metal, perhaps pewter, and is of a condor's wings outstretched in just the same formation as the Angel of my dream.

Gianna and I had been listening intently up to this point, both of us concentrating a lot to ensure we understood the Spanish enough to follow the story. But now all of a sudden, as though a spell has been broken, our ability to concentrate is at an end, the café noises intrude once more upon us. A chair scrapes along the floor. Amuru is standing up, and reaching over he takes both my hands in his, and says to both of us, in his halting Spanish:

'A pleasure to meet you both,' and to me with a roguish smile,

'*Hasta pronto.*' See you soon.

And with that, a smile at Gianna, a nod to Rodolfo, he is gone.

Rodolfo looks pleased, as though he has been given a real endorsement. Wrapping up the class, he praises us for our concentration before telling us about a talk he is giving in a few days on Peruvian mysticism, a special study of his, and invites us both to attend. Gianna, by this time, I imagine having had her fill of weirdo mystical stuff, is already gathering her things together and with a noncommittal nod and a distracted wave, she heads for the door, I'm pretty sure with lunch on her mind.

But I tell Rodolfo I have already seen the poster on the board at the school, and I am planning to attend and indeed am very much looking forward to it. And with that and a further thank you and goodbye to Rodolfo, I too head off on my own search. First to find that bank, and after, to buy some crackers in a supermarket.

Chapter 17

Discovering Qoricancha

Some days later on a free afternoon I am walking to the supermarket along a busy road lined with shops on my right side, I pass by a beautiful, substantial, stone-built building on the opposite side of the street. It sits on a small hill facing into the main street. Curious, I make my way up the little path leading to it and, by skirting round the side, I find the main entrance and a wider open space. I have discovered *Qoricancha*, or the Temple of the Sun. I had read some Inca history in preparation for my visit here, so I knew that like all buildings in Cusco, what was once here has been plundered and built over by the Spanish conquistadors from the 15th century.

Now this building seems quite plain, but I know from my reading that in its heyday it was the most sacred and important edifice in all of Cusco, indeed in all of the Empire. As I look around at the ruined and plain stone walls, I begin to imagine what once had been, all these walls covered in gold and intricately carved.

The stone walls are incredibly thick, which helps to explain how they have managed to withstand the centuries and the earthquakes that periodically occur in Cusco. The extraordinary craftsmanship of the stonework, however plain it looks now, is in itself a feat of engineering to be marvelled at. Some of the stones, especially the foundation ones, are huge and yet they are so smooth and evenly put together, fitting so neatly snug with all the neighbouring stones, and all without the use of mortar. Like countless people before me, I touch these beautiful stones, warmed by the sun, and I am amazed.

I am reading a plaque now. It tells me the Catholic Spaniards commandeered this building – as they did all the others in Cusco – and, leaving a lot of it in ruins, they had then overlaid what was left of this sacred site with a Catholic Church: in this case the church of Santa Domingo. On our way to class that first morning, crossing the main square, Gianna and I had popped into another church: The Church of the Society of Jesus. Rodolfo had bumped into a friend and we had used that opportunity to nip in briefly. Gianna wanted me to see with my own eyes the elaborate and stunning interior – all in gold. Some of this, no doubt, was the very gold that had once graced the interior of *Qoricancha*, now turned into: a huge and ornate cross, a giant monstrance (the vessel where the consecrated host, sacred to the Catholic Church, is carried) and statues of various Catholic saints. I had not wanted to go any further inside. That church, Rodolfo had told us when we resumed our walk to the café where we would have our morning lesson, had been built over what had once been an Inca palace.

The feel of *Qoricancha* is quite different. Maybe it is because a lot of it is open to the sky and there is a sweep of garden on one side, but I love to be here. I try to imagine how the building was before the huge church had been built over the part of the original building that was left standing after the destruction.

There is enough remaining of the Temple of the Sun for me to begin to get a picture. I walk down what looks like one side of a cloister to the back wall. There, the signs speak of a huge gold obelisk disc that used to be in pride of place there, filling the whole wall. The disc was to represent the Sun God Inti.

'*Inti*,' I read, 'issued from the Creator God, whose name is known as *Viracocha*. From him also issued the moon, *Mama Killa*, and the Earth, *Pachamama*.'

Just then, I spot Ralph, the caretaker from the hostel. He is standing with his back to the wall, looking towards the entrance to the site. His thick black hair catches the sun, highlighting bluish undertones, and with his short, sturdy frame, he somehow seems very at home here.

'Ralph, what are you doing here?'

'I volunteer as guide here on my time off. I waiting group. You want I tell you some things? I have time.'

I nod and smile my delight at this suggestion.

Ralph takes me to the end of the chamber where the sign says the huge gold obelisk had once hung. He explains to me that this huge gold disc, long since pilfered, was the central focus for what was effectively an annual ceremony of allegiance. He said there were grand processions, with folk all dressed up in their colourful clothes coming from all corners of the kingdom to renew the social contracts that made the Empire possible. When I ask him how they did that, he takes me round to a different chamber, which is very long. Here, he shows me niches in the walls, lots of them. These, he tells me, are where all the divergent clans in the empire would place their sacred icon; this would be a representation or sacred totem of their clan. The purpose was twofold: in the first place, while this icon resided there, this was a symbol of that clan's allegiance to the Empire, and in the second place, as long as it was being kept there, it signified the continuing protection of the Empire of that clan. In this way, there was a wonderful physical embodiment to demonstrate the treatises in place. Treatises which unified and centralised a system of organisation that enabled the Empire to flourish.

But Ralph's group has arrived now, so he leaves me to go attend to them. I am ready for a rest anyway, and I go to sit down on a bench in the courtyard and begin to enjoy the warming sun on my body, newly emerged from my sick bed. So lovely to breathe the fresh air and sit among these beautiful stones, imagining the buildings as they might have been in their heyday.

I start to ponder what Ralph had been explaining. The social engineering of the whole thing is perhaps something the United Nations could learn a trick or two from. The sacred objects housed by each clan must have been considered more than mere symbols, however potent a symbol can be. In a very real way for these people of old, these Icons left in the niches must have been felt to be part of their very souls, the soul of their tribe. If that were the case, then if the sacred emblems were to be destroyed or banished from the protection of the Temple, this would surely have seemed a potent harbinger of the downfall of their people, something to be avoided at all costs.

From all Ralph has been telling me, the Temple of the Sun was the epicentre, in a very real way, of the Inca Empire. So clever too, was the recognition that ceremony and ritual were crucial. In this way, each participating tribe's allegiance was tangibly demonstrated and, at the same time, the Empire's protection of those tribes – the ones whose Icons were safely guarded in the inner sanctum of the Temple – was made explicit.

But for me, the most fascinating aspect of this social engineering was the role that ceremony and ritual played in reinforcing this social cohesion. And playing into the geography of the Kingdom so beautifully too. Cusco, the Inca capital, was at the epicentre of all this, just as it is physically – sitting as it does in the bowl of the surroundings hills.

In what was very likely the central courtyard of the Temple of the Sun – what is now the central plaza or *Hawkaypata* – is the meeting or crossroad where the pathways from the four provinces or *suyus* of the Kingdom would have intersected. All roads led to and from Cusco quite literally.

The ceremonies of the time enacted this regularly. I imagine pageants on special high days with brightly dressed representatives from each corner of the Empire, arriving and passing through the central point, affirming their allegiance, not simply to the Emperor but to what lay behind him – the

Great Sun God *Inti*, by whose power the diversity of the many peoples was held together.

Despite the enormous amount of plundering and destruction that went on after the Spanish conquest, I marvel that it is still possible to see that chamber whose walls are lined with many niches.

I begin to imagine this mutual allegiance being renewed with great pageants held in Cusco. In the minds of the people, the value of the Icon in its niche was more than the splendour of the gold or silver from which it may have been made.

To be noncompliant and not joining in risked being cut off from the nurturing supply lines of food and textiles, true, but perhaps more seriously, to have your Icon cast out from the protecting niche of the Temple risked being cut off from the spiritual line of nourishment coming directly from the Sun God himself. I let my imagination run free and envision the spectacle back in the Inca heyday. All the walls lined with ornate gold and silver, the carved figureheads and colourfully dressed attendants resplendent in finely woven cloth, entering into the Holy of Holies, the inner sanctum with that huge mandala covering an entire wall in that central room. All that pure shining gold; it must have felt like you were entering into the heart of the Sun God's abode, not merely a physical building – the Temple of the Sun.

Cusco was this central point, the pulse of a mighty beating heart, giving life to all that was connected to it, all that radiated out from it, into the four directions or the four *Suyus* of the Kingdom. Any peoples would have gone to great lengths to maintain their allegiance, for to have your Icon taken down from its symbolic niche would very literally be having your settlement cut off from the life-giving blood of the central heart, causing withering and decay and, in no time, certain death.

I start to envision our modern world creating similar ceremonies to unite divided nations and remind each country of their interdependence. The enormous containers that criss-cross the globe on a daily basis, bringing the wherewithal of modern living from all corners and to all corners of our Earth, are a sign of our need for each other. Most people realise about oil, but what about all the other basic building blocks of our modern world, like salt and sand, copper and iron? How great would that be, if instead of the powerful nations extracting what they need by exploitation, rather took the time to honour the nations and the miners in those nations whose work enables these basic but crucial raw materials to reach the factories of the powerful nations.

My mind is brought back to the present. I am a little exhausted by all this imagining and starting to feel the need for some sustenance. I am wondering about checking out some of today's soup in that restaurant down the road from the school. However, before I head off, I notice a small group of people beginning to gather in front of me. They're in what might have once been the courtyard or garden of the Temple. They are grouping around what looks like a large statue or container hewn from a single piece of stone. As they gather around it, a few of them pull out what look like large pens that then unfold into dowsing rods. I know that is what they are, because I am familiar with dowsing. My mother had been a natural water diviner, which means with the use of twigs, she could walk about in a field and, by the response of the rods, know when water was underfoot. I had given it a try myself while attending a dowsing course in the past, with some success.

One person catches my attention the most. He is a tall, slightly stooped, grey-haired Englishman who has a look of concentration on his face. His eyes are closed, and he is moving his hands in different directions as though making up his mind about something. Crisscrossing them one way and then moving them a fraction to crisscross them another way. He then walks about purposefully with his dowsing rod, nodding and muttering to himself as the rod swivels back and forth as he goes.

The content of the dowsing course I had attended in the Fife countryside of Scotland had told us about ley lines. How apparently the whole world is crisscrossed with these lines, some wider and more potent than others. Where it gets exciting, so it had been explained, is where these lines cross each other, and this is what I think the elderly man is describing as I get up from my bench to join the fringes of the group so as to be close enough to hear.

'The lines all run into this point,' he is saying, pointing to the centre of the solid stone trough. 'They form a cross here as they pass through.' He is placing his crisscrossed hands decisively over the stone, having made up his mind about the exact direction of each line.

I wonder if he is their teacher and they are his students, because they are attending to him so keenly. 'The lines are around forty-five metres wide,' he is telling them. 'Type three pairs crossing each other here. This would make this a sixth order node.'

He stops talking to the group and begins to attend individually to his flock, helping them feel for themselves what he is speaking about.

'While there are many sixth order nodes in the world at sites of special interest there is something special about this node...it has an Emperor Dragon line running through it leading all the way up to Saksayhuaman...' I hear him say as I reluctantly leave them to it, deciding a bowl of soup has to take precedence, as I am starting to feel quite weak. I am still adjusting to the rarefied air.

Back at the school, the days start to settle into a routine. Rodolfo keeps us in class and sticks to the curriculum from then on. I take to going down to the main square every afternoon after classes. The restaurant I'd noticed halfway down the hill has proved a real find. Now, every day I enjoy their freshly made soup with noodles and vegetables and little pieces of chicken, which makes a perfect lunch. Gradually, I am supping my way back to strength. I still have to go slowly up the steep hill back to the hostel, but even the youngsters slow down and do not chatter quite as incessantly as they make their way to the heavy wooden door that gives entry into the school.

Geoff has lent me a book about Peruvian mysticism, which I am studying, and I am eager to hear the talk Rodolfo is due to give that evening.

Chapter 18

Doorways Opening

After a light supper, I make my way downstairs to one of the bigger classrooms where Rodolfo's talk about Peruvian mysticism is to take place.

As I thought she would, Gianna is giving it a miss, and I wave to her as she passes on down the stairs to her night out. She has found a wee dive where she can dance salsa most nights of the week and is having a ball. Geoff was not there at supper, but I see him now passing Gianna on her way out. He's with a woman who I think recognise. Is it Carole, the hard-working lady who had been running the retreat centre in Scotland?

But she looks so different; her shoulders seem to have relaxed several inches down her back. Her hair is still piled up on top of her head, but in a looser bun with flattering tendrils escaping to frame her face.

'Carole? I can't believe it!

Carole, recognising me, smiles broadly. I don't think I ever once saw her smile in Scotland.

'Freya, you wee scone! Whit are you doin' here?' Her voice thickly Scottish to show her delight.

'I wis gonna ask you the same thing,' I switch to the vernacular as we give each other a big hug.

'Weel?' She waits for my reply.

'Och, I'm just takin a wee break,' I answer. 'Is the rest of the Scottish group here? '

'No, not at all,' we switch to our more normal voices. 'there's a retreat centre further down the Sacred Valley in a tiny village called Taray. I'm managing their retreats for them over the season.'

'Yes,' says Geoff, coming up now and putting his arm around her affectionately, 'that's where we met. I went there to see first-hand how an Ayahuasca retreat is run.'

I am thinking what a great pair they make, Geoff with his spiritual gifts and knowledge of Ayahuasca, and Carole with her amazing organisational abilities. Geoff is still assiduously practising his Spanish, so I am not sure how much Carole understood, but it doesn't seem to matter as they continue, arms around each other, up the stairs towards the room where the talk is to be held.

There are quite a few outsiders also coming to the talk; they are being directed upstairs by Ralph, who is at his post by the solid oak door entrance into the school. I can tell by the way he is standing, so proud and being so gracious, is enjoying the buzz. We give a little wave to each other in greeting.

Then I recognise the dowser and a few of the others from my visit to the Temple of the Sun coming up the stairs.

I go up myself and, finding a seat near the door, take a look around. There is Amuru, from the café. He is sitting wrapped in his poncho, his wide-brimmed hat partially hiding his face. He has seated himself up at the front, close to Rodolfo at his right side, facing into the audience, somehow lending potency to the room. Then he closes his eyes and seems to go into an alert sleep.

The talk is fascinating. Rodolfo describes the great ages of what he calls the precessional cycles. This is similar to what in the Hindu tradition are called the *Yugas*. As in the Hindu sacred texts, the Peruvian mystical tradition speaks of multiple ages gone by and the great flood that marked the end of one cycle; how these myths of a great flood can be found all across the world. Apparently, the Earth is travelling all the time through the constellation of the Milky Way, and as it reaches certain points on its journey, we can expect certain things to happen. These Precessional cycles last 24,000 years approximately, and Rodolfo seems to be saying (he is talking in Spanish, so cut me some slack) that we are nearing the end of one such cycle and we must expect tremendous upheaval in the ensuing decades. Also, more fascinating somehow to me, he seems to be suggesting that the Inca ruins that abound, especially around Cusco and the Sacred Valley, were not built in this Precessional cycle but were actually left over from more than 24,000 years ago. That they were built in the previous Precessional cycle. Images of things I had read about, the ancient civilisations of Atlantis and Lemuria, pop into my head. Rodolfo is saying that there was an equally important civilisation of the Pre-Inca era, now lost in the mists of time. He is saying that the Earth – or our sacred *Pachamama*, as the Peruvian mystics refers to our home – has done a lot of shifting, including continents and seas moving and changing hugely over these aeons of time.

All this is fascinating, but it is what he says next that arrests my attention thoroughly. It is what he and Amuru had begun to explain to us in the café when I had been recounting my dream of the golden Angel thumping a great golden staff into the ground, compelling me to travel to Peru.

He is explaining the Peruvian belief of how Cusco was founded. *Manco Cápac*, son of *Inti*, the Sun God, was sent forth from Lake Titicaca, by *Viracocha* the Creator, with a golden staff to found the city of Cusco. In a reverse from the British myths of King Arthur, instead of pulling the sword easily out of the ground, it was the spot where the staff hit the ground with a single blow and sank in that would indicate where the city was to be founded.

The centre of the city was in the heart of the Temple of the Sun, the place that I had visited only a few days previously. Rodolfo is saying that the stone trough marks the exact spot where legend has it that significant blow was struck, the very place where the staff hit the ground and sank deep into the Earth.

This was the place where the dowser and his followers were hovering when I had visited. He is going on to say that this area marks the spot of an important nodal axis, that through it travels what he calls *ceques* or lines of energy, reaching out to link other power points all over the world. I see the English dowser just in front of me nodding and writing in a little notebook.

I feel a shiver go down my backbone at the thought of my golden Angel waking me by banging the golden staff into the ground, propelling me to go to Peru. I had had no idea of the connection between a golden rod and the founding of Cusco. Nor had I known about the golden God Inti and His Temple, here in Cusco, once all lined with gold.

Rodolfo is going on to say that there are big changes ahead for humanity, as we are completing one of the great Precessional Cycles and are about to shift into a new one. According to their traditions and prophesies, this will be heralded by great changes and upheavals for the inhabitants of the Earth. He talks about a messiah figure being born to a young indigenous girl.

This sets my mind thinking. I love how these messiah stories from different religions carry similar themes. After all, Jesus, the Christian Messiah, was born to Mary, a young maiden.

Rodolfo has reached the end of his presentation. I stay seated where I am, frankly, a bit stunned. Amuru and Rodolfo are heads together and Amuru seems to be giving out instructions. The dowsing gentleman has hung back with one of the women he arrived with. She has a lively, intelligent, open face. Carole and Geoff too have hung back, as one by one the others leave. Just then, Ralph comes back in. I can't help noticing his similarity to Amuru, both of them wearing ponchos which bring out their indigenous features. Both have those same melting brown eyes. Ralph with his shock of straight black hair, Amuru's turning silver. He closes the door.

Rodolfo turns to us. Speaking in English, he says,

'Thank you for coming to my talk and thank you for staying. Amuru would like to invite you, if you are willing, to a special ceremony, now, this evening, a short walk from here.

'He believes it is no coincidence you are all in this room together at this talk, and he has taken this as a sign that now is the right time to do a nodal activation that he has known for some time has been required.'

Amuru looks on and nods, trusting his message is being relayed correctly.

Geoff, Carole, and I look at each other and of course readily agree. Then we all hastily introduce ourselves to the dowser, who is a retired pilot from the UK called Graham, and his friend, who is from Italy, an energy healer called Marianna.

Rodolfo tells us we have half an hour to get ready and then meet him outside the main door of the school.

—

By the time we reconvene outside the huge solid oak door half an hour later, the street is quiet, with only the odd figure, head down, making for home. At the bottom of the street, nearer to the main square, are a few stragglers smoking a last cigarette, reluctant to call it a night. Rodolfo and Amuru are not there, and Ralph, it seems, is to be our guide. I am surprised that instead of heading down the hill, he takes us up a little way before diving down a cobbled alleyway to the left. With a few more swift turns, we push open a door almost hidden with ivy and twigs and, trusting our guide, find ourselves in a secret underground tunnel. Ralph doesn't stop and we have to walk briskly to keep up and, as we wend our way, I begin to lose all sense of direction. No one seems fazed, though, as we focus on keeping together and keeping up with Ralph. We are all equally surprised when we find ourselves in the courtyard of the Temple of the Sun. We come out from a narrow part of the tunnel and emerge from behind a tumbled-down pillar and into the courtyard. We are only yards from the central trough and from the spot where I had been sitting only a few days ago. I realise I had not noticed the opening from below because it is obscured by the ruined pillar and scraggly undergrowth.

Amuru and Rodolfo are already there waiting for us. They are standing around the nodal point that has been explained to us is the centre of the node – that hewn stone container. There are two other men with them. I recognise them both from Rodolfo's talk. A young, strong, upright European-looking guy with tanned skin and close-cut hair, and an older man with long hair, also wearing a poncho, although he is not Peruvian. He is tall and thin and has a reverential air about him, and he is deep in meditation. Without speaking, we shuffle about and thus find our place within the circle around the trough.

We take each other's hands in the darkness. I am between Carole and Marianna. Amuru speaks and Rodolfo translates in careful and grammatically correct English. 'Amuru has asked me to thank you all for being here. We are both part of a line of shamans going back through our oral tradition into a time before the Spanish came, keeping alive the ancient traditions and prophesies of our lineage. He wants you to know that this is no accident you have arrived in Cusco at this propitious time. We have gathered you here this night, as this is an important nodal point.

Twenty-four thousand years ago; the time when we shifted into this current Great Cycle; the one that we are now preparing to leave; this site – here where we stand – was one of only a handful of First Order Nodes that existed on land. This very spot too, in the time of the Inca Empire, was the lynchpin of the entire system that kept the Empire together. Radiating out were forty two *ceques* or lines of organisation which connected to over three hundred *huacas*. The *huacas* were shrines: sometimes a sacred spring, sometimes a temple, perhaps a rock or a fountain or dwelling. They were intrinsic to the maintenance of the Social Order.

Our job here tonight is to gather the threads together; to activate this nodal point and in so doing to link up with other nodal points similarly being activated over these crucial days and weeks and month ahead. This is being done in order to prepare for what is to come. This is going to be done all over the world during this next month, when the right people will be called to gather at these special points, at the right time. He says to tell you that we had been planning to wait until the end of December, after our summer solstice on the 21st December, to do this Cusco activation. This would coincide with when Pluto will be crossing the Galactic Centre exactly. But Amuru says that he has taken deep counsel and because of the serendipity of the people who are here now in this group, all arriving in Cusco at the same point in time, we are taking this as a sign that now is the correct moment for this ceremony.'

Amuru speaks some more in his native Quechan. Rodolfo, nodding his understanding, continues to translate his words.

'Pluto is no longer retrograding, and over the next weeks it will become closer to, until it finally aligns conjunct to the Galactic Centre at the end of this month. He says it will go back and forth over this potent point, the centre of our galaxy, for over a year. He says to expect difficult times to come over this coming year and to be prepared. The challenges can come in many forms. This is especially true for those like yourselves who are connected more specifically to the Galactic Centre.'

Amuru speaks again, gravely, and he seems to be looking at me with compassion. Rodolfo continues his translation, 'The Galactic Centre is a potent point; it is from here we believe floods in new energy, fresh beginnings, and new inspirations. Essentially it is a great black hole, full of potentiality, and terrifying too, because here there is complete emptiness yet fullness too. The fullness of all potentiality not yet formed. As always with Pluto comes death and destruction and huge challenges. By connecting to the Great Void, the centre of our galaxy, we invite renewal, although we can have no idea what form this will take.' Amuru nods sagely, then says something briefly in Rodolfo's ear which he then translates.

'Please now take some time to introduce yourselves too.'

Marianna speaks first. 'I feel greatly honoured to be here. I am a healer and live in Italy. My healing practice is on an important node and I believe that is why I get such good results. So, I appreciate the importance of what we are about to do.'

Graeme next. 'I am a dowser from England, and I was here earlier in the week and already picked up that this is an important nodal point with energy generating out to the four quarters from its centre.' The tall man with the long hair and poncho introduces himself as Michael. He has a beautiful way about him, humble yet strong. 'I-I-I I am a h-h-orticulturalist from G-Gloucestershire' Michael begins with a stammer which subsides as he gets into his flow, 'and h-h-have wanted to visit here for a while. S-s somehow everything f-f-fell into place for me to do so now. I have studied much in India and learnt about the yugas and can concur that the sages agree we are about to reach the end of the Kali Yuga – the age of darkness – and shift into a New Age of return to our spiritual roots. It is not a straightforward transition however and some s-s-say we have to p-p-pass through 'The Yoke' and each one face the darkness before we can leave the old ways behind and r-r-reach into the new beginnings. ' Michael finishes what he has to recount and steps back folding his long elegant work weathered hands together in front of him and bowing his head slightly.

It is the turn of the younger man to speak. He tells us his name is Dan. 'I run hiking tours to the sacred sites around here, Machu Picchu and beyond. I have been living here over six years now. I come originally from Israel.'

Carole speaks next. 'I am working in the spiritual retreat centre in Taray, further down the Sacred Valley, helping run things. I've been doing that before in Scotland, but I'm actually from Manchester.'

Now Geoff. 'I am from the USA. I have been living in the jungle in Peru with an Ayahuasca master, learning from him as I want to return to my native country and run retreats bringing this sacred and powerful medicine to help combat some of the ills of our Western way of life. I am currently staying in the same retreat centre in Taray as Carole. I came out of the jungle to improve my Spanish so I can understand my shaman better and also see firsthand how to run an Ayahuasca retreat.'

Now it's my turn; I notice Amuru lifting his gaze, his rheumy eyes looking at me so intently, it's impossible to dissemble. 'I felt propelled to come here by an Angel dream,' I say simply, 'a great golden Angel startled me awake, with wings spread wide like a golden condor. They thumped an enormous staff into the ground with the word ENOUGH! My heart was pounding and racing as I awoke startled, clutching my chest. I felt that a big turning was upon us, that we had to change our ways. Ever since I was a little girl, I have had the sense that everything must change. When people used to ask me, "What do you want to be when you grow up?" I remember being puzzled. Why are they asking me that? There is no point being anything, everything has to change. In fact, I did become something – a yoga teacher. In this way I can stay in a place where I don't have to be caught up in society's values, as they are today. And hopefully I can give my pupils the space to find their centre, to connect to their inner stillness.'

There is a pause and we each of us smile and nod to each other as we take in each other's stories, while Rodolfo relays my words back to Amuru in his fluent Quechuan.

Amuru nods, satisfied. Now we are to move on to the next part of the ceremony. Ralph appears out of the shadows, and he is carrying a big staff. Amuru indicates he is to hand it to Carole, who is on my right. We let go of each other's hands. She, in turn, passes it to Amuru on her right, who passes it to Michael and so on round the circle. Everyone takes the staff and holds it mindfully for a minute, then passes it on. We are all going deeper into ritual space, and I am starting to feel a swirling vortex of energy sweeping around us. A vortex that seems to me to be carrying us upwards. I am sure the others are feeling it too as we all begin to sway gently. I am feeling a great tugging from the centre of the node. I feel an overwhelming desire to step into the centre. My heart starts tugging again in just the same way as it did in my dream. I feel like a dog tugging at the leash, desperate to get outside. I turn to glance at Amuru. He is watching me intently and, understanding, nods his permission. I go to step into the trough, the centre of the sacred node, just as Marianna is handing me the staff. I step fully into the centre, holding the staff high and feeling all my focus reaching up and up into the Great Void. I tune into that place, which in the past has so terrified me. This time I am doing so consciously. Within this ritual context, somehow, I am no longer afraid. I feel the support of the group as I open myself without fear to experience the Void. All that I have pushed away, I let come to me. I feel a spinning in my forehead. I have felt this once before when I was deep in the Scottish

Highlands running a yoga retreat. I was sitting quietly in my room when my third eye, as Indian sages term the energy centre or chakra situated in the centre of the forehead, began to spin and open. It was happening again here in this potent setting. But now something else strange I have not experienced before begins to happen. I feel a second activation, only this time in the back of my head, a great whirling well of energy revolving behind me at the base of my skull. I somehow 'know' this is the place where the Great Void connects into our human frame; but instead of being frightening, it is exhilarating. I feel a flood of energy flowing through me into the third eye centre and flowing out through the back of my head. I feel myself reaching higher and higher towards the Galactic Centre, and a great joy fills my whole being. I feel a huge smile beaming on my face as I slowly turn, holding the staff high above my head. And then, just when I feel I may shatter into a thousand pieces with the blissful joy of it all, I find myself bringing the staff down decisively onto the ground in the exact centre of the node. Everything speeds very fast, like light and energy rushing to

Earth faster than the speed of light, into this central nodal point. Whence from there it is radiating along the *ceques* or ley lines out through all the Earth to every point of the compass. I hold tight to the staff and use all my focus to stay standing upright. Then suddenly nothing and everything goes blank.

Chapter 19

Coming Down From The Heights

When I come to, I am lying on my bed back at the school. I have no memory of how I got here. Carole is beside me, chaffing my hand. I wake up smiling.

'Hey, welcome back – you gave us all a bit of a fright.'

'How did I get...?' I begin to ask her.

'Luckily, young Dan is strong; it was he who caught you and pretty much carried you back here.'

She gives me a cheeky wink, as Dan is a bit of a hunk.

'Behave!' I say, and we're both laughing.

'But what happened...?' I am searching my mind to find a memory.

'Okay, well, we were all in the circle holding the space. I could feel this pull on my heart, and it seemed to me like a vortex of energy was circling around us, connecting us all from the heart centre and then spiralling into the circle where you were and then from there spiralling upwards. It got really intense. You were looking like you were on another plane altogether. You were smiling fit to bust, and I started to worry you might be whisked upwards too. I was ready to grab your ankles,' she jokes. 'But I had to concentrate really hard myself just to hold my ground, 'cos I felt like I might be pushed backwards with the power of the force. And then suddenly the energy seemed to reach a peak, and then all was quiet, and that was when you collapsed onto Dan.' She eyes me sideways as she says this.

'Stop it,' I say, 'what about the others?'

'Well, you were on the floor in a heap being cradled by our hero, and we all gathered round and shared a bit about what we had experienced. Michael described much as what I had felt, and the others all agreed they too had felt that pull from the heart and that same sense of the energy spiralling. Amuru looked pretty shattered and Rodolfo took him off quite quickly, leaving Ralph to get us all out of that place and get you home. We went back through the tunnel. It was a bit awkward, actually, with you an inert heap. Ralph helped me get you up to your room.' Here Carole yawns, and I realise she must have been keeping vigil while I have been out of it.

'Carole... thank you... You must be shattered!' I sit up.

'Yes, but thank goodness you're back. Listen, before he went off last night, Amuru mentioned the high altitude here is hard for your system. So, Geoff and I were wondering if you would like to move down to Taray. It is lower and right by the Urubamba River in the Sacred Valley. It'll give you time to find your equilibrium. The next retreat's not for a couple of weeks, so there's space.'

I readily agree, as Amuru is not wrong, the high altitude is still quite taxing for me. The thought of being lower down, in a tiny village *and* near Carole and Geoff, both of whom I trust and like, is bringing a big smile to my face.

'Okay, well, look, you get some sleep now and we'll set off tomorrow. We'll pick you up after breakfast and drive down there. We'll stop in Pisaq. It will be a market day. You'll like that, it's very traditional.' Carole leaves and I fall into a blessed and dreamless sleep.

I am ready and packed when Carole reappears early the next morning. Ralph is there to see us off as we exit through the sturdy oak door. He had been very solicitous at breakfast, making sure I ate a tasty freshly made omelette and that I drank his green coca leaf tea brew, before he let me drink my Darjeeling brew. And with lots of smiles and handshakes, we go out into the street. A taxi is already waiting for us, but before we can get in, we spot Rodolfo, appearing with Amuru at his side. They are on the other side of the road, a little up the hill, emerging from one of the many alleyways that led off the main street. That must be the way we took to the underground tunnel.

We all start waving and smiling cheerily at each other. As Amuru reaches me, he takes both my hands in his and shakes them warmly, all the while doing that shamanic checking out I have started to grow accustomed to. Meanwhile Carole and Rodolfo are also greeting each other with warm handshakes. Amuru, clearly satisfied with what he has divined about my state of health, speaks to Rodolfo who passes on this message.

'We achieved the nodal activation as required. The *Chakana* or cross is not just on the horizontal plane but also on the vertical. It was this meeting that we managed to do yesterday. You will feel better in the Sacred Valley and be able to enjoy the nature.' At this, he hands me a small object wrapped in tissue paper. I open it and am so touched to see a beautifully crafted *Chakana* cross, the cross of four equal sides, with a square inside the cross. I think it is made of pewter.

'Thank you, thank you so much.' I place my hand on my heart. 'I will treasure this.'

Amuru nods his understanding and then, tugging at Rodolfo's sleeve, speaks gravely to him, all the while keeping me in his sight.

'Amuru says you must be prepared for things to be difficult in the immediate future, as this heavenly transit completes its work.' Rodolfo imparts this news to me. 'We have opened a new pathway into the future, but this pathway needs consolidating. Those who have been prepared to lead the way must walk into the Nothingness of all Potentiality to create a pathway that others might then follow. There will be no signposts. Amuru says in the weeks and months to come, you will be called upon to trust your inner guidance, to follow your inner light as never before. For some reason, you are wired to be susceptible to the energy of the Great Void. This is why you were able to play the part you did in the ceremony last night. Remember, we are part of your circle of protection now. Reach out to us if you need us.'

I turn to face them, bowing gravely to each one in turn. Amuru then reaches for my arm and squeezes it, then with that rheumy smile, he turns on his heels and they are gone, whisking away from us and swiftly disappearing up the street and back down the alley from whence they came.

The cheeky-looking driver is enjoying observing all this and winks at me as I catch his eye. He tells me he is from Taray, the village where the retreat centre is, and his name is José. He speaks in a mixture of Spanish and not bad English. Carole is explaining that Geoff has gone ahead to a sacred site nearby called Saksayhuaman, and we will pick him up on our way down the valley.

José, overhearing this, asks in English if we want him to go by 'saxy woman', laughing at the well-worn pun, rolled out to every passenger, I imagine.

Carole is distracted as Ralph has just appeared from the doorway, carrying a box of provisions she must have had delivered there to take down to Taray. While he stashes this in the boot, I go to retrieve my case, which I had left just inside the big oak door. It's not a big case, I like to travel light, and it's a pretty nondescript black, but with a thick rainbow belt buckled round it tightly. It's actually the one I use in my yoga practice but it is also great at airport baggage reclaim to quickly pick out my luggage. Carole takes it from me. 'Yeah, if we get a move on, we'll be there before any tourist crush.' She stows it alongside the box and throws in her own bag, a woven zipped bag decorated with llamas. She must have bought it here. Both Carole and I go to take our leave of Ralph. His intense brown eyes crease at the corners as he shakes my hand, taking it warmly in both of his, before he steps back, slipping back under cover into his role as caretaker.

'Go in the front,' Carole invites, 'enjoy the view.' I slip into the front seat beside José, putting my neat day rucksack on my knees, and we're off.

The journey takes around ten minutes. We stay high up but as we descend, every now and again I get a glimpse of the road wending its way down into the Sacred Valley below.

Cusco is said to be built in the form of the body of a panther, and Saksayhuaman is apparently seen to be the head of that panther. It is sited a little distance from Cusco and sits upon a long, flattish hill. I have already been knocked out by the masonry in Cusco, but here the stonework is even more extraordinary. The enormous blocks of stones fit so meticulously together, so smooth, so huge and all with no mortar. You could not even put a folio of paper between each layer.

As everywhere else in ancient Cusco, over the three centuries since the *Conquistadores* arrived, the stones here have been plundered and used to overlay Christianity onto these ancient ways of life. In this place, it is mainly the top stones on the upper part of the site which have been removed. Here, where I am standing in the lower part of the site, the stones that I am admiring are so huge they are happily not plunderable. Apparently, what is left of Saksayhuaman – *The Fortress of the Royal Hawk* – was once the foundations of a settlement. In the past, many buildings would have sat atop these solid foundations, supporting many people and a vibrant way of life.

Just then, we spot Geoff. He has climbed right up onto the hill and is standing deep in contemplation just where the sun is hitting the hillside. I let Carole climb up to him and while I am waiting, José points out some of the finer details of the site. He is clearly proud of his heritage, and as I listen to him speaking, I notice those same deep-set brown eyes indicating indigenous heritage.

Geoff safely retrieved, we set off down the winding road leading towards Pisaq, which is to be our next stop. I notice Geoff glancing carefully at me and when he sees that I am none the worse for wear – in as much as I am still in the land of the living – he doesn't ask me any questions. I am grateful for this.

The mountains that surround us are the colour of dry sand tinged with reddish pink. In fact, everywhere looks dry – not in an arid way, there is still plenty of green. But many of the rocks are the colour of ash and the air when you breathe in doesn't have that dampness we are so used to in Scotland. As we start to descend, we get a great vantage point where I can see how indeed Cusco sits in a bowl shape with all the surrounding hills cradling it in a wide enveloping circle. It is very lush and green and mossy. Initially, the trees to the side of the road are stunted, but gradually, as we get further down the valley, they get taller. The more we descend from the great heights, the better I start to feel. I can breathe normally again and don't feel every breath is a labour. And by the time we reach the outskirts of Pisaq, some 1,300 feet lower than Cusco, I feel quite restored. Later, I discover Pisaq is still a good 1,500 feet higher than the point when altitude sickness can kick in, so starting out even higher has been a good preparation – I must have made lots of extra red blood cells by now.

—

Arriving in Pisaq, José pulls the taxi up by a little bridge over the Urubamba river, just on the edge of the little town. As we get out, I notice the river looks quite murky. He points to the other side of the bridge where there is a track going off the road to the right. This is the way to Taray, he tells me. But before we go there, Carole wants me to see Pisaq. José is very happy to wait. A group of men, no doubt fellow taxi drivers, are clustered in front of a rough and ready café over the way, and he disappears into their midst as they greet him. We head into the centre of town to the main square.

Pisaq is bursting with colour. We have arrived on a market day! The main square is alive with stallholders, some still setting up their brightly covered booths, and quite a few folk are milling about looking for early bargains. Many of them are women dressed in the traditional Peruvian way, brightly coloured, flared skirts and wide-brimmed hats, some with babies slung behind their backs secured in wide, material sashes. And there is a woman with her carrier slung to the front, a little llama peeping out. I feel quite gleeful, drinking in the sounds and smells and bustle. I am so pleased Carole insisted I experience this.

Pisaq is a village, or small town. It sits below high mountains which enclose it in a half moon. The mountains are terraced and there are many stone hewn steps which lead all the way up to the top. Even from here I can see there are ancient ruins where people must have lived in the past. They must have been fit, clambering up all those steps, which I can see go all the way to the very top. There must be fabulous views to enjoy from up there. I marvel afresh at the people who have built these structures. Imagine all that clambering up with heavy building materials. I make a note to check with José whether you can get a taxi up there.

The town is bound by the mountains on one side of it and the Urubamba River on the other. The road that we have just lately descended from Cusco continues to take you down deeper into the Sacred Valley, past Ollantambayo and beyond to Machu Picchu.

But today is not the day for vigorous exploring. Instead, we mingle among the stalls and stallholders jostling for customers. Brightly coloured dyes of every hue for sale jostle alongside great hunks of animal carcasses. A stall holder is making me feel queasy, as machete in hand, she makes ready to hack off a slab of meat for a customer. Clearly, butchery skills are not too highly prized round these parts. Everywhere are brightly coloured clothes and garments for sale. Pots of *chica*, a kind of corn on the cob, bubble away. I hand over the required pesos and the lady plucks out one with tongs and wraps it in some greaseproof paper and I enjoy gnawing away on it as we wander. Having finished that, I pass a young woman with a baby strapped to her back, standing at a mini barbecue stall where she is slicing slivers of lamb onto small thin paper plates, adding a small, freshly boiled potato out of a pot boiling at her side before selling it to her customers. It smells tasty, so I go up to her. Smiling, I make the transaction. It is delicious and reviving. I am definitely getting my appetite back. By this time, I have become separated from Geoff and Carole, but now I see her waving to me through the crowds. She comes up to me and takes my arm.

'We are going into Lulu's now to drink some tea, want to join us?'

I cross over the threshold with Carole, where Geoff is waiting for us by the door, and it is as if I have gone into a time warp. I could be back in hippy Wales in the early eighties.

Lulu's Café, what can I tell you? Tibetan-looking drapes adorn the walls, wooden benches line these walls, cushioned with foam covered in some woven Indian looking fabric that makes me think carefully before sitting down, especially when a glance around reveals several hippy-time-forgot types. Some with dreadlock hair and that stoned tomorrow-will-do-fine look in their eyes. I gingerly sit down, choosing a rickety wooden chair over the material seats. There are English newspapers here, albeit a few days old, and a notice board advertising the kind of things that English speakers visiting the Sacred Valley want to do, for instance yoga retreats, obviously run by ex-pats, as yoga is not exactly part of Peruvian culture.

Lulu herself comes up to serve us. An energetic woman in her fifties, she loves a new face and has come to meet me, which is fine by me as we take a shine to each other. I am curious to know her story, and while Geoff is getting tea at the counter, she explains to Carole and me that she is an expat American who arrived in Cusco some 15 years before and fallen for some local Peruvian. They had married, and although the marriage had long since died a death, she had stayed on, moving down from Cusco to the less rarefied heights and easier climate of the Sacred Valley.

Carole gets up to help Geoff with the tea things, and Lulu confides in me that she had rather burnt her bridges by selling up her property in the States to finance her move, which had made it problematic to move back. Whatever, she has clearly made a go of it here. Her café in the main market square has become a hub and a haven for English speakers. She has WIFI and an international telephone line, which is highly sought after. This is still the early days of the internet, and WIFI was not a given on every street corner. Travellers mainly have to log into an Internet café to communicate back home. As a wee side line, Lulu also takes in laundry, for which service she charges a reasonable sum. She is able to employ quite a few local Peruvian women to help her run all of this, and I could see for myself they were being kept busy hanging out piles of that day's washing in the sunny backyard and folding the dried clothes up ready for collection. Additionally, they help her behind the counter and in the kitchen, making and serving up copious green tea and flapjacks to her many customers, hungry from clambering about the extensive ruins overlooking the town.

The climate in this part of Peru in the Sacred Valley, being so incredibly dry is great for drying clothes out of doors. The sun, when it shines – which it does most days – gets so hot that it is possible to put even soaking wet jeans out in the morning and they will be dry by early afternoon. By the end of the afternoon, any washing can be folded up and be ready for collection later that same day. Lulu told me she did not need an electric dryer to make her laundry viable.

Notwithstanding, we are not going to need to avail ourselves of this efficient laundry service, as apparently the retreat centre we are heading to, over on the other side of the Urubamba River, is well equipped.

After all the external stimulation, I suddenly begin to feel the need of some quiet. Carole must have noticed the look on my face because she says, 'Come on, let's get on the road and head to the retreat centre, it is only a few miles to go now.'

I smile, grateful that she has noticed, as I am waning fast. We swig back the rest of our teas and start to head back to the bridge, where we left our driver. As we pass down the side street, I notice a small juice shop, and Carole waits for me as I nip in and order a fresh banana, mango and papaya. She doesn't want one, and laughs at me as I come out of the wee shop with a very large smoothie.

'I see you are making up for your loss of appetite!'

Undeterred, I slurp away happily at the tasty concoction and feel the better for it.

Having found José and all bundled into the taxi, we set off along the dirt road that José had pointed out on our arrival in Pisaq. Barefoot children with jet black hair are freely roaming, as well as pigs and slightly scary mongrels. All need to be carefully avoided, but José takes it all in his stride, and without mishap, we reach the tiny village of Taray.

Here, even this dirt road comes to an end as we arrive in front of a huge main square around which the villagers' houses are closely clustered. Facing us at the far end of this square is an enormous white painted church which totally dominates this tiny village. Behind it and on each side are clusters of simple houses disappearing into a thicket of greenery and trees. A steep slope leads up the hill, but there is no road out that way. The only way to leave Taray by car is to retrace your steps back along the mile and a half of dirt road we have just driven along. Looking to the left of the big church, I notice a steep slope, which Geoff tells me wends all the way up to the main road back to Cusco, but only for travellers on foot. Behind us, the Urubamba River continues its journey, bubbling and brown with mud. I am a little disturbed to see that a lot of debris – mostly stuff made of plastic: old bowls, discarded household items, torn plastic bags – all have been flung into the water with impunity. Environmental protection is clearly not a thing here yet. Pondering later, it occurs to me that the inhabitants of these houses, many of them with dirt floors and the ubiquitous slate roofing made from baked mud, would have used clay pots before the advent of plastics, so their lifestyle would have been quite biodegradable. Clay pots and mud tiles would in time have been absorbed back into the river with no damage. Unfortunately, now the debris in the river is mostly plastic, and it isn't going anywhere.

As the road has petered out, we take our bags and walk the short distance behind and to the left of the big church to reach the retreat centre. Geoff is leading the way, carrying the box of provisions, and Carole has taken my suitcase. Some stunted trees in the main square offer a fun climbing frame for the village children, and one girl, her pigtails dangling, is hanging upside down.

I smile at them all and the small band of them stare as we make our way towards a wooden sign which is hanging by a chain above the entrance to an enclosure. As I get closer, I can make out the word *Picaflor* carved onto the sign and a small hummingbird insignia painted at the bottom. It looks just like the pictures I've seen of one of the Nasca lines. I am so enjoying the air being more breathable, and the quiet too is a blessed relief. Carole takes me through the high gate and leads me along a narrow crazy paved path to the right where there is a row of simple barracks-like buildings made of wood, each with their own door. She leads me through one of the doors, and we are in a room with a high window open to the sound of bird song through which I can see gently swaying tree tops. The room is clean, with a scrubbed wooden table where I lay my bags.

'You get some sleep now, Freya, and I'll wake you for dinner. You'll be fine here.'

Carole gives me a reassuring hug and disappears to attend to her many duties now that she is back at work.

I need no second bidding. Having found the little bathroom block along the corridor and washed the travel dust off my hands and face, I go back to my room, get right under the covers and fall into a deep and peaceful sleep.

The following days pass pleasantly. The cost of the centre is similar to the school, so I am staying within my budget. They are not due to have another retreat for a week or two, so there is no pressure on me. I simply relax. The centre has a garden which runs between the long, thin buildings and the stream. It is very verdant with a delicious smell of the warm, dry earth, and I especially enjoy time spent swaying gently on a hammock outside in this garden. I like to gaze up at the tall, thin trees also swaying gently, their leaves translucent against the backdrop of the soft blue sky. There is a profusion of little garden birds, and I enjoy hearing their chatter, especially in the early mornings. But my greatest joy is to watch the native hummingbirds, which I have never seen before, some so tiny, flitting back and forth you could almost mistake them for dragonflies. If I keep quite still, they come feed on the tall showy flowers that surround the hammock. Each day, coming closer and closer to where I am idling. Only yesterday, one fed so near to me, its tiny wings working so furiously as it supped on the nectar they almost disappeared. I felt sure I could have touched it if I had stretched out my hand.

Meals are pleasant and nonintrusive. No one asks me about what had happened up in the cloisters at Qoricancha. I'm glad of that because I'm actually not sure myself.

On the third day, Geoff comes to sit by me on a neighbouring hammock.

'Hey, how ye' goin', Freya?' He is speaking in English, so this chat is not a Spanish practice.

'Good... so peaceful... really well looked after...' I pat my stomach, indicating the delicious food served up here.

'My body tho'... so achy...' I begin to stretch,' just want to sleep... and sleep.'

'You're a somatic,' he proffers. I look at him, puzzled. 'Someone who processes things through their body,' he explains.

'I can help you uncover what's going on for you by what we call in the trade "enquiring into the discomfort you are feeling". Are you up for that?'

'Okay...' I say. 'How d'you do that?'

He jumps nimbly out of the hammock. 'First of all, let's move!' he says. 'Come with me to the top of the hill, there is a beautiful waterfall I discovered hidden among the trees at the head of the valley.'

Taken aback by his sudden change of pace, I am swept up in the idea and, without thinking about it, find myself following him. He makes his way swiftly up the side of the steep hill thick with small trees and bushes. We have to stoop and dodge. It is all so beautiful, green and lush, and the earthy smells are heaven to my senses. We spot little birds darting ahead in the dappled light, a flash of hummingbird, iridescent blues and reds.

My breathing is getting laboured and I am forced to breathe more deeply. All those freshly made red blood cells are paying off. I get a second wind and with one last push find myself, laughing delightedly, sprawled on the mossy ground. I am by a huge boulder at the top of the cascade which is tumbling down below us. Geoff sits nearby, letting me enjoy this fabulous feeling of being among this most splendid of natural settings, feeling the sprinkle of the waterfall occasionally splashing my face.

After a while, Geoff says, 'Just stay as you are and feel into your body, and then describe to me what you are feeling.'

I do as he says and bring my awareness to my body, and particularly the back of my neck, a place where I habitually feel tight and constricted.

'It's my neck,' I say, 'it feels so tense and kind of stuffed.'

'Good,' encourages Geoff, 'now go more deeply into that feeling. Describe it a bit more.'

'Well,' I say, warming to my theme, 'have you ever seen a dressmaker? When making a collar, they turn it inside out and with a blunt, thin instrument, they stuff the collar fabric into the point before turning it right ways out?' Geoff nods, as he is clearly imagining what I am describing.

'Well, that about describes how my neck feels. Stuffed and compressed, like I'm surprised I can still turn my head. I'm so used to it, though, that I don't really notice. I mean, I do now 'cause I'm tuning in, but it's usually when there's extra stress that it just gets a bit much. And then it goes into one of my migraines and I'm out of action for days.'

'Do you get regular migraines?' Geoff asks, his tone attentive, yet matter-of-fact.

'Well, yes, I do actually.'

'Mmm,' he says, like a doctor diagnosing, 'probably the only break you ever give yourself.'

I am about to protest, as the horrible need to lie in a darkened room and not being able to face the smallest task is not my idea of a break, but actually, I can see he has a point. I certainly drop all my tasks when they occur. It is the only thing that keeps me from teaching my yoga classes, for instance; otherwise, whatever was going on, I would always show up. Break-ups, deaths, colds, aching body, tiredness, I work through them all.

'Wow, I never thought about it like that before.'

'Okay,' Geoff jumps up with decision, 'I want you to let yourself sink into the ground, just give your bodyweight to the Earth. See if you can get an image of how this stuffing into the neck happens. A situation where it might be ratcheted up.'

I do as I am told. It is so easy to sink into the warm mossy stone, I feel held and safe, the sound of the waterfall in my ears, and the little splashes playing with my face.

'I see my brother Leo,' I reply.

'Tell me how you see him.'

My voice is soft, the image is clear in my mind. 'He's 17, I must be 18. So beautiful, his hair... long, free... wild... like his gypsy soul, he'd never hurt a fly.' I'm smiling at the memory.

Despite my smile, Geoff must have noticed a shadow crossing my face, as he leans in even more attentively. 'He's so thin. I see him at the table. There's a lot of us – I come from a large family.' I offer this to Geoff by way of explanation. I fall back into my reverie.

'So many of us sitting round a crowded table in the kitchen, the noise, the stress, an atmosphere of tension. Something, probably quite trivial, tilts the balance, my father is exploding in rage. Leo is stopping midway to bringing some food into his mouth, he can't eat, he can't stomach it. His fork lowers back to his plate, his face almost imperceptibly pinching behind that great golden mane.'

I sense Geoff listening to my every word, which seems to extract the memory more vividly from my store.

'Now I see him again. We're in the street. He is coming towards me, a few inches taller than me, thin as a rake. "Freya, I've dropped to 7 stone. I should go to the doctor. Can you chum me?" He has nobody else to ask, everyone is preoccupied with their own survival in that overcrowded top-floor flat. And I can't go either. What was the reason, I don't remember now?'

I feel the tears falling now involuntarily, trickling into my ears and down onto the mossy rock that holds me.

'Was I down on the rota to cook that evening? Did I have to finish off some Physics or Chemistry homework? Or was it Maths? Maths was the best subject to lose yourself in, so ordered the numbers, you only had to learn the rules, and they never surprised you, never jumped out on you, gaunt and like a shadow needing your help, help that you couldn't give.'

Geoff continues to sit quite still, listening without comment. The sun plays with the canopy of trees flickering leaf shadows across the big rock and over my eyes, as though to find and then chase out these internal memories and pull them into the light of day. I carry on.

'It's a bit later now. I go into the kitchen, I think I was the first one to go in. It is the day he went mad. He's made a great mountain of everything he could find, emptied jars of beans, cornflakes, porridge oats, all our big catering-size packs. And then he had poured cooking oils over the whole big heap and then attempted to set it all alight. He'd pulled some postcards from the wall and added them, although I notice that he has not touched the wooden crucifix that hangs over the mantlepiece. He must have found some left over paint in the cupboard. I read the words he has daubed on the walls, "Everything must go except God and Oma" – Oma was our grandmother; she was living with us then. God and Oma.' I break from my reverie and open my eyes wide, half sitting up.

'Were these the only powers that were greater than the power of our mother? That snaky hold she wove around us all? I never thought of that before.' I tell Geoff.

'Who was Oma?' he asks.

'My mum's mum. Now I think of it, she hid the births of some of us from her. She must have been scared of Oma scolding her and my dad for their reckless procreating.' The thought amuses me slightly, but Geoff encourages me to settle back down on the mossy stone. I shift to an area where the sun is shining, fully lighting up the greens and hints of red of my temporary mattress.

'So, go back again and tell me how many were there altogether living in the flat?' Geoff enquires.

I take some time to recollect the space. 'How can I remember?' I answer, perplexed. 'Sometimes, someone left home, but then a bit later they might come back, bringing with them a spouse. One of my sisters lived there with her husband and new baby for a while, it was always pretty full. Maybe 18 people at times.

What I remember is the perpetual rounds of shopping, cooking, cleaning, collecting dirty clothes, sorting them into lights and darks, washing them, hanging them on the pulley in the kitchen, the window always left slightly open to air them, ironing them, folding them up and putting them away. All the while trying to keep up with my school work. I had a determined sense that doing well in my exams would be a way out for me. And then finding time to slip away from these endless household duties, visiting Leo in the hospital where they had started to pump him full of chemicals.' I have sunk deep again into the painful remembrance.

'And where was my brother gone? I watched him become bloated, perpetually moving from one foot to the other due to the effects of the drugs administered. They said he had schizophrenia. You know what he told me recently?' I open my eyes, looking at Geoff, who is still there with that quiet attentiveness.

'That they'd asked him if he heard voices and he had said yes, to see what would happen.'

I smile to myself ruefully. I suppose that *was* a bit crazy, my dear brother, choosing that moment to display his mischievous, anarchic spirit.

'He didn't come home for months and months and when he did, he was no longer recognisable; he'd grown so huge and bloated and never could sit still, always moving from one foot to the other restlessly due to the discomfort of holding all that heavy medication in his system.'

I sit myself up, hoping to somehow alleviate the pain, so full of emotion that I am rocking myself.

'And how did that make you feel, Freya?' Geoff persists with his forensic approach.

'Feel? How did that make me feel? Perhaps a fury so great I could pour out my breath and scorch the land.' I was shouting now. 'He didn't need to go to hospital, he needed a rest cure in the country. Couldn't they have taken him somewhere to run wild and eat good wholesome meals and strum on his guitar and be away from the relentless grind of everyday life? Instead, I had to see my brother's life become blighted with his label, see him tread so carefully in everything he did, afraid to take a step that would lead him back into hospital.'

'And what about now?' Geoff asks gently, 'How is your brother doing now?'

I take a while to bring myself back to calmness.

'He's actually okay,' I smile wanly, 'he's doing okay. He's always blocked from promotion by his medical record, but he's doing okay, works in the civil service. He got married and has two great kids.'

'That was a lot for you to handle and you were still a teenager yourself. Would you like to let some of that go? Give it to the ground?' Geoff is calm and focused.

Let some of this tension go? Is that even possible? my look seems to say. But Geoff is implacable. And in the face of this, I acquiesce.

'Okay, yes, I will give it a go,' I say sincerely, settling myself back down onto the rock.

'Take off your shoes and bend your knees so you can feel the soles of your feet on the moss of the rock.'

I do as he asks and begin to feel the connection to the rock through my feet through the spongy softness of the moss.

'Okay, so just notice your body lying on the ground and follow your breath.' Geoff continues to guide me into a deeper relaxation.

'As you breathe in, take your awareness to your feet and then as you breathe out, let the weight of your feet fall more heavily to the ground,' Geoff carries on in this way, 'feeling your legs become heavy, your hips, the base of your spine.'

I feel myself sinking more and more heavily into the mossy ground. I feel safe and supported, I hear the sound of the waterfall and imagine the running water beginning to wash away my tensions.

'Finally, release your neck, let the ground take the full weight of your head.'

My neck starts to soften, but then I resist this release. Geoff seems to intuitively understand why.

'Don't worry,' he says, 'whenever you need that level of alertness, it will be there for you. But like a warrior, you are allowed to put your spear down sometimes!'

We both laugh and in that moment, I feel a huge weight releasing from me, as if quite literally I am giving a great burden to the Earth. Taking a deep breath, I shake myself and sit up, still chuckling and grinning. But then I have a thought. 'Is it okay to give our burdens to the Earth, won't we burden the Earth?'

'Well, no,' says Geoff, 'for the Earth, it's compost, and like compost, it will break down and be recycled into harmless and nourishing components.'

Being a bit of a gardener myself, I have seen first-hand how food waste and weeds and so on can be broken down over time into gorgeous-looking soil ready to be used to grow more plants, so this makes sense to me.

'Geoff, thanks so much, I feel so much better.' The sun has begun to sink behind the mountain and there comes a chill into the air, heralding the start of evening. I lean over the stream where it is bubbling near my legs and splash my face with the pure water, enjoying that distinct fresh water smell I have loved from childhood. Cupping some into my palms, I bring my face close, inhaling deeply a few times and then gulping down several scoopfuls – so delicious. Then I run to catch up with Geoff as he has started heading down the steep slope, back to Carole and dinner.

—

It is one afternoon, about a week into my stay, when the Israeli guy, Dan – the one from the circle we had formed at the Temple of the Sun in Cusco – who had apparently carried me home, shows up. Carole is on a break and we are hanging out at the back on the hammocks, drinking coca leaf tea. We are all pleased to see each other, and he goes to sit in the centre of a spare hammock while Carole pours him some tea. I steadfastly refuse to catch her eye and only slightly blush when he asks me solicitously if I am okay. Having ascertained that yes, I am fine, he goes on to say he has come to tell us he is running a trip to Machu Picchu the following week and is wondering if anyone wants to come along. I am certainly up for it, and I text message Gianna, who is still up in the language school in Cusco. Her planned trip has just fallen through, so she is enthusiastically up for it and apparently with the two of us, his quota is now full and so we are all set. The next days are spent preparing for the trek and I get a lift up into Cusco to pick up some provisions. While there, I take Gianna to meet Dan in his smart office off the San Blas. With him is a blonde-haired young lass whose proprietary glances at us and back to Dan give us no doubt it's hands off. Ah well, I decide, he's a bit young even for my proclivities, and notwithstanding, we sign up for the trip and get all the details. I don't suffer any altitude side effects from the day trip to Cusco, and on my return to the retreat centre it is clear my days of recuperation and being molly-coddled are finished, as when I arrive back everything is bustle. Beds are being made up, provisions got in, local ladies are in the kitchen busy chopping vegetables in preparation for the arrivals the next day. But I will be gone by then, having booked my taxi for a very early start the next morning.

Chapter 20

Trip To Machu Picchu

The trip is wonderful – four days trekking in unspoiled country. Not even passing gaggles of noisy tourists on their return journeys can spoil it. Some of the younger sprightly ones in our party, including Gianna, enjoy to race each day's journey. But I prefer to go more slowly, so often I walk alone, which is bliss. I love walking through the mossy, gnarled forest floor with trees providing dappled shelter and not another soul in sight. The second day is hard, as it is a very steep uphill walk to the high pass, the highest point I have been to so far. It is a good bit higher than Cusco, at 4,215 metres compared to Cusco's 3,399 metres. Our guide, Cal, who works for Dan, had been assigned to carry the oxygen specifically to help strugglers at this point. But Cal is nowhere to be seen, having joined the fast ones in competition to reach camp first. I consider sitting and waiting, as I suppose at some point someone will come back for me. Yet by dint of going step by step, breathing slowly and carefully, I make it to the top of the pass, where I rather alarmingly see the big sign reading 'Dead Woman's Pass'. Well, not this one yet awhile! I take a moment to enjoy my triumph and survey the view from this dizzy height, before beginning the welcome descent to the less rarefied air. Halfway down, I spot a brook sprouting out from a deep underground spring. I take a moment to commune with the water and the land. I love the sound of the bubbling water, so pure and clear, and cup some into my hands to drink. I savour the delicious smell. Looking back down the trail, I spot Cal heading back up the pass towards me. He is looking rather worried and carries the oxygen cylinder and a flask. As he comes within earshot, he looks a bit flustered and out of breath.

'Are you okay, Freya? We were worried you'd got into problems on the pass.'

I refrain from telling him his administrations are a bit late, and I do drink some tea from the proffered flask, which is very reviving, and we amble down to join the others making camp near the bottom of the valley. The tents are already pitched and the porters are now busy building fires in preparation for cooking up dinner. We all help look for firewood, then I go for a wee rest before dinner. Gianna, whom I am sharing the tent with, indefatigable as ever, is showing some salsa steps to Cal.

The third day, we have to climb again a bit before beginning a steep descent. The way down is by way of well-worn hewn stone steps, which have been here hundreds, if not thousands of years. The porters, when they pass you, small and loaded up with their packs, fly past, sometimes only with sandals on their feet. After an hour or so on the trail, everyone has passed me, racing to be the first to arrive at our final night's pitch. I enjoy simply being alone in such a magnificent place. I love the stone under my feet. Trees are growing on either side of the path. And then I remember years ago, once running through a forest just for the sheer joy of it. And inspired by the porters, I decide to try it and begin to run down the steep stairs, trusting that my feet wherever they land will know how to adjust to whatever uneven surface they find. As I run, I gain in confidence and soon I am flying down the steps, round one tight bend after another. It is exhilarating, and all too soon, I see the others up ahead. I stop running and walk up on them nonchalantly, and so enjoy the look of bewildered disbelief in their faces, to see me all caught up with them.

Arriving at Machu Picchu in the early hours of the following morning, we find a slight mist over the buildings. Because we are so early, we are going to be able to enjoy the ruins to ourselves for nearly an hour before the tour buses bring the first early batch of visitors up from the *Aguas Calientes* train station.

Wandering around on my own, I find there is also a Temple of the Sun here in Machu Picchu. Apparently, it is aligned in such a way that the sun will shine through the entrance way at their summer solstice. Some say this would have served a useful purpose, being a helpful way to alert them to optimal planting times. Continuing to explore, I notice a half cross or half *Chakana* forming part of a wall which looks out towards the higher peak of Hauyna Picchu further into the site. The shadow of this half *Chakana* falls onto the stairs below, which I notice are also in a half *Chakana* shape. It seems to me that together they form a complete equal-sided cross.

It must be that the stairs were carefully sculpted to also follow the pattern of the *Chakana*, so that with the shadow, a whole cross would be formed. Seeing this symbolism reflected here is making me understand how important the message of the *Chakana* is. As above, so below; as inside, so outside. I find my fingers reaching to touch the *Chakana* I have been wearing round my neck ever since it was gifted to me. Clearly there is a lot in this symbol, more than I have understood.

I get up and start to wander about. The air is warming up and our party has spread themselves about, exploring as they will. The site has attractive notice boards with relevant information to help make sense of what I see as I wander round. Great mystery shrouds the knowledge of what exactly Machu Picchu has been. It lay empty for centuries until it was rediscovered in 1911 by a European explorer by the name of Hiram Bingham. At this point, it had already been abandoned by the Incas for several hundred years, as they left shortly after the Spanish conquest in the sixteenth century. When the indigenous peoples did leave the site for good, they disguised the paths leading up to it, and it was actually never discovered by the Conquistadors, but only much later on by the said Mr Bingham. Historians argue that it was built in the fifteenth century, but this I find hard to believe. Standing gazing at the amazing feats of engineering, the huge stones smoothed and so skilfully crafted and placed, I find myself on the side of those who say that this collection of buildings is a remain of a previous Yuga or age before this one; a remnant that was used by the Incas until the Spaniards arrived and the way of life was destroyed. Yuga is a term which comes from the ancient Hindu religion and refers to repeating 24,000-year cycles in Earth's history. After the end of this long period of time, the Earth is destroyed and has to be rebuilt. Many sages and seers argue that now, in 2006, we are approaching the end of the latest Yuga and we should expect catastrophe and unravelling to come.

Machu Picchu sits at a mere 2,430 metres so, although it towers over the neighbouring valleys, it is not as high as Cusco, and I am having no trouble breathing. In fact, it is very pleasant to be here. So much so, I decide to head up Huayna Picchu. This is a sheer mountain top just beyond Machu Picchu with no safety rails and a vertiginous view from the summit. I decide to do the climb as a mini vision quest. By that I mean that I will take a few moments to centre myself before climbing, and ask that some sign or message about my path in life be given to me on this climb. I don't have any trouble scampering up the first set of hewn stairways. Then all the safety walls end and climbers are completely exposed to the gorgeous panoramic views of the surrounding mountaintops. Unafraid, I leave behind many who are clutching these walls and deciding they have gone far enough. I find my way to the very top, and standing there with the wind blowing through me, overlooking Machu Picchu, I feel like a great eagle, or condor. How delightful it would be to soar off the ledge and circle around the splendours of the ruins beneath me.

I am struck by the incredibly inhospitable terrain and feel in awe that people could survive up here at all. We know that they did because there are remnants of buildings even up here on this craggy top. It could only have been because of the tremendously careful and well-thought-out organisation of Inca society that such a thing was possible.

Up here on this peak with nothing between me and the great rolling mountain range in front of me, I think about how the most recent manifestation of the ancient indigenous Peruvians, the Incas, had survived some 400 years. Their Empire had spanned some 2,000 miles, reaching all up and down the coast west of the Andes.

How did they manage to bring together the many disparate groups of people who made up the extensive Empire? I thought about what I had been learning while here. Part of it was the massive amount of physical infrastructure that was built; roads, outposts, water channels and terraces, to name but a few of these things. I had seen signs of some of these with my own eyes on the arduous trail over the last few days. Hewn stone water channels, high up where the snows come, sending that melting snow tumbling into the lower terraces warm enough to grow crops. What I see is only a small part of a vast complex of irrigation canals bringing life-giving water from the high mountains down to the valleys below. We also pass abandoned and ruined storerooms even higher up, where the cold, dry air makes it possible to store what is grown lower down without it spoiling.

From my lofty perch, images flood into my mind's eye, being in the terrain makes sense of my reading about the Inca Empire. Sturdy and reliable roads traversing throughout the Empire. Strategically placed barracks, interspersed with sentry boxes and constant streams of messengers or runners passing regularly between the sentry boxes and the barracks on the upper highways, receiving messages and information while delivering messages from the controlling administration. A huge physical internet highway of its day, buzzing with information and an extremely effective way of enabling compliance and cooperation.

Every new town or city brought under the aegis of the Empire was invited to join forces with the Empire and when they acquiesced, storerooms were built high on the mountainside that would be clearly visible to the inhabitants below. Filled with food and textiles, the message to the people below was clear: 'Align yourself with the Empire and you will never go hungry or unclad.' The reason being they would be joining a highly organised and effective system providing the means of not just surviving but surviving well in good times and in bad.

The steep mountain slopes create hugely different terrain. High and dry and cold is not good for growing, but it is perfect for storing and freeze-drying food, which can then be stored reliably for many years. Meanwhile, the lower south-facing mountain slopes were carefully terraced for crop growing. I had learned all about this on a visit to Moray with Gianna while still at the language school. Moray, a couple of hours' drive from Cusco, is a huge, terraced amphitheatre. The archaeologists studying the site believe it was used as a laboratory for experimenting with which slopes facing where and at what height produced the best crops, chosen from the likes of the many varieties of beans and potatoes and maize that can grow well in Peru. So, these terraces that were dug into the side of the mountain were built in a considered way. First, an inward slope prevented the earth being washed away. Then they were filled, first with rocks, then gravel and sand, and finally topsoil was carted up from the fertile valleys below. During the day, the rocky mountainside would heat up and the slow release of this heat during the night would be enough to mitigate against frost. It was quite a precise science. Successful crop growing would have in turn meant that the populations would not have been so at risk of the vagaries of the weather from year to year. All further reason to be happy to throw in your lot with the overarching Empire.

I think of the band of native Peruvian men who had carried all the accoutrements of our camp up and down the Inca trail for us. They were not tall, but sturdy and strong with tremendous stamina. Much like their ancestors then. An image of an abandoned village in a lonely spot perched on a clifftop comes into my mind from Mull in Scotland. This was a place I had loved to take my children in the summer, when they were small. Somewhere wild, where they could be in nature away from the city. In the old days the people from Mull had also had to walk long distances as a matter of course. Perhaps it only seems so impressive compared to the ease of our modern life. But then my mind vividly pictures the Q'eswachaka Rope bridge in Southern Peru. Gianna and I had visited it on another of our excursions from the language school. It had been quite a long trip from Cusco, as it is in the district of Quehue near Huinchiri. We were told by our guide, a native to those parts, that this was one of the only surviving rope bridges. It crosses over a dizzying deep gorge. I experienced it first-hand when I crossed over it. It was swaying and narrow and rather precarious with a clear view, if you made the mistake of looking down, of the plunging gorge below. It took a bit of courage for us to cross, it has to be said, so now imagine how they even built it.

Apparently, once again, the spirit of cooperation was evoked and the surrounding clans from either side of the gorge would come together. Coarse grass would be woven and by dint of working together, the rope bridges could be made. In this way, the bringing of goods back and forth could go on throughout even the most remote regions of the Kingdom. Damaging the bridges in any way was punishable by death. And the reason we were able to see it and cross it is because, in honour of their ancient history, the locals to this day come together to renew the Q'eswachaka.

The contributions a settlement was required to make in the grand scheme of things would depend in part on the height of the settlement. The warmer valleys, being free from frost, would be ideal for growing maize – one of the mainstays of the Incan diet – as well as other lowland crops. The middle-terraced slopes were perfect for growing potatoes, and up in the higher zones, llamas could graze, providing wool and meat. The higher cooler regions were also perfect for storing grain, grown lower down where it was warm, which could then be redistributed as required throughout the Empire. Even the abundant fruit from the rainforest could be dried and stored in the high altitudes of the mountains. In this way, with such intricate and interwoven mutual cooperation, the entire Empire could flourish and thrive in peace. And added to that were the annual rituals and ceremonies I had learned about in Cusco. All in all, it was a pretty cool way of organising things, ensuring many more people could survive and flourish than if they had simply tried to go it alone.

As I gaze across at the mountain range in front of me on my perch so high – no barrier between me and the canyon below – I wonder, is there something for us in the modern world to learn from this system? After all, we have come to such a pass in our modern world that we are not going to be able to realistically move forward and thrive and survive unless we recognise our mutual interconnectivity and work together. Somehow we need to put in place the structures that will include everyone, so that everyone can see the advantage of cooperation and understand the penalty and danger of trying to be an outlier. Though it may well be we will have to test the 'Me First' path to near destruction before we pull back.

The breeze is beginning to pick up, the sun goes behind a rare cloud, and there is a distinct chill in the air. I am brought to awareness of the precariousness of my perch. It must be getting late. I better go down to join the rest of my party. As I turn, I notice a few people behind me with slight concern on their faces. I must have been stood here so long they thought I was planning to jump. I smile as I turn and the little group disperses, glad no action on their part is required. It is very wild and rugged up here, with no officials to be seen.

I have not gone far into my descent when I notice a man clinging to the rock with the sheer drop clearly visible to him. He has a look of terror on his face and his eyes don't seem to be registering anything. Clearly, he is having a blind panic attack. I approach him casually and put myself between his eyes and the dizzying edge he has been surveying.

'Hi,' I pause to give him time to let his gaze focus on my face rather than the steep drop at my back.

'I find it helps to sit down.' I say this to him casually, keeping hold of the eye contact to steady him and encourage him to sit on his bottom. I don't want him to lose face though, so I keep it light. His terror gradually finds its way to my gaze and as if catching it, I indicate with a barely perceptible movement of my head to slide down. He follows me and, very slowly, we both slip to the ground. My eyes keep level with his as we slide to the rocky ground.

'Great, put your hands on the ground now too. Can you feel how steady the rock is beneath us?' I say encouragingly with a smile.

'Let's crawl, like kids, come on,' I say in a tone of play. In this way, step-by-step, I begin to slide us down the precipitous mountain. It is as if I am drawing him in an energetic tow to follow in my wake.

'Look at the rock, there are loads of handholds, aren't there?' In this way, I succeed in getting him to look right and so drawing his attention away from the steep drop on his left. I can feel him starting to calm down. With more of his body in contact with the ground, he is already feeling safer. We continue to slide down, round and round the spiral path until we find ourselves on a wider platform. There are more people around and I am conscious he does not want his fear to be known. I know from here on there are rocks and handholds on each side of the descent, and the view of the side of the mountain dropping sheerly away is not visible from here on down, so it is not going to spark him off feeling giddy again. I stand up, and he follows suit. We nod and smile a little to each other, giving him time to recover himself more fully. Down below, I see his family – two young children and a pretty wife who is eyeing our interaction curiously. I smile and indicate the way down, which he takes, pushing one hand firmly into the rock on each side of the descent. I watch him as he arrives into the hugs of his family and wave to him as he heads off with them. *Is this the answer to my vision quest?* I ponder. *To be there to steady folk who are having a panic? Help them to safety?* I shrug, then seeing Gianna waving to me, I run nimbly down the remaining slope and back into Machu Picchu to join the rest of my party. We have to get going to be in time to catch our train back to Cusco leaving from nearby Aqua Calientes.

Chapter 21

Last Of The Summer Rays

It is well into December and time for me to be thinking about returning home. Geoff has gone back into the jungle and Carole is taken up with running the retreats. I have moved across the main square in Taray to a simple apartment owned by a local lawyer and his wife who live most of the week in Cusco. It was José, the cheeky taxi driver, who had put me on to it, and it suited me perfectly. To enter the apartment, you need to go through a small doorway in a hefty gateway. The gate is thick wood and reminds me of my convent school days when we entered each day through a similar door. There is a peace and safety inside, as there is a lovely inner garden with little almond blossom trees that hummingbirds flit in and out of constantly. Like the other villagers, I have my outside sink for washing clothes. I love that, hanging them out dripping wet in the dry sunshine, and being able to take them in quite dry by late afternoon. The downstairs apartment is reserved for the lawyer and his wife for their weekend visits. My apartment is up a short stairway. I like to stop at the doorway to look over the mud tiles of the neighbouring houses towards the mountains in one direction, and the Urubamba River – if I stand on tiptoes – in the other.

My lodgers will be going home soon, but I am enjoying my time in the little town of Taray. I feel at home here. I've made friends with a Peruvian family in the village, not to mention most of the children we first encountered climbing the trees in the main square the day I arrived. The head of the family is Alcides. He runs the little grocery shop; though that implies something grander perhaps than the rough counter on a concrete floor with wicker baskets and piles of onions, potatoes, maize, and a desultory collection of odds and ends of stationery and plastic sundries, bowls and suchlike on display. His wife is a teacher, as is his daughter Anna.

Alcides always greets me like an old friend when I arrive for a chat, as I do most afternoons. He invariably invites me through the back to the garden. There they have rigged up a running stream flowing to a pond. There are fish to harvest for food and also in the garden is a caged area for the guinea pigs. *Cuyu* are widely eaten in Peru – a detail I won't be sharing with my young daughter, who actually keeps them for pets. He brings out a little tripod stool for me to sit on and waves his hand, and somehow tea is brewed and brought out to us. Our friendship was cemented some weeks ago. I had lent him my reading glasses and my copy of the latest broadsheet newspaper that I'd had with me. I could see he enjoyed perusing it and my glasses seemed to be the right prescription. So, the next time I was in Cusco I bought him a cheap pair of readers and gave them to him, along with a wee pile of newspapers, when I next visited. That consolidated my place as family friend.

It feels safe here in this village under the protection of Alcides and his family. What a joy to sit here chewing the cud with him, as he periodically goes through to serve a customer when the bell in the shop tingles.

They are poor by our standards in the West, I daresay. But from what I can see, they have everything they need and more than most in the UK.

The house is basic, and the cooking is outside in a covered terrace where they also eat. The terrace is also where most of their life is conducted. There, near an almond tree, is their big sink with cold running water where the clothes are washed out and hung to dry on the copious washing lines strung back and forth across the garden. The dry atmosphere and the fierce sun make light work of drying the family laundry.

On this particular day, I am chatting to Alcides when José comes in with a big happy face. He lives with his wife and child behind his parents' home. He has just got back from his *finca* where they grow maize and potatoes, and he looks so at ease and happy with his morning's work. I think of the hustle of even getting to work experienced by so many commuters on buses and trains on the daily grind in the UK. Okay, they have expensive trainers and phones and computers and flats even, but the simple delight of being in the fresh air and attending to your allotment would be a luxury – assuming you had managed to make it up the seven-year waiting list and been allocated one. After that, finding the time amid the daily grind might in itself prove a challenge.

It is then I notice the ungainly youth, Marco. He is across the garden cleaning out the guinea pig cage. He is dressed shabbily with flip-flop-type sandals and a torn T-shirt. I had been puzzled as to who he was until one day I had asked José and he had explained to me he was a *creado*. That word resonated with me. It was what Bembe had told me he had been. When I quizzed José some more, he explained that *creados* are distant relatives who are orphaned. You have some duty towards them, but not to the extent of them being a fully paid-up member of the family. They have to work for their keep, and that was what Marco was doing. My heart went out to him and to Bembe. A harsh way to be brought up, always a second-class citizen. I begin to understand better the stories Bembe had told me of being brought up by his uncle by marriage, husband to his father's sister. He had been raised, but clearly on sufferance. From when still really small he was put out to tend to the goats and the sheep and collect the firewood, as well as a dozen other small jobs, in exchange for his board and lodging. He was allowed to go to school it's true, but there were always lots of after-school jobs to do before supper. He told me meal times were very strict. His uncle, having been high up in the Batista regime, came from a well-to-do aristocratic family and was rigidly adhering to traditional standards. He had served a long spell in prison, a political prisoner, before being released to live out his days, his authority gone, on a small holding near Santa Clara. It makes me smile as I mull this over. Bembe, the big strong agricultural worker, being brought up with such refined table manners. And yet it also suited the side of his nature that was delicate and sweet, a side not given much chance. Whatever the ins and outs, he always drank his tea with one pinkie raised!

My thoughts are brought back to the present by the excited calls of the children when they discover I am here.

'¡Vamos a jugar!' It is the children of the family: Esbeen, the youngest son of Alcides, clearly an afterthought, and Max, only slightly younger, the son of José. They have got used to me being something of a playmate to them. They finish their lessons for the day by lunchtime and have got into the habit of knocking on my door to collect me to go out to play! These are delightful interludes, taking time each day to decide what to do. *'Vamas a…'* as we agree on: a trip to the river, or helping them with their English homework, or exploring up the hill. Sometimes when I need to go into Pisaq to check my email in the local Internet café, to their delight, I take them both with me. We pick up a three-wheeler cab which is waiting in the shade of the trees in the main square of Taray. I pay the few pesos needed so they can have a go on the computers – still a novelty back in the mid-noughties in the Peruvian countryside.

I love this place and I begin to wonder whether it would be possible to live here permanently. Something about this place has gotten under my skin, not least that the dry atmosphere, so different from damp Scotland, is making my body feel so good. I have not had one ache or pain or niggle, which you grow to expect in Scotland. When I mention such a thing to Alcides, he surprises me by telling me he has two plots of land he could sell if I liked the idea. I agree to meet him the next afternoon so he can show me.

The next day, I go out and stand in the shade of the main square, looking over to the huge church in front of me, to wait for him. I am standing quite near to the big communal oven, which is where the locals in the not-so-distant past would have brought their pies and pots to be baked after the baker had finished with the oven for the day. It is built into the wall, although I have not seen it in use since I have been there, but José tells me it is still fired up on high days and holidays.

There is Alcides now. We greet each other companionably, and I follow him a short distance down a side street. I say street, but you have to imagine a narrow, dusty dirt track. Alcides hollers a greeting to whoever is inside, and the rickety high wooden gate is opened and we find ourselves in a courtyard. We have entered a family's sitting room. A young child sits on the dirt floor with their schoolbooks and pencils around them, doing their homework. I don't want to go any further inside. I feel like an intruder, so I leave Alcides to talk to his tenant. I don't like the idea of turfing someone out of their home so I can live there. But actually, as Alcides walks me round the outside of the property, I see that there is more room at the back where you could build a house from scratch and not have to evict anyone. We talk prices and building costs, it would be doable. But am I ready to abandon my life in Edinburgh? Mainly, my daughter, who is still young, can I really do that to her? What is it about this place that has so captured my heart that I would even think about it?

Chapter 22

Christmas At Home

Notwithstanding my love affair with Taray, I confirm my flight back to the UK. I have delayed everything up to the last moment, and it is the day before Christmas Eve when I do finally fly. The plane is blessedly quiet, most travellers preferring to be already ensconced with their loved ones.

I feel quite at a loss to understand the enormous pull I feel in my heart as the plane takes off from Lima airport. While I had gotten fond of many people during my time in Peru, it was something more that was pulling me. The very land itself, perhaps. I allow myself to stay in a dream state. Maybe that was it, the enormous freedom for the mind to range freely. It was something I had experienced before, when travelling back from South America. If you want to put it into mystical speak, I felt an enormous freedom for my crown chakra to expand right up to the sky.

———

As I am pondering these thoughts, I am startled by this interior sensation of having hit a density, like an actual force field. This happened to me before. I glance up at the aeroplane map showing the position of our plane and sure enough, we have just entered European airspace. Welcome to the world we live in every day in the West, with our legacy of two world wars and the holocaust hanging like a density in the atmosphere. I want to halt the plane, turn it around and take me back to where my brain, my mind, my spirit is able to range free. Clearly I know that South America is full of its own traumas: murderous dictators, drug wars, and the legacy of mass extinction and disease from conquering Europeans. But for some reason, those things do not impact me, unlike the holocaust trauma, which seems to have seared into my soul.

—

It is a joyous homecoming. All my lodgers have left and, complicated co-parenting arrangements notwithstanding, my children are waiting in the house to greet me. They have plotted together from their respective fathers' houses to be able to meet up beforehand to bring in a tree from the local plant nursery and dig out the precious tree decorations and festoon the house with tinsel and a huge 'Welcome home, Mum' banner! It is wonderful to see them and experience them creating for me the traditions I'd carefully nurtured with them over the years. We have a delightful and merry time together and they love their Peruvian knits – flappy knitted hats and woolly llamas were *de rigueur* that Christmas.

PART III

For the most part, you live your lives neither knowing the bigger picture playing out, which is affecting your actions, nor how those actions then become part of wider reverberations which then go on to reach far out into and through many planes of existence.

While you are struggling with seemingly mundane issues, these battles, which may seem little to you, contribute to success in the bigger, more obviously heroic struggles going on in the Heavens.

You count your lives as successful when all is going smoothly, and don't realise that these are periods of rest, and that the true work and purpose of your lives on Earth is when you are faced with struggles and difficulties. These can be when you offer your energy to be a helper or enabler for those with their own onerous tasks to perform. It is merciful that you do not see all the ramifications of your lives and dilemmas as they play out, as it would give you overwhelm. But from time to time, when it will help on an individual level, you are given glimpses of the greater cosmic wheels and gears which are ever whirling and turning.

And then there are times, such as are upon us all now, known by us in the Heavens as Times of Great Turning, when the shifts and clunks of the changing gears are so momentous that many more people than in quieter times get wind that something is afoot. That something other than their personal life is playing out. Indeed, some might sense correctly that their own actions, the very particulars of their own life, have become implicated and drawn in to become part of the forming constellation required to enable the transition to occur.

Naturally Freya has not viewed her life in this way. Her lonely childhood, the intrusion of The Great Void from age 12, the constant hovering of it at her shoulder – even the inviting of Bembe into her life – all this is a preparation. I give you this background because I would like you to understand that it is when you are struggling most darkly that you are doing your most mighty work. Constructing who knows what edifices on the inner planes. Edifices that those souls coming after may use to climb the self-same path that has been such a struggle to you – only they will be able to do it with much more ease, your own struggles having cleared an easier path for those coming after. So, hear this and take heart, all you who are in struggle.

Chapter 23

Darkness Descends

Come January, my daughter has returned to her boarding school and my son to his life in London. In February, we contrive to reconvene and snatch a joyous, posh hotel afternoon tea at half term to celebrate my daughter's *quince años*, her fifteenth birthday. I decided to copy this Latin American tradition, and celebrate my daughter blossoming into her womanhood. I gifted her a delicate freshwater pearl necklace which I had purchased in the Cusco shopping cloisters off the main square.

Celebrations behind us, with the light returning but not the warmth, as is typical in Scotland, I find myself struggling. Ever since the weird experience in Cusco at the site of the nodal axis, when I had felt drawn to enter into the centre of the energy point and had drawn down, as it seemed at the time, some Galactic potency, I have felt on edge, out of sorts, and a seriousness seems to have descended on me which I can't shake. I remember the words of the old shaman Amuru, that I should expect life may be difficult going forward. What have I activated, not just in that sacred site, but within myself?

The feelings I had first experienced as a child of twelve began to recur regularly: the feeling of being disassociated from the world around me, of the unreality of what we normally take as the real world. It is as if I am being slowly yet inexorably encompassed by the Great Void. It begins to take all my resolve to go about my daily tasks, to teach my yoga classes. One Thursday evening in a regular weekly class, I go to the loo. I feel completely surrounded by the darkness. The image of the presence of one of my long-term pupils, like a faithful lieutenant turning up week after week, keeps me from disappearing entirely. Previously, when I had experienced the Great Void, it would last only minutes and I had always been able to scramble back, by dint of will power, into the everyday consensus. But now, this is off the scale. I am completely encompassed by the Abyss. It seems to me as though I am walking through pitch darkness. There is nothing solid under my feet, there is no direction, no up, no down. The words of Starhawk, the author of a book I'd cherished back in the eighties called *Dreaming the Dark*, come back to me again and again. 'You must stand up in the darkness.' And this, it seems, is what I must do. Bring the light of my own being to guide me forward, step by step.

I dream of a great chasm that must be crossed. Of an old way of being, an old world order falling away, and in a very real sense a bridge being formed over the Void. A bridge that is needed in order to be able to enter into a new, better-adapted future. Words from the Bible come to me: *Straight is the way and narrow is the path*. I sense rather than see that narrow path and image myself picking a way through this hazardous pass, inch by inch. All is complete darkness, no ground beneath, no sides, no above. I also sense other souls also about this task, not many of us, but there are others. I remember Amuru saying to me, 'Remember, you are not alone.' Crossing over the Abyss, building a bridge into a new imagining, a new creation, a new beginning. I have this image then of many beings, in the future, many souls being able to pour over this bridge we are now creating, easily streaming from one world order to the next, the hard work having been done. I feel exhausted all the time. The process seems to go on and on for the best part of the year. I give in to it. I stop trying to get back into 'the real world'. It takes all my concentration anyway to keep up the step-by-step walk through this Great Nothingness. Somehow, I keep myself alive and attend to my classes. In the middle of this process, I struggle with my resolve to keep Bembe out of my life.

It is one thing when he is in Cuba, but he is in Edinburgh now, and he has asked to meet me for a coffee in a local café. The morning we meet, by now mid-March, it is surprisingly mild. The welcome sunshine is even warming the air a little. We have arranged to meet in a café on the main drag close to my house. It is on the sunny side of the street in the mornings. This morning, although the March wind is sharp, the buildings are providing shelter, creating a welcome sun trap outside the cafe. There he is. I see him across the road: Bembe, sitting at one of the little tables they have set out optimistically on the pavement. He is wearing a vivid green T-shirt showing off his beautiful arms and those muscles hewn by a lifetime of hard work in the fields. His smile devastates me, once again. My lonely heart cannot resist him and the warmth of his Cuban spirit. I sit opposite him, enjoying the feel of the sun on my skin and so proud of this gorgeous man and to be sat there opposite him. The beauty of his complexion, that milky coffee brown. His skin always blows me away as it is so smooth. I want to reach out and touch his bare arm, but instead I order a green tea. We chat, he remembers to ask after my mother, my brother Barnie. He makes me feel like he is family. And I know for him, I am as close to a family as he gets while he is in the UK. I know I make him feel safe. I ask after his son. I know I am a convenience for him, but I can't accept that – I am not ready to see that. And there is another thing: stupidly, I feel a responsibility for having brought him from Cuba, which in a way has initiated a lot of the dilemmas he is now finding it hard to resolve. Why I should feel it is my job to shoulder that, I cannot explain. Perhaps it is my upbringing, where it was always my way to take on responsibility for way too much. And maybe in a family overflowing with children and competing needs, that was my way of not disappearing.

He has been doing okay without my help. The owner of the Latin American restaurant wasn't able to find space for him in the rota so he has found work in a large hotel kitchen and is currently staying on the edge of town in a run-down housing estate with a Spanish family he has befriended. He is near the sea, which he loves. I know he likes to wander by himself along the shore and ponder and think about his lad back in Cuba.

'Let me move back in with you, Freya. I will pay you some rent. I will be closer to my work. I have very early starts, you know.'

His beautiful brown eyes, in this moment, so gentle and warm, the timbre of his voice... I am powerless.

And so, before another week has passed, he has moved back in with me. Javier, my boarder, is back too and he watches in silence, though I know he thinks it's a bad idea.

Bembe has his own room and, to be honest, I am glad of his company at first. He goes off early each morning to work. The kitchen boss is impressed with him and Bembe enjoys the work. He is a cheerful workmate. Could he make something of himself here, build a career? But that would mean him giving up his life in Cuba, the months, and even once a full year, spent back in Cuba. Would he think about throwing in his lot with Britain – with me? That same false hope, still not extinguished, has me considering these questions. Obscuring from me the truth I am still trying to hide from myself. His centre of gravity is not with me; it is back home with his son and the mother of his lad.

Even my capacity to deceive myself is challenged, as it is becoming clearer by the day that Bembe's heart is not with me. He is phoning home a lot more and is religiously sending money back to Anna, his boy's mother. I had always encouraged him to stay in touch and respect her. She was the mother of his child, and he had always been careful to send the regular stipends home. But this is something else, hiding while making calls and an urgency and surreptitiousness. Also, Bembe does not seem happy and he begins to overeat to a degree that has him putting on a lot of weight.

Looking back, it is easy to see he was uncomfortable with the lie he was living, trying to make out to me he wanted to be with me, while all the while saving as much as he could for Cuba, where his heart still clearly was. I confess I phoned Marco, a friend of Bembe, a retired businessman who Bembe often used to help out at home or in his garden. I knew he had just got back from Baracoa. He had been married to a Cuban woman himself, so he knew the terrain.

'Is he with anyone else in Cuba?' I ask.

'The only one I saw him with was Anna, the mother of his child.'

So, Anna. It finally dawns on me, they had gotten back together. Possibly as early as when we first got our legal separation? But we are only legally separated, not divorced yet. I need to talk to him.

I find him in the box room, where he is sleeping on a futon on the floor. I go to sit down beside him.

———

'So, you and Anna, you got back together? It's okay, Bembe, you don't have to lie to me.'

He isn't denying it.

'But there is something else, isn't there? What is it? For goodness' sake, you can tell me.'

This, as he looks at me from the other side of a canyon he doesn't know how to bridge. And then I get it.

'Oh my, so Anna is pregnant?!'

He looks amazed, as if I have just thrown a lifeline, a rope across the chasm between us which, if he holds onto tightly, will keep his world stable. Like a guilty child realising the world will not cave in if his secret is known.

'We got back together a while ago when you and I legally separated, and this last trip away, she got pregnant. I came over because I need to earn money for her, for my family.'

'Finally, you are telling me the truth, Bembe. I suppose that is something.'

—

That would have been a good conversation to have, but all those words were in a miasma between us, and my own need for him to be here because he missed me, because he wanted to see me, was too strong to allow the words out. So instead, I ask him if he wants to come down the allotment with me. He agrees readily, as he has by now discovered that he enjoys helping me out there.

And so we come to an uneasy truce. Him sleeping in the box room, going off early to work, usually eating at work, coming back to sleep. Us being decent with each other when we do meet. But the underlying tensions are growing to the extent they are becoming unbearable for me.

Bembe, on the other hand, is made of sterner stuff. In a war of attrition, he is always going to win. Nevertheless, one morning I go to him.

'Look, this is not working. Why don't you go back to live with your friends and let us have the space we need?'

'But you forget, Freya, that we are still legally married and I have the right to live in the marital home, and I didn't sign any papers renouncing that right.'

Oh my, so he has done his homework then. For the first time, I know fear. What have I got myself into, what tricks and cunning is this man plotting against me? What else is he planning to throw at me?

He is right of course, and I know it, and I curse the wretched lawyer who omitted to tell me about this little loophole.

I flare with anger.

'You know the reason you are still living here is because you are stronger than me. I hope that makes you feel good about yourself.'

Bembe the peaceful bull has been pushed too far, I see his anger rising and him not being able to control it. He rushes out of the room after me as I move into the hall and picks me up by my arms and starts to trounce me up and down.

'Let me down!' I am shouting in rage, unable to do anything, my feet bouncing up and down off the floor like a rag doll in his strong arms, until Javier comes rushing out of his room: pulling us apart, pushing Bembe back into the sitting room, telling him to stay there, taking me into the kitchen and rolling me a cigarette from a wee stash I use when tensions get too much.

Javier, lighting my cigarette, says, 'Calm down, Freya, *dios mio*, do you guys want to kill each other?'

I take deep drafts of the cigarette, feeling myself calming a little. Javier goes back out of the room and into Bembe's. I hear him talking in a cool-headed way with him. For the first time, I contemplate the home life Javier has come from. He is seventeen years old – he has no right to be so damn good at reconciliation.

By the time he comes back in, I am calmer.

'I'm sorry, Javi, this is not your fight, but thank you for helping.'

He gives that cool grin of his, skinny body and short-cropped black hair with his handsome pointy face, and we both start laughing. The door opens and Bembe comes in, under control again.

'I sorry,' he says, 'You okay?' I nod and indicate with my head that it's okay, he can go.

'I go work now.'

'Yes, okay, see you later then.'

Crossing the Meadows on my way to teach, I attempt to compose myself. Could he push things to the extent he could claim half my house? Would I need to sell up? Is my very security jeopardised? Then the survivor in me begins to form a plan.

In class, I roll up my T-shirt so all can see the bruise marks, still fresh. I note just who comments and make a memo to myself in case I should need them to be a witness. I didn't want to pull Javier in; that would not have been fair to him.

I don't have to wait long. After a few days, a letter arrives from a lawyer Bembe has instructed. Clearly Bembe failed to let this lawyer know that we had made a settlement in order to get a legal separation and that Bembe had accepted this settlement and had signed it. I take some relish in penning a reply. I point all this out, and also the fact that Bembe is exploiting the loophole of his right to live in the marital home while we are still not officially divorced, but that he can be violent and I have witnesses to bruising caused by such an episode. I did not lay it on too thick, but clearly thick enough, as shortly after Bembe's return visit to his lawyer, the case against me was dropped. He was not going to be able to milk his catch anymore.

Should I be more outraged, more angry with him? I know someone must have been nipping his brain and telling him he could take me to the cleaners, and against his better nature, he had had a go at that. And he had failed. I might be an emotional sap and susceptible in times of weakness to unscrupulous men, but luckily I have a clear mind when I need to, and this has helped me overcome this particular hurdle.

But it is this same mind that makes me feel compassion for him. I know what it is like in Cuba, his home country. And from things he has told me, I know how hard he found being a *grinjaero* – a peasant – with all the stigma attached to that position. Contrast that with his status when he visits Cuba with hard cash – with dollars. He would be greeted like a conquering hero. However, once his supplies were used up, I imagine he would suffer a loss of status. He would hate that. He is a proud man, and at heart, he wants to provide. Just, sadly, not for me.

It is a few days later. Bembe is at home that morning, working an evening shift. The sun is catching the window seat where I sit to catch the rays. I roll a cigarette and begin to smoke it, calming myself. He comes in and sits down at my feet on the folded futon we unfurl at times for overnight guests. We speak in his native Spanish.

'I want to explain things to you about Anna.'

'I thought you said she'd moved on, had a boyfriend?'

'Yes, she did, but when I was sending the regular stipend home, I got certain rights. And the first time I went home, I was not happy that my young son was starting to call this man Papa. I made this clear to Anna, and she dropped the boyfriend.'

Cuba is such a poor country that I could understand the regular remittances were something she needed to support her son, and she did not want to risk antagonising the sender – Bembe.

'After you and I legally separated, Anna and I got back together on my next trip home.' During this last year that I have been in Cuba, she became pregnant. The baby is due soon and I need to earn money for her – for my family.'

So, he hadn't wanted to come back; if he could have earned money in Cuba, he would not have come back. That was the stark truth. But I am still not ready to face it.

I certainly can see the world from his point of view – his status in the eyes of Anna depended on him having money. He would want to look good in her eyes because she was quite a catch for him: she was from Spanish descent, well educated, and had a professional standing working in a bank. For a *grinjaero* from the hills, she was a real prize. However much of a melting pot Cuba is, it is not egalitarian. The middle-class professions are given more status and those posts were generally held by those from Spanish descent. And they had the early access, before those from the more menial professions, both to the internet and to email.

Look, it all sounds so straightforward reading it like this, but whatever words Bembe says, that's not what I hear. I still hold out hopes for us that we might have a future. What story I tell myself in my head to justify it, I can't say. The truth is that I need him near me. Something about Bembe makes me feel safe and protected. Despite everything, we actually make each other laugh, and Bembe is a great raconteur. Both my daughter and I, when she is home, enjoy his funny expressions like "I Fidel' when he is trying to say, 'I feel ill'! And we are genuinely fond of each other. There is a connection between us which somehow transcends what is happening on a more mundane or surface level in the unfolding story of our lives. A strength and weakness of mine has always been to be able to see the potential in a person. This has enabled me often to lend encouragement to someone at a helpful time. But as far as my love affairs go, it isn't so helpful. And on top of that, I have a wonderful imagination and can easily invent a lifestyle together with even the most unlikely of men. So, I decide to overlook all I have learned of

Bembe's double life and put it down to life with a Cuban man. What can you expect?

That's not quite true, I do not entirely overlook it. Bembe is still sleeping in the box room. We are still officially separated and he is living under forbearance on the understanding it will not be for long, and as soon as he can he will be going back home to Cuba. But that established, we soon settle into a rhythm. Our natural harmonious connection reasserts itself. The fact of the matter is we actually like each other. And, I see it now, we had this in common we could neither of us could ever really belong to another person. The experiences of our early childhoods had taught us both that self-reliance which wasn't about to bend. So perhaps it is simple expediency, that now and again, when he calls me into his room late at night, neither of us regret the deep satisfaction we both experience when, throwing everything aside, we simply enjoy the sheer pleasure of our two bodies connecting. Even still, we both know it is temporary. And it helps that Bembe is not much at home. He goes off early to work and he is also beginning to take the odd shift back with Mohammad in the Latin American restaurant working as a commi-chef. Javier is here during term times and back home in Spain for the holidays. He is in Spain the evening I get a worried call from my brother St John.

St John is the eldest of my unwieldy family. He left home early, so my memories of him are mainly from when I was growing up. I always loved it when he and I would be put on the rota to make the evening meal together. He always made everything so fun. He'd come in at the last possible minute, spreading a bag of provisions on the kitchen table, shouting out the menu and my instructions, and like an early version of *Ready Steady Cook*, we would wildly chop and fry and stir and bake, all the while singing loudly, 'I could have danced all night…' That was our favourite, taking turns with the parts. 'I could have spread my wings…' 'Do as you're told, it's time for bed…'

And like magic, come 6 pm when the queue was at the door, all would be ready, table laid, no fuss. Sometimes, on first arriving home, before we would start cooking, he would slap a wad of notes down on the table. 'Just a little bet that came off.' He had this gruff, roughie-toughie way of speaking. Yet once I opened the door into the sitting room and surprised him where he was lying in the dark by himself on a cushion on the floor watching TV. The cat was resting on his chest, purring, and he was gently stroking her. When he saw me, he flung the cat away, trying to make out it had only just arrived, but I knew better.

He has done well for himself working as a software inventor, and has travelled a lot all over the world, but now he is settled in London. He once told me he used to dream solutions to his software problems and he put a lot of his success down to that. He still gambles on the horses and keeps a running profit on his shrewd guesses. He has done his best to take our brother Barnie under his wing, keeping in touch via their shared love of horse racing. He invites him to stay from time to time, even when I know it must sometimes be hard work for him and his partner.

He never really phones me, but whenever I phone him his great voice always booms out enthusiastically, 'Freya! How delightful to hear from you, and how're things going for you?'

His voice is not booming now. I hear fear behind his words.

'It's Barnie, he's flipped, gone manic.'

His voice is anxious, he's out of his depth. Barnie's high is too close to the bone for someone used to running by the seat of their pants. What fine line tips one into success and another into the locked wards?

'Barnie's been here, Freya,' St John makes an effort to clarify the situation. 'I just thought I ought to warn you that he left this morning. We put him on a train north, but he's quite high and out of control.'

Barnie, the second victim of what our family have named, in our blackly humorous way, that helps us to cope with our inherited lot, 'the mad gene'. Leo, meanwhile, as I told Geoff back in Taray, is quite recovered. Albeit living carefully and always a little nervous that he might be catapulted back into another episode that will land him in hospital again. Barnie hadn't seemed to be a contender. He was glorious in his teens, very popular with the girls, and clever. He'd achieved a law degree and was working his articles when he succumbed in his mid-twenties, when I had been happily safely out of it in Wales. But now back in Edinburgh, I was very much in the thick of it.

'What happened? What was the lead-up?' I try to inject a calm I don't feel into my voice.

'Well, he'd come for the weekend and we were having a drink last night, but he had already turned manic and was ranting and raving. We only finally got him off to sleep in the early hours of the morning. Then we just put him on a train to Edinburgh, but he's really off on one,' explains St John.

'You didn't want to phone the psychiatric services down your way?' I question him.

'Well, no, he was adamant he wanted to go north where they know him in the hospital in Edinburgh.'

'Well, that makes sense, okay, thanks for the alert. Don't worry, St John, we have been here before,' I start to say the comforting words, said to me by one of the mental health nurses many, many years ago, when I still used to get completely distraught when my brother took one of his turns. Like a mantra, I intone,

'Remember he has been here before, and he always gets better.' And it is true that the umpteen times my brother has had a manic fit over the years, he has always recovered.

It worries me, the fear I note in my brother's voice, that having to deal with a manic brother is too dangerous for his own mental health.

'Don't worry St John,' I say again in an attempt to reassure him, 'he has been here before, it will be alright, we just need to get him to hospital.'

We end the call and I am left feeling somewhat deflated, realising my big brother, whom I have always looked up to, is not in a position to give me comfort. Rather, I need to stay strong and be the one dishing out the comfort. I suddenly feel very alone and very tired. I don't have time to indulge in this for long, however, as shortly after I put down the phone on St John, the phone rings again; it is the police.

'We have apprehended a Barnie Banks. He is giving you as his contact. Can you confirm?'

'Yes, that's correct. I'm his sister. Where is he?'

'He got as far as Crewe on the train north from London, but he's out of control and frightening the other passengers.'

'Would you be able to accompany him up to Edinburgh? They know him in the hospital here; that's why he is so keen to get north.'

'Yes, it would probably work, but unfortunately, we don't have the manpower to spare someone to travel with him, so he is being transported to the local psychiatric hospital – it is fair to say, with some resistance.' The policeman reports this to me over the line.

I can't help laughing at the image of my indignant brother protesting at not being allowed to continue the journey he had paid for back to his hometown. Especially since he was willing at that point to go quietly into the hospital that he knew.

'Oh dear,' I manage, 'thank you so much for your help and I'm so sorry for the bother you've had.'

I phone my sister, who lives around the corner from my parents so she can go round and let them know personally.

It is not one hour later that the police are phoning me again.

'Your brother has absconded from the mental hospital in Crewe and we don't know his whereabouts.' He gives me a number to call if I hear anything.

My best guess is he will be heading for our parents' house. I text my sister this time to say alert moved up to red.

As it happens, I'm correct. Barnie has headed up in a taxi to my parents, but they have not let him in. He is very frightening when he is in one of his manic rages and they are elderly. No one tells me of this development, however.

It is early the next morning, and Bembe has already left the house as he's on an early shift in the hotel kitchen. I am just packing my little rucksack with what I will need to teach my yoga classes this morning. I can't find my water bottle, which I need to rinse and refill. I go into the front room, maybe I left it in there. I see the lights of a car as it is drawing into our cul-de-sac.

The doorbell rings. Going to the door, expecting the postman, I hear rather than see that it is a taxi which has brought my brother to my door. It is reversing now back up our dead-end street. And there my brother is, coming towards me like a bat out of hell, flying at me with his fist to land me a knock-out punch. Lucky for me, I am ninja quick, my reflexes honed by years of body discipline. I sense the punch and jump backwards. Throwing my arms up and back, I bang them hard against the frame of the door, badly jolting my shoulders. However, the blow when it lands, barely glances my face. Pulling myself together, I shut the door against my brother and phone the police. There is only one place for my brother when he is out of control like this and that is the psychiatric hospital. I lean against the door. I am trembling; I phone Bembe at work, something I would never normally do.

I have to phone the hotel kitchen, and as I wait, I hear the echoes and footsteps of the corridors.

'Freya, ¿que pasa?' What's happened?

'It's Barnie,' I say, 'he came to the door, he's punched me. I'm quite upset,' I'm crying now.

'Wait there, I come now.'

And they let him out from work and sure enough, to my surprise, he arrives half an hour later, calm and competent. His implacability, his physical sturdiness, strangely calming.

I see another side of him. The side I am sure he can more easily play in Cuba: the protector, the carer, the provider. I get a sudden insight into how all my helpfulness towards him has driven a wedge between us.

But in this moment, he is on sure ground. Money and status are not an issue in this dilemma. Issues of sanity and madness cut across culture and social status. And when I see his benign look of calm, an amused smile wanting to flicker across his lips, I realise HE IS NOT AFRAID and it is as though a spell is being broken. And we both start to laugh, hesitant and slightly uncertain on my part, it is true, and verging on crying, but as we laugh I can feel the carapace of fear beginning to crack and break down. A fear my whole family has lived under, for so many years. When will the mad gene land on me or, worse still, my children? The stigma and shame of having a brother so relentlessly affected by his manic depression he can barely live a life of any kind. And any life he does build up is shredded and thrown away when high in a bout of aggressive and unrelenting late-night calls and manic spending, wild gambling and costly long-distance taxis. A life out of control.

And as I lean into Bembe and allow myself to be held, I sense the implacability of this man. The very thing about him that has nearly broken me is the very thing that is in this moment sustaining me. I know he has seen as bad, if not worse, in Cuba, he has navigated a lot to live the double life he juggles. And none of it matters right now, only the great relief of being able to see the funny side in this moment with a big reassuring hunk of a man who is here right in front of me just when I need him most.

He finds my eyes as he reaches to hug me again, this time a brief, yet big, warming, reassuring embrace.

'You okay now; I go back to work? Yes?' And as I nod, he heads off imperturbably out the door and down the road, back to his hotel kitchen to finish out his shift.

I am still in time to get myself to work if I am quick, so I rush off to teach my class, cycling through the park, taking the time to allow the beauty of Arthur's Seat in the morning light and the spaciousness of the Meadows to calm me. Whether any of my pupils notice anything untoward, I can't say.

But as we are tidying the mats away at the end of the class, I get a further call from the police. They have picked Barnie up at his home in Edinburgh, and he has now been admitted to the locked ward. They've had to break down the door, the policeman explains, as he had not been answering, but they have since had the door made safe. This is important to know, not only to protect my brother's things, but also because, for my sins, I am my brother's landlady. This had come about when I had access to some funds and used them to house my brother in a modest flat in a central part of town. That this had probably saved his life is no exaggeration, but it had also caused me additional headaches with managing the tenancy.

This reminds me of a previous occasion. Just before Barnie was about to go manic, he gave me £350 and asked me to keep it safe as he knew he would just blow it once he got high. Like an idiot, I took the money rather than helping him put it into a post office account. A few days later, at 3 am or so in the morning, I was alone in my flat, which is on the ground floor. Barnie was at the door banging and shouting like a man possessed, demanding the money. I was so relieved neither of my children were staying with me that night. But I was also furious he should have risked frightening them. I opened the door with a fury that quite matched his mania and indeed topped it.

'Go away, how dare you come here waking folk up in the middle of the night! If this is how you mean to behave, you can leave my flat. I wash my hands of you.'

My brother was stopped in his tracks and went away with only an enfeebled muttered, 'Well, it's my money,' as he sloped off back down the road.

A few days later, I had seen him and he had apologised, in control of himself once again.

'You said you would kick me out of the flat?'

'Yes, and I meant it, if you pull a stunt like that again.'

'How many warnings do I get?' he had asked, ever the chancer.

'You just had it,' I replied, my voice rock solid.

I saw something interesting then. My brother looked relieved. As though, having been given a non-negotiable line, he could relax. Whatever devil was playing havoc in his life would have to find another boundary to push against, as this one was not for budging.

I thought back to when he was a boy. Like I've said, he was my mother's favourite, always sitting on her knee, even when no longer a small child, and she would nuzzle him. For a sensitive lad, boundaries there were not. What a terrible price he seemed to be paying, tangled still as he is in her web.

Returning home from teaching my yoga classes, feeling the need of a bit of pampering to steady my nerves, I book an appointment at the hairdresser's. As my normal hairdresser is not free, I accept his colleague John, who turns out to be just the tonic. John keeps his own hair really cropped and has a put-together neatness about him. A man who could hold his own in any rough situation even in the most run-down estate. He has a quiet dignity about him that commands respect too from folk higher up the social scale. As I relay the morning's events, he tells me about a cousin of his, who was similarly at times scary and out of control. The middle-aged lady in the next chair, silver foil highlights in her hair, overhearing, starts to chip in with her own story. The man waiting in the next chair talks about his father's crazy bouts when drinking. I start to relax as I realise our family is not alone, how many people are also touched with people they are close to manifesting bouts of crazy, out-of-control, scary behaviour, even at times violent. John could not have been more skilful if he had been a top psychother-apist. I relax, the other customers relax. I think we all feel it that afternoon, the protective, supportive acceptance of each other and the realisation that mental illness is part and parcel of everyday life and not something shameful that needs to be hidden.

When I leave that afternoon, while it may be the case my haircut is not quite the way my regular hairdresser would have done it, nevertheless I feel lighter and more carefree than I have in weeks.

Chapter 24

Barnie Asks For Help

After my trip to the hairdresser, I feel calm enough to contact my sister, the one living nearby my parents.

'Oh yes, he was here and when Dad didn't let him in, he headed off for Edinburgh.'

'Yes, Barnie came to my door earlier this morning and tried to knock me out.'

'Oh, I am sorry. I should have told you he was heading back to Edinburgh! I should have alerted you.'

Well, yes, I think wryly, that would have been very helpful, but I only say, 'Don't worry. I'm okay, just shaken. How are Mum and Dad?'

'Oh, you know, Mum is all in a twitter and wants to go to the hospital to visit him. He's her son, she can't abandon him and so on.'

'Well, I think that is a really bad idea. She is old now, she needs to look after herself and Dad. Barnie is in the best place he can be right now. You know none of us can handle him when he gets out of control. Look, I need to go, let's try and keep each other in the loop, okay?'

We ring off, my sister to go tend to her beautiful allotment and let the worries blow away in the brisk Berwick breeze. I, to chop vegetables for the evening meal.

Meanwhile, Barnie is safe and out of harm's way to others and to himself in the locked ward.

We all enter a period of downtime. I am surprised by the arrival of my sister Amanda. She lives four hours away by train, and yet she arrives like an angel of mercy to stay with me for a few days. She is concerned that I have been attacked. I am touched by her support. An older niece joins us too, for a few hours. We three of us sit at the table and drink tea, not solving anything but simply showing up, being there for each other. I am comforted. Amanda goes to visit Barnie, who is still high at this point, and she doesn't get any sense out of him. I don't go with her. I have learnt to put my lines firm, and speaking to Barnie when he is high, to me, is not a productive way forward. I hate the psychiatric hospital; I find it extremely disconcerting. I am so grateful to the staff who are able to work there and care for my brother and others in need. My sister, job done, returns home.

After she is gone, one of the psychiatric doctors phones me.

'How is he?' I ask.

'Well, it is washing out of his system,' she explains. 'When he gets high, it's a bit like a dose of the flu – it has to run its course. In your brother's case, I am expecting it to take around three months for it to do so.'

'I am sorry, but I can't visit when he is high, and I have been telling him I won't take any calls after 7 pm at night.'

'Don't worry about that,' she says sympathetically, 'you must do the right thing for you. The most important thing for someone who is manic,' she stresses this point, 'is to have clear boundaries. You are absolutely on the right track with stating them clearly and sticking to them.'

I am reassured by the doctor's words. But however much I might be setting my boundaries, how do I get the memo out to my unwieldy family? I know quite well that my brother, when high, goes through his little black book of family members and as we are so numerous, it is like trying to slay the many-headed hydra. As you teach one to put a boundary up – 'Don't accept midnight calls,' 'Put down the phone when he becomes abusive' – another is drawn in by his skilful manipulation: a young niece or nephew feeling sorry for him, inexperienced and out of their depths, being bothered and very quickly upset by his demands.

Notwithstanding, I am buoyed by the unexpected place of laughter I have found with Bembe, and the solidarity I experienced in the hairdresser's, not to mention the support of my sister and niece.

In this way, we wait it out. And the weeks turn into months. Short conversations with my brother and news from family members and occasional updates from the hospital help me chart his progress. From belligerence to blame, through anger to remorse, until finally he plunges into a deep depression.

This is not an uncommon pattern, but this time it seems the depression is something different and more profound than anything he has experienced before.

The doctor calls me again.

'The mania has run its course,' she says. 'He is very low. He is deeply sorry and mortified for having attacked you, especially since, he says, you have been the one to help him the most, providing him with a secure flat he could live in.'

This was true; it was unlikely another tenancy would have lasted through the vicissitudes that might have seen another landlord throw him out years ago. And at the time, I had tried to do it as a joint family venture, but not one of my siblings had wanted to touch what might so easily have become a poisoned chalice.

'He would like to see you, to apologise in person,' the psychiatrist continues.

There is a silence as she waits. I know I have to do this.

'Okay, yes, tell him I will come in a day or two.'

And so, I steel myself. I drive to the car park, find my way through the maze of buildings to the locked ward: ringing the bell, giving credentials, being taken in through the double door system, being locked in a kind of decompression chamber alone while the nurse goes to check out the feasibility of my timing. And then the second door to the inner ward being unlocked, following the nurse through the corridor, with people milling about. One young inmate is eyeing me curiously, his reserve abandoned, he calls out loudly,

'You here fer Barnie?' Most however are averting their gaze, lost in their own worlds and thoughts. Eventually, we reach a small ward. The nurse stands aside for me to enter and there he is, my beautiful brother Barnie, sitting on a chair facing me. He is grossly swollen in face and body, a side effect of the antipsychotic drugs he has been prescribed. I feel like weeping but try not to show my shock at the look of him. I should be inured to it by now.

I sit down opposite him; a hospital table between us and the easy chair he is sitting on.

'Freya, I'm so sorry.' His speech is slurred and slow as he looks at me. I catch his eyes and it is as if I am plunging into the depths of his soul. Being sucked as though into a vortex, into the Great Void. He is only barely hanging in there. I hold firm. I know this place. I know we can stand firm in this place.

'Freya. Please. Help me.'

He holds my gaze. The moment is charged and potent. I return his gaze unflinchingly. Something is being agreed, some pact is being made and sealed. No words are exchanged. Only that terrible gaze held, the unfathomable depth of nothingness faced. How close he has become to being irretrievably lost.

I reach out my hand, slowly and deliberately. He also slowly and purposefully reaches across the table to mine. Our hands meet in the middle and clasp, all the while we are maintaining that gaze.

'Yes, I'll help you,' I say.

He slumps back in his chair.

'Rest now,' I say, 'it's going to be alright. Get your strength back. I'll not desert you.'

I go round to his chair and put my hands on his shoulders gently and lean into him almost imperceptibly. It is all this sensitive and brave, crazy man can endure by way of an embrace. Who are we to make judgments on those who, from craziness or courage, sail so close to the wind? Or those who, like Icarus, with his foolhardy, brave recklessness, fly too near to the dazzling sun, only to crash and burn.

Chapter 25

Walking Out Of The Void

Barnie is discharged in early spring. He comes to my home on a regular pre-agreed basis in the mornings and we climb out of the window and down the steps into the shared back green, where we sit on a rug in the morning sunshine, not saying anything in particular. It is enough to sit, to simply be. The March weather is kind to us and the garden protects us from the wind. The journey is slow, the task clear, to reach into that dark place where Barnie had found himself and, inch by inch, walk him out to a place of balance, to a place where daylight can enter. Where he can begin to re-establish an equilibrium.

And so begins the long and slow process. Step by careful step.

I give thanks for that warm spring that enables us to sit every day in the garden. The honeysuckle spread along the railing hanging above where we sit has buds tightly closed, branches bare.

My task is clear. I must sense into the dark dense place where he is trapped and very slowly, by degrees, bring him out. I guess there is a real risk of being frozen into inaction by the intense chill, but I will give no truck to the immensity of the Abyss, threatening at any moment to engulf us both. My mind is totally focused on one thing only: find my brother, bring him out of that darkness. And so, I travel without fear right into the very depth of the Void. The place I have run away from all my life. My job is to turn and face into its heart. In the end, it's not difficult. There is no space for fear. My total concentration is on finding my brother. At first, all is complete blackness, but gradually I sense his form, there in the darkest corner of the deep – crouched and frozen in that most terrible of places. He is sensing he is not alone anymore, that he does not have to stay in that place. I stop long enough to be sure he is coming with me, then inch by inch, step by step over the long weeks, I bring him out of that place of misery. Emerging gently and safely into the welcome warmth of that Scottish spring. By degrees, the chill that has very nearly frozen us both begins to melt away in the light of the day. And as the days and weeks pass, the honeysuckle too springs into welcome leaf.

I am remembering a book that made an impression on me as a teenager. *The Pilgrim's Progress*. Bunyan writes about how people can fall into the Slough of Despond. But it is only a place, you do not have to stay there. And real as I know the great Chasm, the Great Void to be, I also know we are not meant to live there. And therefore, it is with confidence I can walk my brother and myself out to safety.

To begin with, the task was arduous it is true, but day by day, week by week, as Barnie by degrees steps away from the deep, the mood becomes lighter. We begin to start to talk about ways of managing his condition rather than simply being swept away with each fresh bout in a chaotic way.

In time, a working group is set up. This is made up of his doctor in the community, Dr Sharma, his CPN community psychiatric nurse, Hannah, myself, and Barnie. We start to meet regularly. Often there is an intern present at our meetings, which Barnie does not object to. I have to overcome my reluctance to have any truck with psychiatric mainstream. The traumatic treatment my brother Leo had endured when he had needed help as a teenager was still vividly alive for me. But the staff are human beings and I find Dr Sharma a caring, if rather careworn doctor, and the nurse a formidable and strong person who wins my respect from the beginning. Hannah, the nurse, has been on Barnie's case for quite a number of years, and I sense she is really pleased to have some support. Between all of us, we come up with an idea to create a 'management of a manic episode' plan.

We gather a circle of protection around him. In the first meeting, Barnie's case files are sitting on the desk. They are nearly two feet deep, representing 23 years of my brother yo-yoing in and out of hospital. I ask if they have ever been collated.

My brother is very willing to be honest and shows an encyclopaedic knowledge of the different drugs he had been administered over the years, some, while an inpatient in hospital to deal with the manic attacks, and others when he was back in the community, the purpose of which was to keep him from having a manic episode and thereby having to go into hospital.

I observe that the motivating factor for the medical team is exactly that – to keep him from going into hospital. That is what is counted as a success from their medical viewpoint. Very little, if any, weight seemed to be given to the effect the drugs prescribed to my brother have on him. I feel, as a family representative, that my position has to be to support Barnie to gain some quality of life in between his manic episodes There seems to be little appreciation of Barnie as a person or of the impact the illness has on his life, almost as if he has to forfeit all rights to consider his quality of life because of his mental illness.

I point out that when Barnie does go high, when he is at his most frightening, is precisely when he is the most frightened and, looking at his life, there is usually a trigger that sets him off. From what I have been able to observe, every time he has a blow up, there is a good reason for him to be agitated. His natural chivalry and philosophical nature make it really hard for him to accept his human feelings and emotions, like anger, for instance, however justified. Hospital, where we can seal him off for his own safety and protect him when he needs it most, is not a failure; rather, it is a necessary safety net.

And it is true, Barnie has a real charm and wit and intelligence when well, and we all can recognise that.

We discuss, over the weeks and months of our meetings, how with each manic attack it is becoming harder and harder for my brother to recover any semblance of a normal life. The problem being that each time he is manic he shreds up so much of what he has managed to build up while at home. All it takes is one out of control and abusive phone call while ill, to alienate a would be ally. Not to mention the reckless spending, which leaves him in debt. We also acknowledge that each time Barnie gets well again, he has always worked assiduously to clear these debts and has always managed to do so.

It is Hannah who formalises the outline of the management plan. It will not be unlike a birth plan. One you might make stating what your ideal is when your time comes to go into hospital to have your baby.

We thrash out the details of it between us, with Barnie fully on board.

Barnie agrees to accept to have his phone and credit card removed from him on admittance to hospital. This will save him building up debt with any wild betting and reckless spending and also prevent him making those damaging phone calls when high.

We recognise that just before he dives off the deep end, Barnie has a short window of insight when he can realise he is feeling unwell and tipping into a manic episode.

We realise we have to be alert to when that happens and act swiftly to bring him into the safety of the hospital. There to take away his credit card and phone, before he moves into the belligerent phase when he is ready to fight and take on the world, and certainly not willing to comply.

As the plan falls into shape, we ask Barnie if there is anything else we should be considering.

'Yes, I don't want my mum to visit me when I am in hospital, it only adds to my stress as I worry for her safety as I may not be able to protect her from other patients. It causes me a lot of stress and anxiety, when I already have a lot to worry about.'

I am very struck by this and see that here is a very clear way to see how much our mother can respect her son's wishes and boundaries.

All the while we have been thrashing out the management plan, Dr Sharma has ordered an intern to wade through Barnie's files and see whether we can see any patterns that may help us. Barnie admits to often dropping the preventative medication when he is no longer under a section and obliged to take it. But we also discover that he equally gets high when he is religiously swallowing his lithium, so it seems when he is going high, the preventative medication is not able to stop that happening. Barnie also details which antipsychotic drugs actually help him, and which are not helping, and I realise he is the expert on his own illness now, having lived with it for so many years and seen out many a doctor and nurse, so long has his affliction been in place.

While the medical team look into finding patterns, I set myself to the task of beginning to work out how to train the family to set their boundaries as far as Barnie is concerned, and to become assiduous in sticking to them. Rather than lacking compassion, they will be doing the very thing that will help him the most. *Feed the person, not the mania* is a wee mantra shorthand which helps me, and in my mind I see a distinction between the mania – which I personally will not have any truck with – and Barnie, who I have stepped up to assist.

I know that trying to teach my unwieldy family will be very hard. When manic, Barnie, the chess player that he is, is always able, when one boundary is fixed, to find another pawn to use in his chess game.

I know from personal experience how hard it is to distinguish between the natural compassion towards my brother's predicament and the need to put up the boundary against feeding the mania. But I have also seen firsthand how it is the very thing which he most needs and also what the medical profession advocates.

Little by little, a structure is put in place, and little by little, the wider family begin to realise we can work better as a team with a consistent approach rather than managing alone off-piste.

———

It is a few months after the first meeting, while the early beginnings of a management plan are being formulated to support my brother with his mental health condition.

I am visiting my parents in their little house in Berwick. Dear Muma, sitting at her kitchen table, which sees so much action due to the plethora of children entertained there. The gallery of family photographs, carefully curated by my dad all along the hall corridor and up and down the stairs. My mother who, long after her retirement as a primary school teacher, carried on tutoring youngsters with literacy or numeracy issues. She has a gift with even the most difficult of children, one might say especially the most difficult of children. Perhaps she was aligned to them. My favourite childhood story of hers was the one where she jumped out of a window to get more quickly into the playground, rather than keeping her place in the slow line of girls filing down the stairs to reach the door. Unfortunately, this got her into trouble as she landed on top of another pupil! Muma, who had such an ability to listen and hear and understand the little dilemmas of life. That was when you were able to catch her attention of course, as with so many children, she had always to be busy about one of them. But Barnie was her Achilles heel. He was her pet, you might say her security blanket. He was the one she cuddled on her favourite rocking chair long after his early childhood was past. But today she is thinking ahead, and she is thinking of him.

'Before I can die peacefully, Freya, I want to make sure that Barnie will be okay.'

'Yes, we all want that, Muma.' I say. She still has not yet been able to acknowledge the fact that the modest little flat he lived in was my doing and was so far keeping him from homelessness.

I know there is no point going there. Muma wants to be the Kingpin, or rather the Queen pin. She wants the world to revolve around her, the ideas to be generated by her. But she is very old now, and even her formidable powers are waning.

'We are working together with the medical profession to make a plan to help Barnie manage his condition,' I introduce the idea gently.

I can feel her inwardly bristle as she is excluded from this – that this is not of her doing. Not of her instigation. Which will win? Her genuine desire to see her son protected, or her need to be at the centre of the drama? I wait a few moments.

'He has asked that you do not visit when he is in hospital...' I begin. She lets me go no further. 'But I am his mother, he is my son,' she exclaims melodramatically. 'I can't abandon him; he is my business. I will go to him when he is in hospital!'

I look at the relish with which she says this and I am struck uncomfortably with the impression that my mother feeds off the drama of my brother's illness.

I say no more. I retreat back. I see clearly that my mother will not be able to get behind helping Barnie get some kind of control over his regular bouts of mania. For that very reason, this journey will involve helping him break the umbilical cord with which he is still attached to his mother. A cord which she has, in an unhealthy way, come to depend on in order to feel engaged and alive. I don't see that she has it in her to let go in order for this transition to happen.

I realise that I will be on my own in pushing this through, as no one will want to back me up if it risks upsetting their mother. 'Don't rock the boat' was one thing, but I felt my brother had the right to his own autonomy. I also had a pretty shrewd idea that part of my brother's problem was his compassion and this innate chivalry, which precludes him from getting angry with – in this case – his mother. Instead, he always seems to store up his frustrations until they get too much, and then like the proverbial pressure cooker, everything erupts in a scary, aggressive manic attack. Vituperative recriminations come pouring out at these times. I am often put in mind of the hero Prince Rilian, who features in CS Lewis' *The Silver Chair*. When the fit was upon him, he was tied to the eponymous chair, from whence the truth of who he was and his enchantment would tumble out. Speaking freely until the episode passed, he would then return to the status quo and forget all he had said during his 'fit'. Barnie could not bring himself to be angry with his mother, although he had a perfect right to be. She had tied him to her, to assuage her own insecurity – isn't that always why mothers hold too tight to their offspring? And indeed, lovers to their partners? I think back to the fury he had displayed that day he nearly knocked me out. Had he flown at me and tried to hurt me because he could risk doing to me what he could never do to his own mother?

It is a terrible thing to be a witness to; my mother, nearing the end of her life, her power waning, struggling to be relevant, holding onto the drama created by her son's illness as a means to enable her to feel she still has skin in this game called life.

I am facing a horrible impasse.

But I have made my choice. I am choosing for my brother. He still has many years of life ahead of him.

I realise I am right about being on my own. This will take a lot of determination and strength. I close my eyes and hope I may be equal to the task ahead. I feel an overwhelming sense of the blackness of the Great Void descending, and a great aloneness. But there is no going back now. The only way is through. I must keep walking and hope a path through this darkness may be found by simply concentrating on the next step in front of me. Walking into that Void, with no certainty there will be a way through.

'Are you okay?' says my mum, wondering at my profound silence and closed eyes.

'I'm fine, nothing for you to worry about,' I smile towards her reassuringly. 'Come on, let's make a cuppa!'

I decide to draw back from trying to bring other family members on board. The family dynamic is just too convoluted for this to be the right time. So, without keeping anyone else abreast of the developments, I carry on working with Hannah, Barnie and Dr Sharma. Little by little, the management plan is put in place and tightened and adjusted, and Barnie is happy with it. There will be time enough to involve others when things are more established. I sense the resistance pushing back against me. A great force which I have to withstand. One of my sisters encapsulates the family position when she says to me:

'Don't upset the applecart, Freya, don't upset Mum.'

My mother's spiritual force is still formidable and I begin to feel myself caught up in an almighty tussle. I hold firm. I can begin to see a way through. In my mind, it is as if I am moving towards a narrow pass, with insurmountable boulders on either side. I get a sense of this struggle not only being about Barnie, my family, my mother, but something else, about being freed from the fear that keeps us clinging to unhealthy ways. The fear that keeps the bond of the umbilical intact way beyond the time of a healthy cutting. Of walking the difficult narrow path that will lead, it seems to me, into a breakthrough, into another way of doing things, into a way of living that is not distorted by fear. Fear of being alone, fear of death, the very fear of even being in existence. All these fears I am having to face myself, inch by inch, walking through the narrow pass. I somehow sense there are others too about this work. Not many, but others helping to prepare this bridge, this pathway, from one way of being controlled by fear to another possible way – that of trying a new path.

The tussle with the unconscious family dynamics seems to bleed into the struggle I have been having ever since my return from Peru and the unsettling experience at the nodal axis point in Cusco.

At times, it is as if the rest of the world disappears and every iota of concentration goes into this all-consuming task of preventing myself from being swallowed whole into oblivion. Amuru warned me things might get difficult for me. Was this what he meant? I also remember him telling me, 'Call to us, we are part of your circle of protection.' And I do. In my dreams, I see myself joining a sacred circle, seemingly suspended in darkness where I take my place with the others. I recognise some of the circle, but many I don't know. Are these also the bridge makers crossing destinies by overcoming fear? And so, I do know I am not alone. And is that really my mother taking her wizened place in that dream circle of souls? It is true that on some deeper level, it feels that the role my mother is playing in all of this is necessary too, and part of a greater configuration that is enabling some shift to take place. My overriding sense is of crossing into an enormous black hole and having to find a way through. A way out the other end. Is that even possible? I sense a narrow pathway emerging with high impenetrable boulders on either side. Step by step progress is being made, a pathway is being forged. A pathway bridging into a new world. A world turned upside down, a world turned inside out. A world altered profoundly.

It is at these times, when I feel overwhelmed with the task, with the complexity of my family and the feeling of being drowned in the mire of it all, that I turn to Bembe. It is an extraordinary thing, something about his strength and his dispassionateness towards me actually helps me. When I go near him, when we get close, I feel like I am brought under a pure and cascading waterfall, and washed clean, my spirit renewed and refreshed and able to keep going at this seemingly endless and apparently thankless task.

In the event, back in the real world, despite my mother's unwillingness to comply with Barnie's wishes not to visit him in hospital, in time her own failing health lends a hand. It is a full two years later and Barnie has managed to be out of hospital all this time, which is itself something of a miracle. When he does next succumb to a manic episode, and is readmitted into hospital, dear Muma is two years more frail, and even she has to surrender to her fading strength and does not attempt the journey into town to visit him. Nevertheless, she does take advantage of an offspring visiting with a car to make a heroic effort to appear at the tribunal where Barnie is contesting the section he has been put under, aiming to overturn it and be allowed home. Setting up these tribunals, we start to observe, are a regular occurrence and are a sign my brother is emerging from his manic state and returning to equilibrium. And dear Muma, managing to conjure herself there uninvited, slipping in on a compliant offspring's arm. But very much in the background, a spectre, a very old lady, watching from the sidelines, finally realising the reins are no longer in her hands. That she has no choice now but to let go.

It is a few months after this tribunal. Barnie has now been released from hospital. We are all very pleased that the management plan put in place some years ago has worked and that he has not accrued huge debt. His cards had been removed from him on admission. Although to be fair, he did kick up a huge fuss at the time, his mania having by then taken full control. They were able to do this as he had signed the agreement previously as part of this new management plan. Similarly, he had managed not to upset so many people, as again his phone had been taken from him while he was being admitted to hospital. He had kicked against this too, but the staff had held firm and emerging on the other side of his attack, he was pleasantly surprised to find the aftermath was a fraction of what he usually had to manage.

—

All our hard work has produced some really positive and tangible results.

My mum is gently fading, she is well past 90 by this time, and doesn't always know who people are.

Bembe had liked my mum straight away when they first met all those years ago. He had admired her beauty which, with her beautiful cheekbones and facial structure, she maintained to the end. He had liked her mischievous and rebellious spirit. They had both taken a shine to each other. And so, when I suggest we go visit her, he readily agrees, which in a way surprises me as Bembe was never one to be persuaded to do anything he didn't want to do.

We arrive after lunch and my mum is resting in her room, but she wants us to come in. She is a very social creature and happy for a diversion. My mum recognises me but has no idea who Bembe is, only that she is hugely glad to see him. She shines and is all wreathed in smiles and joy, drinking in his vitality and faith in life. She has eyes for no one else, in her mind, he is here for her and that is all that matters. Bembe seems to totally understand the situation. He reaches his big hands to hold both her frail ones in his. It is as if they have a prearranged appointment and there is something to be discussed between them.

'Shall I leave you two?' I query, seeing their absorption. Bembe glances at me and nods. He's got this. I go out to find my dad and sit with him in the room opposite.

We hear the sound of quiet talk, the sound of laughter, and we wait.

After half an hour, Bembe opens the door, indicating we can come in.

Something extraordinary has happened, something has changed. I see in her face a peaceful acceptance of where she is in her life. On the threshold of crossing. No longer with the power and influence she used to wield. Not the power over the hundreds of pupils that have passed through her care, nor the power over her numerous offspring. Something has shifted in her. Accepting these facts is somehow enabling her to realise the potency of the place where she now stands – so close to the threshold of life and death. I feel as if she has turned her face to where she is going, instead of where she has come from. This acceptance has given her an assurance, a peace, and so it seems, a strength. It is as if he has broken a spell. She looks so happy. Quite radiant.

I look questioningly at Bembe. 'What just happened?' my look is asking.

Bembe, with a grin of self-assurance, says simply, 'She have trouble to take off her crown.'

And he would make no further comment. Subject closed. Job done.

But looking at my mum wreathed in her happiness, I can see he has found a way to help her let go of all she has been, and to do that without her feeling her spirit diminished in any way.

And why should it be diminished? My mum is an amazing spirit, a great mystery, I always call her. She is more than what she had been to so many in this life. And I know her great spirit will go with her into death and beyond and there are plenty of adventures yet for her to come.

How strange then that this man, plucked from obscurity from a little Cuban village and brought here with all the drama and vicissitudes entailed, should be the one, should have the exact skill set, the exact compassionate humanity, insight and faith and above all humour to render this service to my mother at such a crucial time of spiritual crisis for her.

How humbling to realise that when we think we are in charge and one thing is happening, unbeknownst to us there is another narrative at play, beyond anything we even realise. I remember then something Bembe said to me, some time ago, that he felt he had a mission to perform here and that was why he kept coming back. Perhaps this has now been accomplished.

—

It is several weeks after that in the early morning. I am gazing out of my study window, sipping tea, enjoying the green of the spring trees and the blue of the sky, when out of nowhere the clouds floating by form themselves into the shape of a bird flying off. I have a sudden instinct that something is happening with my mother and I must go to her. I suppose it sounds strange put like that, but I had long since learnt to trust my intuition, and so I cancel my day's plans, jump in my car and drive the hour to my parents' door.

When I arrive, the house is quiet. I have my own key so I can let myself in. I shout *'ollie ollie'* – our family call. No answer. I go upstairs and there is my mother lying very still in bed. My father is sitting quietly in an armchair nearby. He looks up and gives me a smile of greeting. I sense something is happening. My mother is very far away, not really sleeping but not present in the room either. I feel she may be dying. I am surprised no one else is here, as it is unusual to arrive at my parents' home without another family member present.

My father senses it too. He has his rosary beads and is quietly saying his *Hail Marys*. He has always been a deeply devout man.

'Shall I call in the priest for the last rites?' I suggest.

My father nods his agreement. So, I go to the church, which is very close, and ask if the priest will come and attend to my mother. He says he will come as soon as he can and I go back and wait in vigil with my father. We sing some hymns together companionably, hymns that we know my mum likes.

Virgin most pure, star of the sea, pray for us sinners, pray for me.

It's a long time since I sang any hymns, but the words and tunes come back to me easily.

My mother seems to be sinking further and further away. Deeply and peacefully going into her own space. My father is calm. I begin to think the priest will be too late, when the doorbell rings. I go down to open the door and, bringing the priest upstairs, I usher him into the bedroom. My father and I leave the room as it seems an intensely private moment. From next door, we hear the priest intoning. It sounds like he is saying a mini mass. And then he calls us in. My mother has rallied; she opens her eyes and is present again. It seems she has come back from the shades of death.

I prop her up, my father has gone to make her some tea, which she drinks thirstily when it arrives. But something is not the same and this day marks a new phase of her life. A phase of forgetting. A forgetting of all she has been in this life. A release from all the trappings and intricacies of this lifetime, a dropping away of the cloak amassed with all the details of this current lifetime. And yet she is still very much there, very much present, her essential self, just as glorious as ever it was, even if remote from us all now. Eventually, she is to forget all her children, forget that she is married even. But always that joyous lighting up of her face when one of us comes before her, recognising a kindred soul, albeit not knowing she'd birthed us moons and moons ago.

Meanwhile, Bembe is still saving hard in order to go back to Cuba, but he is getting restless. Although he is doing really well in the hotel kitchen, being a genial employee, willing to work hard and always cheerful, despite the menial job he is doing. He himself refuses to allow himself to be regarded as a menial.

He has been telling me for days that the dishwashers are not working properly, which is giving him a lot of extra work ensuring the plates are clean before being put back on the shelves. He has taken this matter up with his immediate manager and then, getting no response, with the one above him as well. Nothing was done, the dishwasher was still not fixed. On this day, the 'big boss', as Bembe calls him, has come down into the kitchens to give a little pep talk. Bembe is telling me this story with great relish, his natural gift as a raconteur coming to the fore. I am reminded of meal times in Santiago de Cuba, sitting at table with his extended family, how he would hold everyone's attention and have them all laughing in their seats.

'This hotel's excellence depends on each of you doing your best and in that way, you contribute to the excellence of the hotel.' The man was pontificating.

'I said to him,' Bembe tells me, 'unfortunately, I cannot do my best in my job.' I can imagine the wide-eyed innocence with which he would have said this.

The man had turned to him, eagle-eyed, ready to trounce him like a hapless Oliver Twist orphan.

'And why is that?' he had roared. But Bembe is more than equal to this man.

'Because my dishwasher is broken and therefore I can't make sure the dishes are washed good.' Bembe tells me he had replied simply.

Needless to say, the very next day, a maintenance team arrives and fixes the machine pronto!

His next in command was red-faced and really annoyed to have been shown up. But it was water off a duck's back to Bembe.

'It his fault he not listen me.'

Despite, or indeed perhaps because of, showing up the kitchen management, the head chef is very taken with Bembe's skills, and seeing his potential, has started to give him commis chef jobs to do.

'Why don't you stay here and I will train you up to be a chef?', he offers.

But when Bembe tells me about it that evening, I can see he won't do it. His heart is not here with me it is in Cuba. Even I can't miss this glaringly obvious truth. He misses his son. And now he is concerned for Anna, the boy's mother and her growing belly.

'You want to go back, don't you?' I say.

Bembe's eyes light up as he sees he won't have to be the one to broach this conversation.

'Yes, I want go back, I save money, I go when I buy ticket.'

And that is my dilemma: What is the point of living with someone, however much you love their being, their energy, when you know their heart is elsewhere?

Finally, I reach that point I never thought I would reach. I realise I'd rather he went sooner than later, prolonging this impasse, so we make a deal.

I will pay his flight and, in exchange, he will sign the renunciation of the right to live in the marital home. It is still too soon to get a no-fault divorce – in these days, you still have to wait a full two years.

And so, in pretty quick order Bembe packs up and leaves. As well as the usual clothes for his son, he packs little baby clothes. I look, but I don't say anything.

Chapter 26

A New Beginning

Luckily I do not have a chance to brood on Bembe's departure. Barnie is taking my attention as he becomes increasingly able to walk along this new trajectory we are co-creating to help him manage his terrible affliction. A way that can bypass the unhealthy psychic pull of our dear mother.

Barnie, his deep, dark depression well behind him now, has become interested in picking up the pieces of his life again. He has re-joined his chess companions at his club and begun going out on hillwalking expeditions which are organised as part of a therapeutic programme he has signed up for. He doesn't need to visit so regularly or so often. My role falls back to one of attending the now less regular medical management meetings. My attendance at the meetings has given my brother a context as a member of a family, not simply a medical problem. It seems to me he is beginning to be treated more as a human being and less as a statistic who must be kept out of hospital at all costs, in order to tick the correct box to fulfil some arbitrary criterion. Together we are creating a new pathway in his treatment.

There is to be no instant cure for my brother. But gradually, little by little, the work we have begun by working as a team begins to filter out to my family. As the chaos and unpredictability subside and a new pattern for management of my brother's condition starts to emerge, they in turn are gradually able to reach out to him in a more sure way. My compassionate brothers and sisters, finding ways that are possible for them, ways that, while maintaining the boundaries necessary for their own mental health, can start to bring him in from the periphery. We can start to create a circle of care around him while letting him have the autonomy to find his own way. A walk in the park, a coffee meet-up, a shared football match, all these give Barnie an incentive to keep the plan in place.

One day, when he and I arrange to meet in a local café, Barnie shows me a postcard he has worked on in a therapeutic group he has joined. On it are three different photographs, each of a man engaging in an activity, with a caption beside each activity. 'One man has a serious mental health condition, one man is a chess champion, one man is a loving father,' and on the flip side of the card, 'They are all the same man.' It feels really poignant. That my brother has the right to be seen as more than his illness feels like something of a miracle to me.

We are finding a more humane way forward, which is recognising Barnie as a person. It might seem obvious reading this from another day and age, but there is at this time so much fear around his condition. To be able to perceive Barnie as something other than someone to be feared and shunned and chemically coshed feels like an enormous breakthrough.

To recognise that when he is at his most scary and frightening is the very time he is the most scared, most frightened. Going forward, hospital can be viewed as a sanctuary for Barnie when those times arrive, to protect him from his manic excesses, not a punishment and not something to be ashamed of, neither by him nor his family. Taking away his bank card and his phone when he is in the grip of a manic attack, again, is not a punishment but a means by which we can prevent or at least mitigate against the worst effects of him shredding up his life while under the influence of his manic attacks. A life that had been taking longer and longer to rebuild between episodes.

All this will take time, years and years of it, but we are at the beginning of forging a new way. And I can sense in the wider family a collective exhalation, a relaxation of the tension of waiting for the next out-of-control attack, a relaxation from the fear of being overcome and infected by the chaos previous attacks had provoked.

In my mind comes the image of a card, one of the tarot cards. The ten of swords. The image is from a particular deck, *The Mythic Tarot*, that uses imagery from Greek Mythology. So here, in a darkened landscape, stands Athene calm and strong – in her hand, a sword. She is holding the furies at bay behind the other nine swords which are plunged into the ground, forming a cage-like barrier. For the time being, at least, the Furies' power is spent. Their energy restrained. Meanwhile Orestes, completely done in, lies unconscious on the ground. This is exactly how I feel too. And behind them all, in the far distance over to the right, the dawn has begun to rise on a new day. Unbeknownst to

Orestes, worn out by his efforts, the battle is won and night is giving way to the light of a new dawn.

This describes how I feel most perfectly. Totally rinsed out and not able to quite believe that the long night is past. Whatever task was upon me has been completed. The over-whelming force of the mother tamed. And whatever task put upon those of us at Qoricancha, the Navel of the World; feels now to be, too, completed. I feel like I have been let off the hook.

—

Then out of the blue, Dave arrives.

Australian Dave with his earthy practicality and humorous grounded-ness. We know each other from attending the same healing courses a few years back. It had been a regular monthly event over two years and we've had plenty of time to get to know and appreciate each other and become good mates. Darling Dave, he just happens to be in Edinburgh; he has a few days free en route for some massage conference or other further north. I don't pay much attention. I am just so grateful for the miracle of such a dear friend being there at this moment of need, the timing could not be more perfect.

He comes like the rising sun of the tarot card. He cooks me some tempting and tasty wholesome food, and he lets me talk. He cradles my head in his lap and administers a deli-cious fizzy ear candle treatment, enabling me to so deeply relax on that trusty kitchen futon. Feeling the reassurance of his physical presence, my blood gradually starts to warm again as he helps pull me back from the chill of the Deep. Inch by reassuring inch, he brings me back gently from the terrible and non-human realms where I have been travelling.

Dave is not able to stay more than a few days and while I could have got used to a bit more pampering, those few days have been enough to turn the tide and put me on the path back out into the bustle of the marketplace of life.

I teach my classes as before, but now full colour has returned and what had felt frozen is thawing beautifully as my life begins to flow once more in a reassuring and familiar way. I start to go out again and reconnect with my salsa crowd and generally re-enter the land of the living.

—

It is one night a few weeks later at one of those salsa nights. I am enjoying seeing some old pals, noticing all the inevitable shifts and changes in the dance scene. The new students arriving in Edinburgh taking lessons and showing promise, strutting their stuff, looking gorgeous. Orlando, the hunky dance teacher, has a new Spanish girlfriend. She is watching him severely from the side-lines, so he is only asking the older women or the not-so-attractive to dance. No chance of a dance there then. My pal Ken is there. He is the only Scottish man I have found who can actually dance, and that, I imagine, is to do with his Italian ancestors. We enjoy a few dances together and he tells me he too has a new girlfriend. She sounds very high maintenance and, to be frank, a bit neurotic, and it is true, very shortly after that we lose Ken from the salsa scene.

My friend Carmen is there, she's having fun dancing with one of the new intakes, so we simply wave to each other across the dance floor. I also know her from yoga as she's been coming to my classes for ages. She is a Spanish language teacher at the university. The department is a stone's throw from one of the classes I teach so I have got to know quite a few of these vivacious Spanish teachers. The thing I most love being in their company is the way they praise each other. '*Que guapa*' when one appears in a hot new outfit, or a fun new hairstyle. Not like the British women who, if you look good, immediately worry that your beauty will diminish them in some way. Perhaps that's why they often seem to adopt a somewhat sullen and suspicious look when I'm around?

Then I notice Marco arrive on his own. Marco is the one I had phoned before, a local businessman of advancing years. He was the first person I knew who had got married in Cuba and brought back his spouse. She was now his ex, to be fair, her ambitions quickly exhausting his modest means, but they had stayed friends, and Bembe told me she looks after him when he needs it, despite her having moved up the social scale to a slightly younger and wealthier beau.

I wend my way through the twirling bodies on the dance floor and make my way towards him at the bar. He greets me warmly.

'Freya, hi, can I get you a drink?'

'Oh, just some water, thanks.' I'm thirsty from the dancing.

'I'm not long back from Cuba,' he tells me.

'Baracoa?' I ask casually.

'Yeah... I saw Bembe,' he adds carefully.

'Aye,' I give him space to say more.

'And the new bairn. He was very proud to show me his wee boy.'

Marco throws me a sympathetic look, but knows better than to say anything more.

'Sure you won't have a drink?' he eventually ventures.

'Yes, why not!' I rarely imbibe, but just in this moment, it could help.

'I'll have a Glenmorangie,' I say, noticing the malt displayed behind the counter.

I drown it in water just the way I like it and knock it back.

'Cheers, Marco. D'you know what? I'll see you around, I'm going home.'

And that is indeed what I do.

—

When I get home, I take the time to notice how I am feeling. The hurt and disappointment of a love affair that didn't work out. Why am I taking it so personally? From what I have pieced together, Bembe had unfinished business with Anna. Perhaps his coming to the UK was simply him running away. And now it has all gone full circle, and he is back where he needs to be? If so, maybe I should be proud I helped him. And after all, he helped me by supporting me when I needed it and by being so able to understand what my mother was going through.

Why do I feel so damned abandoned, miserable and alone?

My mind goes back to the exhilaration I had felt at the node in Cusco. Such a difference to this place I am wallowing in right now. Then I seemed to be linking in with a potent force – to the great cosmic Galactic Centre – which is, after all, a black hole. But then I hadn't felt afraid. I had felt such joy. Weirdly, in a way I can't begin to explain, I knew what I was doing. I felt a sureness of purpose. But then, it is true I had blanked out. In fact, I don't remember what happened, only the others around me said I'd fallen to the ground. That I had passed out. But what if I could consciously reconnect with that space now? Couldn't I in some way balance myself and be healed from this misery? My curiosity alive now, I spring into action.

I settle myself, sitting upright on the bed with my back supported by pillows. Closing my eyes, I bring my awareness to the back of my head, just around the nape of the neck. I imagine the whirling of that great energy centre – the medulla oblongata – just as it had opened for me that first time in the ceremony in Cusco. It is not difficult for me to do, and soon I feel the hugeness of that force, feel the great nothingness of all potentiality opening up behind me. Holding my ground, I take all of my feelings of disappointment and abandonment and upset and I place them into the black hole. And then something extraordinary happens. All in a trice, I feel quite myself again. Quite well and happy. Every trace of bad feeling has simply disappeared. Wow, that was fast. I take the time to carefully close down the chakra, and then to scan my body. Everything seems quite in order. I am fine, absolutely fine.

PART IV

Chapter 27

Insights Abound

And now another Christmas had come and gone. My two children and I have navigated the complexities of their two separate fathers and their two second home lives. We have become pretty expert, mainly involving seeing Christmas as a movable feast and not being hung up on the 25th December as the only day that counts to be together. We had had our lovely time, the three of us, that was precious to us all.

And now we are in the days following even our extended Christmas. It is that fallow dark time of year, the solstice well behind us. Christmas has come and gone but life has not yet restarted, despite the turning into the New Year

My son has gone back to his life in London and my daughter is with her father.

I find myself on Facebook. I had posted some wonderful pictures from Peru some years previously: the high Inca ruins and the stunning views.

My inbox pings.

It is an old friend, Aryeh. Years before, we had met at the same spiritual exploration workshop back in the early

1990s. I suppose we were the vanguard of what was to come, a few people beginning to reach out to understand life from a less materialistic perspective. This workshop had been led by a Denise Lyn, and was held in a church hall in central Edinburgh, tucked away behind a shopping centre. A hundred or so people from different walks of life had attended. She had put us all into a meditation and walked round, I suppose sensing our energies. When she came to me, she bent down and whispered in my ear, 'Your head in the stars and your feet on the Earth.' Later we had been divided into groups of around six or so, and Aryeh and his friend Octavia and I had been placed in the same group.

Denise had got us all to sit in a circle on the floor and to take turns to really look at each person in turn and then to go round the circle and say what we saw that person being in a past life.

When it was my turn to be scrutinised, quite a few of the folk told me they saw me as a dancer. Well, I could relate to that. I enjoy a lot to dance salsa and have devoted my life to teaching yoga. When it was the turn to scrutinise Aryeh, I got such a strong image of us as having been married for a lifetime, an old peasant couple scratching a living in some remote outback in Eastern Europe, for all the world like an illustration out of that children's story, *The Great Big Enormous Turnip*. To me, he was a benign, friendly and familiar presence, and I liked him. He didn't have that effect on everyone, though, and someone in our group said they thought he'd been Genghis Khan!

Following on from that workshop, there had been some attempt to form a meditation group. We had enjoyed the workshop and in those days there were not so many outlets for spiritual exploration, so when a small group of us were chatting together at the end and someone suggested the idea, Octavia volunteered to host the first one. She was definitely unfamiliar with the spiritual New Age world. She was young, smart and beautiful, lived in a gorgeous flat in an expensive part of town and dressed immaculately. Her vibe was corporate world and as we arrived at the appointed hour, she was at the door handing us all big glasses of white wine from a silver platter! Not quite the meditation vibe we had decided on.

I had stepped in to circumnavigate our meeting from turning into a drinks party. I took the tray from lovely Octavia, who was happy to have some direction, this being her first time hosting a meditation meet-up. I put the drinks tray to one side for later. I indicated to everyone to form a circle on the floor. Octavia was not the only one who seemed not to know what the form was, so I took the initiative, having had plenty of practice with leading circles of people into peaceful states. Then once we were all seated, I led us all in a simple meditation. It was very beautiful, as I remember. And then we had drunk the wine and chatted, and had a lovely time, but we hadn't carried on meeting. That was all a very long time ago now.

I had bumped into Aryeh here and there over the intervening years. We had chatted in the interval of a concert or met at a poetry reading or a friend's play or in a bookshop at a book launch. And yes, we were friends on Facebook.

'Loving your photos of Peru,' pings my Messenger inbox.

'Aryeh, hi, nice to hear from you! Yes, I fell in love with the place where I was staying, Taray. It was hard to come back. I got myself up Machu Picchu too. And other extraordinary things. Then when I got back, I had the hardest year of my life.' I answer him.

'I can help you make sense of all this,' he replies straight away.

'How do you mean?' I query

'I work with something called the *Optimum Path*. If you like, we can set up a session. I work from home and we can look into what is coming up for you.'

I hesitate only for a moment, as it seems so unexpected and out of the blue, yet perhaps a way forward to understanding all that has been happening. Perhaps it is the feeling we were old friends from that other life that made it easy for me to trust him. Whatever it was, I reply.

'Okay, let's arrange something.'

And so, it is the following week that I find myself driving to my appointment. Aryeh lives in a different part of town to myself, in a top-floor flat with stunning views over a city park. His consulting room is also his living space and it is full of interesting oddities and statues and unusual pictures on the wall. The sofa where he directs me to sit is comfortable with rugs and a sheepskin to cosy up in.

I feel very at home in this apartment and Aryeh soon brings me a cup of herbal tea with a good spoon of honey in it. I get

comfortable on his sofa, large and soft with loads of cushions and throws ready if needed. Sipping my tea, he settles
opposite me on an ornately carved wooden chair with a thick
upholstery cushion, his face alert and impassive, yet with a
ready compassion.

The first task in hand, he explains, is to establish a means of
checking everything said in this session for veracity. He explains that he has guides or Angels that he is able to check
in with and who give him insights while he is working with
a client, insights that will help in the process, help to keep
him right. They will let him know, he tells me, if what he says
is not exact; he can then modify what he speaks to achieve
pinpoint accuracy.

Even as he is speaking, I can see him doing that, looking
upwards momentarily and pausing, waiting for an invisible
nod, or not, before carrying on.

He wants me to find my own connection to my own guides
or Angelic helpers, so I can also check in with them to get a
confirmation or not as we go along.

This doesn't sit so easily with me, though. Some years back,
I had spent more than eight years working with a spiritual
teacher, Mike Robinson, and he had this expression: 'Why
go through intermediaries when you can go straight to the
boss?' He had encouraged us, his pupils, to connect directly
with our own inner guidance, and I had developed something of a facility with this.

Basically, if I was tuning in, I could tell immediately whether
something was right or not when someone was talking to

me. It had cost me friends, no doubt about that, and also whether or not I acted on this knowing was another thing, as my adventures with Bembe have certainly demonstrated.

So, I explain I do know what he is talking about – that checking into some inner knowing – but I don't need to conjure up a guide or an Angel to do that, as it is more instantaneous for me.

Aryeh seems a little surprised but says, 'As long as you feel able to feel for yourself the truth of what emerges in our sessions, then we are good to go.'

I love the feeling of the space being created here, and so I settle in as Aryeh launches forth.

He talks a tremendous lot; much of what he is saying is going over my head, but I am patient. I can sense there is something important here for me. And also, it is as if his words are taking us more deeply into the space where insights and understandings can be discovered.

What resonates strongly with me is when he explains that each of us, as we grow into our lives, makes adjustments in order to survive whatever the difficulties are that we find ourselves faced with, our own particular predicaments.

In the case of myself, he intuits correctly, my need for attention was at odds with what was available to me growing up a middle child in a family of twelve children. My thoughts go back to that night. I am a child, perhaps only four or five, waking up in great discomfort with raging tonsillitis, my throat so sore every swallow is a torture. I am about to cry out in the night, to call for help, when I remember my mother has not long come home from the hospital with the latest newborn, and I stop myself, not wanting to disturb my mother's sleep. I suppose that was not very fair on a wee lass, come to think of it. No one to comfort her. To comfort me, my little child.

Over time, he explains, I became the carer, meeting other people's needs, but in so doing, eclipsing my own to the point I no longer know that I have any and certainly not what they are.

I begin to feel a little despondent at this encapsulation of my life. I know what he is saying is true. I had never heard it presented so starkly, though. But Aryeh continues gently, explaining to me that this had been my way of not disappearing, my way of maintaining my right to existence. Making myself useful and therefore also popular gave me a specialness I needed, but it also presented me with a problem in my life, as I was not living true to my nature. By being forever attentive to the needs of others, I have not been paying attention to my own needs.

He pauses to let me assimilate these hard truths. I think of what I knew of astrology, of my moon in Leo. A Leo moon likes to shine and be the apple of the eye of the beholder. Leo is not made to be a drudge for sure. I am brought out of this reverie by Aryeh suddenly saying apropos, it seems of nothing, 'Remember that time when we did that meditation at Octavia's house? You took control.'

'Yes, of course I remember, it was either that or we'd all have got sloshed out of embarrassment,' I say evenly. 'I just helped what we had agreed upon to happen.'

'Yes, true,' agrees Aryeh. 'It's just that when you were sitting there, I saw you as a Tibetan master with all your chakras opened, all shining and perfectly aligned. I was envious. How could this be, how could you do that?'

Chakras are the energy centres in the body. They are connected to different emotions and different organs, and they radiate colours appropriate to their purpose, and some people are able to see these colours, these spinning vortexes of energy. Aryeh was clearly one of these gifted few.

I smile wryly. Whatever state of balance and composure I had been in then, all those years ago, I did not feel in that space now, or I would not be here seeking his counsel.

I bring the conversation back to what I am trying to get insight on now.

'When I was in Peru, I stayed in a healing centre for a while and I found myself in such pain in my body. One of the people also staying there – a really cool guy called Geoff – helped me. He said I processed my emotions through my body and he got me to tune into what my body was feeling, I connected to all this anger. It shocked me – the strength of it.'

I describe to Aryeh more fully what had happened up on that mossy stone by the waterfall back in Taray. Aryeh nods sagely. None of what I am saying is a surprise to him.

'We make choices when we are small. Whatever the reasons are, it is hard to be ourselves, in your case, being one of a huge family where your needs could not be met. We choose an adaptive strategy in order to survive and what you chose was to become the helper. The one looking after everyone else. This was your way to justify your existence – to not disappear. In this way, you did fulfil that need to shine, albeit that shining was while in service to others.' He is simply saying in a different way what he has already said, but I clearly need the time to really let this sink in.

Aryeh pauses, giving me the space I need to digest his words fully; to check in with my own inner knowing, to process and then evaluate the truth of what he has said.

Pondering his words, I consider that growing up as one of twelve is always going to have its challenges, wherever your moon is placed. But then I suppose that these challenges will vary from child to child depending on their own makeup. With that moon in Leo, my need to be special, particularly in my home environment, is instinctive. What chance of that was there? Who was noticing? I get that by being super helpful, that would have got me attention, I would have become important by being needed. But where were my needs in all this?

My dad also has this placement of the moon. He too liked to be acknowledged, especially when he returned home after a day's work. When we were children, his arriving home from work coincided with the Children's TV slot. It wasn't possible in those days to put a programme on pause. Notwithstanding, he would come into the room and stand right in front of the TV. It was a little ritual; we all knew our part. We would stand up and give a little bow. 'Good evening, Father,' we would say in unison. After that, he could go off happily to find his wife. Sometimes he would bring a bag of oranges and he'd then roll them dramatically into our midst and enjoy the scramble as we picked up this special treat. That's a happy Leo moon. They definitely want to be noticed when they come home. I had myself adopted a similar ritual with my own children when they were younger. When I came home from teaching evening classes, they seemed to know how to keep Muma sweet, to come to the door, to greet me warmly and welcome me back. Leo moons can be generous too. It is just that we need to be appreciated for what we do. That is enough to keep us purring happily.

I thought back to my own childhood. Generosity is one thing, but self-effacement is never going to sit comfortably on a Leo moon. And yet that is what happened to me, being a wee helper, but who is paying any attention to what little Freya wants or needs? Nobody – least of all myself. When you know your needs are not going to be met, rather than face the disappointment of nothing happening to fulfil them, you squash them down and very soon you don't even know you have that need at all.

Aryeh is waiting quietly for me to figure all this out before inviting me to share my thoughts.

'What you are saying rings true,' I begin. 'I find it really hard to know what I want or need in a given situation. I am always looking for what the situation needs. I suppose, too, that is a throw-back to childhood, as my father could kick off into scary anger and even at times violence if things went the wrong way. So, to avoid this, I would work out ways to placate him, I guess. I was always hyper-vigilant and pre-empting problems, for instance, by looking after the needs of my younger siblings, so there would be a calm in the house. To be fair to my poor dad, it must have been super stressful having to provide for so many. And when did he ever get enough of the attention his Leo moon craved?'

'Indeed,' continues Aryeh implacably, refusing to allow me to wander off subject.

'Let's stay with the impact that this has had on yourself though.'

I bring my focus back to his face as he continues.

'So, the strategy you adopted for survival in a difficult environment was to shut down your own needs and to attend to the needs of others.'

I nod my agreement ruefully.

'By burying your own emotions so successfully, they don't just disappear; they have to come out somehow. For you, it is through physical discomfort.'

That made sense of the enormous pain I was under whenever Bembe had been living under my roof in Edinburgh. If only I had had the sense to listen to my body!

'It takes a lot of concentrated effort to continually bury such a huge part of ourselves. And to make sense to ourselves as to why we keep putting in the effort, we turn it into something shameful that has to be buried. This huge and quite natural part of ourselves is not happy being put into the dungeons. CG Jung, the great psychologist, wrote about just this, that when we put the dark secret side of ourselves, what he called the shadow – those aspects of ourselves we feel have to be kept out of sight at all costs – into the basement, our shadow grows larger and more fierce and more angry with the treatment it is enduring.'

'Oh yes,' I agree eagerly, 'I devoured Jung's collected works when I was studying at university, and the shadow in the cellar was an image that had imprinted itself on me.'

'Indeed,' continues Aryeh, refusing to be diverted. 'And so what started as a natural need of a little girl to be noticed, to be praised, to be encouraged, grows into something we feel to be huge and terrible and shameful, which needs to be hidden from view at all costs.'

Aryeh pauses to let me take this in. My eyes open wide in excitement.

'Oh, my goodness, that reminds me of this dream I keep getting!!'

Aryeh is alert, there is an electric tingle in the air. This is important.

'It's a recurring dream. This monster, I call her the elephant woman, is making her way up the stairs towards me. I am standing at the top of the stairs outside my front door of our old family home. She is so deformed and all swathed in bandages, like a ghastly Egyptian mummy on the loose or a hideously deformed elephant woman. She always moves slowly and with great difficulty because of her deformities.'

Aryeh is still all attention, which encourages me to continue.

'I don't want her to come any closer; she is so disgusting and scary, and yet each time I dream of her, she is inexorably making her way step by step closer to where I am standing.'

I pause. I feel somewhat exposed having revealed this frightful dream image but Aryeh is unfazed and he asks me,

'Would you like to work with this image today, Freya?'

I take a deep breath, snuggle into the cosy sofa and pull the blanket higher around me, considering. I sip the delicious honey-sweetened herbal tea. I look at the impeccability of the man before me. I have felt nothing but safe with him. If I cannot trust now, then when and with whom will I ever trust?

'Yes, I am ready.'

I put the cup down on the cork coaster on the low wooden table. I cross my legs and sit up straighter, allowing the sofa to support my back, and close my eyes.

'Get an image of this creature, Freya, and then tell me when you can see her clearly,' Aryeh says.

'Oh, I see her,' I say, 'she is never far from my consciousness.'

'Then, where are you?'

'I am at the top of the stairs at the front door, the door is barely open, and I am on the doormat. She is further down the stairs, all hunchbacked and deformed and grotesque. She repels me.'

'Will you ask her to approach? Will you invite her in?'

My immediate reaction is revulsion at this suggestion, yet surprisingly, almost immediately, this changes to something else. I am curious now. Invite her in, instead of always repelling her? That is a new idea.

I nod my acquiescence while keeping my eyes closed and, in my inner mind, I ask this creature to come in. Aryeh does not disturb me. However, his presence and attention are supporting my inner journeying. She has reached the top of the stairs now and is standing right in front of me. I have to open the front door really wide to let her in. This is because she is so wide where bits of her body stick out at unfortunate angles, and even so, she has to shuffle sideways in order to come in through my front door. And now she is inside the hall. I invite her to follow me into the sitting room. It is a large room and there she is, finally, inside my house.

Then something strange begins to happen. Her body is still swathed in rags like an Egyptian mummy, but now she starts to peel off these bandages. I gird myself against the thought of suppurating sores being revealed. I always am so squeamish. But no! It is a bright golden light garment which starts to become visible. The great humps at her shoulders as they are freed from the constraints of the swaddling begin to spread out and unfurl, as I stare in astonishment. Transforming in front of my gaze, this hideous creature, who has haunted my nightmares for so long, is transforming into the golden Angel of my dream!

'It's my Angel, my golden Angel!' I say in disbelief.

Aryeh is bubbling with glee at this revelation, that what I have been ashamed of and striven so hard to keep hidden and out of sight, is actually a glorious light-filled being who means me no harm at all. This leaves me feeling completely dazed and flummoxed.

I am actually in tears now. But my tears are tears of relief.

'I can't believe it!' I say.

And yet, little by little, I feel something that has imprisoned me for so many years fall away. My puzzlement subsides and very soon, I too am feeling fantastic.

Both Aryeh and I start laughing uproariously, and we spontaneously give each other a big, joyous hug.

'I think that calls for a fresh herbal tea,' says Aryeh.

We take a refresh break. I go to the loo and splash my face with cold water. This is such a huge revelation for me.

When I go to settle myself back onto the comfortable sofa, Aryeh calls to me from the kitchen.

'Do you want honey in your tea again?'

'Yes please, make it two big dollops could you? I need it for the shock!'

We both laugh and, with fresh tea steaming before us, prepare to wrap up our session. Aryeh has some things he wants to tell me following on from this revelatory session.

'Angels by their nature are quite conspicuous when they walk among mortals,' begins Aryeh.

I am glad, that Angels are already part of his awareness. He speaks about them so naturally.

'Yes, so you can understand there is a sense in hiding that part of oneself. The thing is to be in charge of choosing when you hide, and when you reveal, rather than denying a part of your very being.' Aryeh pauses.

'Yes,' I agree, 'I can allow this part of myself to unfurl without the need to ever again swathe her away to such a degree that she becomes deformed.'

'But at the same time,' I continue carefully to make sure I am getting this right, 'it is fine to hide her from view, if I feel the circumstances demand that. But also, when I so choose, when I feel safe to do so, it's good to let my Angel spread her wings and shine her fabulous and glorious being out into the world.'

Aryeh is grinning.

'It's like that quote from, is it Martha Graham?' I say, 'about what you are most afraid of is your light, not your shadow. I can see where she was going with that one.'

And then our session is done. We are both quite rinsed by now. I glance at my watch. It is more than three and a half hours we have been on this journey of discovery. As I head down the stairs and into the light of the fading day, I decide to take a little walk in the nearby park before driving home.

Sitting on a bench as the sun is beginning to set, my coat wrapped around me against the evening chill, I enjoy a feeling unfamiliar to me. My body feels utterly relaxed. I remember my lion when I took the Ayahuasca. My lion, who was also showing me it is okay to be in your body, you simply have to exist, be in your body, and all else will follow.

As an experiment, I allow the great golden wings to sprout from my shoulders. I imagine my golden robe and just for those minutes in the park at the fading dusk, I experiment with being fully myself in all my glory. Nothing bad happens; the sky does not fall in.

Two young lads walk past, no doubt looking for somewhere to have a sneaky puff of something illicit. They glance my way. I smile, and to my surprise, they nod back to me as they hurry on their way. An old man comes by, slightly shuffling, and he too glances at me, and smiles a greeting.

'Nice evening we're having,' he says.

'Yes,' I smile back. 'It's truly glorious!'

———

And so there we will leave Freya, smiling broadly and freely and feeling for the first time completely alive and joyous and herself and unafraid. Most importantly, unafraid.

Oh yes, there will be challenges and difficulties to come; most especially in this time of Earth's shifting cycles; but as she goes forward, she will be more than equal to each one.

Further Resources and Links

Lucy can be contacted at enquiries@lucyemhunter.co.uk

Website: www.lucyemhunter.co.uk

www.authenticartists.co.uk to find out about the work of Kath Burlinson

www.galacticastrology.co.uk to learn more about our Galactic influences and the work of Julia Balaz.

www.roryduff.com to learn more about leylines and nodes much information can be discovered here.

If you are moved by this book or inspired or feel others might enjoy reading it, it would be so great if you could leave a review on Amazon or Good Reads, in turn the author will aim to leave a personal reply on each post.

Acknowledgments

This book might not have seen the light of day had I not attended one of Kath Burlinson's transformative *Authentic Artist's* workshops. Given space to read out to the group what I had previously kept hidden, my words were echoed back to me and I was encouraged to dance. This was a profound experience and helped me take ownership of my story.

It was my two besties, David and Joe, repeatedly urging me to finish my book, that led to the search that found Nicola Humber at The Unbound Press. One Zoom meeting with her was enough to galvanise the process. It seemed I had found the missing ingredient – a place to land. After that, I didn't look back, and with the support of Nicola's regular check-ins and fortnightly meetings with Siobhan and Sally, in our cwtch writers' group, I ploughed on to a completed draft. From there, deep thanks are due to Joe Harney for his careful and thoughtful feedback on an early draft, which was extraordinarily affirming and encouraging.

To Sophie Cooke; whose structural edit with her customary and consummate professionalism, generosity and depth of insight; had me looking at my story in new ways and pushed me to improve my writer's craft.

To Rory Duff for his kind encouragement and helpful tips; to my sister Mj for believing in me; To the professionalism of the staff at The Unbound Press, particularly awesome Em; to Hannah Mello for picking up the packaging further down the line; to Will Ingham for his masterful cover, which hits just the right note. And to all the many people who I have shared this dance of Life with especially those who have provided inspiration for some of the characters in this book, my deep respect and thanks are due.

Lastly and always, deep gratitude and love for her superb final edit and for all else: my steadfast and unfailingly supportive daughter, Jacinta.

About the Author

Of the inspiration and purpose behind her books, Lucy says:

'My books are an attempt to make sense of many strange and at times unsettling experiences I have had from a young age, which led me to explore deeply the world of metaphysics in its various guises. We are, it seems, as a collective, on the cusp of some big shifts, and much of what I experienced seems to be a harbinger of this. Before these things were widely available or talked about, my journey of exploration led me to study with some notable healers and spiritual teachers and to delve deeply into the inner worlds of past lives, chakras, plant medicines, astrology and more. In my writings I attempt to distil some of what I have learned and experienced. I have chosen the format of fiction, which hopefully my readers will enjoy and be entertained by. And if anyone should find themselves identifying with what I write, in a way that is helpful to them, then that would indeed be a source of great satisfaction.

Always liking to keep things grounded and to find the humour where I can, my books may appeal to those on a similar journey of exploration, who are not attracted to the often 'holier than thou' approach of many self-styled new age prophets, whose goal seems to be escaping the everyday world. I firmly believe that our job in life is to become fully embodied, endeavouring in this way to bring heaven to earth. And have some laughs along the way for sure!'